CW00868194

STRANDED IN THE SWAMP

WADE DALTON AND SAM CATES MYSTERIES
BOOK 3

JIM RILEY

To the Most Beautiful

You Always Were and Always Will Be

1 SATURDAY MORNING

EVERGREEN, MS

"Hello."

"Hey, Kenny."

"Who is this? Do you know what time it is?"

Kenny tried to focus his bleary eyes on his bedside alarm clock.

"Kenny, it doesn't matter who this is. All that matters is that I heard you've been talking about the Evergreen Project."

Kenny's eyes popped wide open and his upper body sat erect in the bed.

"What did you say?"

"Don't play dumb, Kenny. You're not good at it."

"Okay, I told a few friends over drinks. So why call me?"

"Because it was our secret, Kenny."

"There's nothing to it yet."

"I know. But I also know what's gonna be there once you guys take care of the Evergreen Plantation."

"We shouldn't be talking over the phone."

"Don't worry, Kenny. Mine is a throwaway. Untraceable."

"But you never know who might be listening."

"You're right again, Kenny. I tell you what. Let's meet."

"Where?"

"Go down Burned Down Road right past the Evergreen Plantation. As soon as the high fence ends, there is an old logging road that leads down to the creek. We'll meet at the creek."

"When?"

"One hour."

2 SATURDAY MORNING
EVERGREEN PLANTATION

THE AROMA OF THE STRONG BLACK COMMUNITY Coffee permeated the den in the Lodge at the Evergreen Plantation. Wade Dalton loved that smell.

"Where are we going to sit this morning?"

Mindy Thomas put her arms around him and gave him a hug.

"Am I gonna hunt with you again? I thought it was my turn to sit with Mandy," Wade nodded towards Mindy's twin sister.

"We share almost everything, but I'm not sharing my hunting buddy with her. She's gonna have to sit with Daddy again."

She tightened the grip around his waist.

"Bruce! Help me. You decide which one I take hunting this morning."

"I'm only the City Manager. I'm not paid to make big decisions like that." Bruce laughed at Wade's predicament.

"You girls decide which one goes with me and which one sits with your daddy. We've got plenty of time. Let us know in the next, oh, thirty seconds."

"I already told you, Wade. I'm hunting with you and Mandy can hunt with Daddy."

Mandy nodded her head in agreement.

"She can have you this time, Detective Ranger. But only if you promise you won't do anything with her you won't do with me later."

Both twins laughed.

Wade grabbed a thermos full of coffee and a couple of Danish rolls.

"Just in case one of us stays awake this morning."

"Last time, I fell asleep. But I woke up in time to shoot that big ol' Axis buck."

"I still don't know if you were asleep or were faking it."

"And you never will!"

After assigning stands to the other guides and hunters, Wade helped the twins load their gear onto the ATV. Mindy wedged next to Wade in the front seat, and Bruce sat in the rear seat with Mandy. With several thousand acres and over one hundred stands to choose from, Wade thought about where he picked for Mindy to find a big whitetail buck this morning.

We could go to the ridge behind the winter pea field. The deer usually travel along it to get back to cover to bed up for the day. We could sit in the stand in the narrow strip of woods between the winter oat field and the cornfield. Deer love getting the last bit of sweet corn before laying down. No, the best place is the one I've chosen. It's above a white oak bottom at the edge of a deep swamp thicket, perfect cover for an old buck to chew his cud out of sight of any human predators. No matter where the old bucks eat at night, a lot of them prefer to retreat to the swamp for the safety it provides during the day. Their favorite route is through these white oaks that produce the sweetest acorns of all the oak trees. It's quite a walk from the main trail for the hunters, but that's also an advantage. Most of my hunters are way too far out of shape to hunt there, so we'll have a stand that rarely gets hunted.

Slamming on the breaks, they saw a majestic elk standing in the middle of the four-wheeler trail. interrupting his thoughts. All four occupants of the all-terrain vehicle stared at the incredible animal.

"He's not in a big hurry to move, is he?" Mandy whispered from the back seat.

"If I was as big as him, I wouldn't be in a hurry to get anywhere until I was ready to go," Mindy giggled.

"Man, he's nice." Bruce could not take his eyes off this magnificent animal.

"Which reminds me, Bruce. If you see that white elk, our deal is still on."

"Fifty thousand, if I remember right."

"That's it. And I'll throw in a whitetail buck for lagniappe."

Bruce beamed. "I've already selected a spot over my mantle."

Wade observed the old bull amble off the trail. After he completely disappeared, he steered the ATV deeper into the woods.

"You can't ever tell about these old bulls this time of the year. Sometimes, the smell of a female, even a human female will set them off during the rut and this ATV is great, but it isn't a match for an angry nine hundred pound bull elk."

"I'm with you, Wade." Bruce nodded from the back seat. "No use taking any chances."

Wade grinned as Mindy's eyes grew wider and wider as she searched the darkness along the trail for any angry bulls.

Her hip squeezed almost underneath Wade's in the small seat.

Wade put Bruce and Mandy in the same stand where they had previously seen a majestic white elk. Wade had not even known the white elk was on the ranch prior to that hunt, but a picture from Mandy's phone provided all the proof needed. After dropping the pair at the stand, Wade and Mindy followed a meandering trail to the rear corner of the property in the lowlands next to the creek and the swamp. They parked the ATV in some brush on the other side of a ridge from the stand and eased through the white oaks in the veiled darkness before dawn.

Reaching the ladder leading up to the stand, Mindy handed Wade her rifle and most of her gear. As she climbed the stairs, she glanced back and smiled at Wade. He knew exactly what that smile meant.

Yes, I know you're enjoying the view from right behind and right below me. Keep climbing.

Mindy reached the top of the stairs and slowly inched the door open, attempting to make as little noise as possible. Wade was still absorbing the pleasant view when Mindy let out a blood-curling scream and bolted over Wade down the stairs. Barely catching a hand on a rail, he hung on as Mindy tumbled on the ground, rose to her feet, and raced toward the ATV.

The blow temporarily knocked the wind out of Wade, and he struggled to get words out.

"What's wrong, Mindy? What did you see?"

But Mindy did not slow down to answer questions. She crashed into small trees and brush in her frantic attempt to get as far away from the stand in as short of a time as possible.

What the heck did she see that spooked her like that? Whatever it is, I'd better be careful.

Wade's nerves tingled, and the hair on the back of his neck stood straight up as he chambered a shell in his rifle. He took a step up the ladder with his right foot, and followed with raising his left foot to the same step, always keeping the business end of the rifle pointed at the door of the hunting stand. Mindy had left the door slightly ajar in her haste to get away.

Man, this ain't right! What could be in that stand? A bat? A snake? Squirrels? There's no way a skunk could get this high. Must be a bat with babies. Uh-oh. The smell of death. That unmistakable smell of death. If I can just ease this door open a little more—

Wade stared at the object in the stand, and then almost leapt from the platform to the ground. He immediately grabbed his cell phone and hit the speed dial at the top of the list.

3 SATURDAY MORNING
EVERGREEN PLANTATION

Luckily, my fiancée is the Sheriff of Evergreen County, or I wouldn't have her at the top of my contact list.

"Sam, you awake?"

"I am now. What's up?"

"Well, get awake and get some of your deputies awake. I found Kenny Thigpen dead in one of my stands. One of the twins, Mindy, found him."

"Kenny Thigpen? Dead? That must have shocked her. Are you sure he's dead?"

"Yes, so there's no hurry with the medical examiner. Unless I need him for Mindy. She took off and there's no telling where she'll end up. Probably in the swamp unless I can find her soon."

"I wasn't expecting this kind of wake-up call this morning. So he's in a stand along the creek bottom at the swamp?"

"It's the old stand at the edge of the cedar swamp in the white oak bottom."

"That's one of my favorite stands. Those big ol' bucks will sneak in and out of the swamp all day long. If I remember correctly, there is a gate in the fence not too far from the stand."

"Yep, that's the one."

"Give me a few minutes to find a uniform and get dressed. I'll call Gus and roust him, assuming he went to bed last night. We should be there in about thirty minutes."

"If you don't mind, come to that gate by the stand so you don't disturb the other hunters. I've got to go find Mindy. She took off like a scalded cat."

"No problem. Just don't track up the scene like the hunters did last time. Did you determine the cause of death?"

"I didn't stay up in the stand that long. Besides, you need to have something to do so you can tell the press about it."

"We'll have plenty to tell the press. Kenny is well known. He was the other City Councilman on the fringe of the Rachel Chastain murder, but he wasn't as involved, if that's the right term, as the others."

"If you mean he was the only one that didn't confess to having a relationship with a teenage girl, then that's the right term."

"All right, be safe until I get there. I don't want to have to worry about you."

"Don't worry. Mindy and I are the only ones back this far."

"That's what worries me, Dear." Sam hung up the phone.

Wade followed the wide trail of debris Mindy left in her haste to escape. The upturned leaves, broken branches and patches of bare dirt where her boots slid going up the hill were as plain to Wade as exit signs would have been to motorists traveling on Interstate 10. Within four or five minutes, even in the morning darkness, he found her cowering next to a huge live oak on the other side of the ridge from the stand. Wade sat next to her and put his arm around her shoulders.

"I wish I could offer you something stronger than coffee, but that's all I have."

"I—I'm sorry, Wade. I wasn't expecting to find someone in the stand. Especially a dead someone!"

"If it makes you feel any better, I wasn't expecting to find anyone either."

"He is dead, isn't he? I mean, he looked dead and smelled dead, if you know what I mean."

Wade tilted his head back until it rested against the oak tree.

"Mindy, that is a smell you will never forget no matter how long you live. Most people, fortunately, have never had the experience. But for those of us that have, we'll never forget it."

"How long does it take to go away, Wade?"

Wade sighed, exhaling almost all his breath before answering.

"I wish I could tell you, Mindy. With me, it has never completely gone away."

Mindy laid her head on Wade's shoulder and openly wept, no longer making any attempt to restrain the tears built up inside. Wade could think of nothing to say that would ease Mindy's tension, so he held her a little tighter as they cuddled under the oak. Eventually, the tears ebbed, and Wade helped her daub the few remaining ones beneath her eyes."

"Who is he?"

"Kenny Thigpen. He's one of our City Councilmen. At least he was."

"I know him. He used to stare at my butt. That didn't look like him, though."

"He won't be staring at anyone's butt anymore, Mindy."

"How did he die, Wade?"

"I don't know that yet."

How long has he been there?"

"I'm don't know that either."

"Why is he in your deer stand?"

"I'm afraid I don't know the answer to that one either, Mindy."

"Boy, for a Detective Ranger or whatever you are, you sure don't know much, do you?" She stared at Wade and then laughed through her tears.

Wade broke into a broad grin.

"Can we get out of here, Wade?"

"I called Sam, and she's on her way. She'll need to talk to both of us to find out what we saw and heard."

As he finished the sentence, Wade could hear the sirens in the distant, drawing closer and closer. The morning sun rose over the horizon, bringing hope of a better day ahead for the pair leaning against the tree on the damp ground. Wade eased his grip on Mindy's shoulder and let his own body relax a few seconds before rising to his feet.

Holding Mindy's hand, Wade approached the hunting stand, watching Sam and the deputies gathering evidence from inside and around the blind. He motioned for Mindy to sit on the ground and he sat next to her in silence. Eventually, Sam noticed them and walked over and knelt beside them.

"I didn't see you walk up."

"We've just been here a minute. I didn't want to disturb you and your guys while you're working. What have you found?" Wade nodded toward the hunting stand as he asked.

"Not much." Sam shook her head. "Somebody killed him in the middle of the logging road. It looks like he drove here to meet someone else because there's another set of car tracks out there next to where Kenny's car is sitting. From what we can tell he was taken out of his car, killed in the road and then dragged from the road to the stand. One set of footprints along the drag line, so we assume there is only one perp."

"How was he killed, Sam?"

"Looks like one shot to the back of his head with the projection indicating he was below the shooter. You know, kind of in a kneeling position."

"So it was an execution."

"That's how it looks right now."

"I was hoping we were through with those."

"Me too."

They stopped the conversation as they watched the deputies bring the body of Kenny Thigpen down the stairs of the hunting stand in a body bag. Several of the deputies carried sacks of material back toward the logging road.

"Tell me what you guys saw when you first got here."

"Mindy went up the stairs first. I didn't see anything or hear anything until she discovered the body and—uh, let me take the lead."

Wade winked at Mindy.

Mindy nodded.

"I got to the top of the stairs and opened the door and turned on my flashlight before going in. You know, in case there was a bat or a squirrel in there. That's when I saw Kenny. Only I didn't recognize him, slumped over in the chair. It was obvious he was dead and I kind of lost it and jumped back down the ladder and let Wade take over."

"Okay, and Wade, I assume you went on up and opened the door again to see what frightened Mindy." Sam so subtlety let Mindy know that she was aware how scared Mindy was.

"I eased the door open with my rifle barrel and peered inside. As Mindy said, Kenny was slumped over in the chair, but there wasn't any doubt if he was alive or not. Neither of us went inside the stand, so nothing in there should be disturbed."

"Excellent. We have an uncontaminated crime scene for once. I don't know what to say."

"A '*Thank you*' would be appropriate, don't you think?" Wade grinned.

"Yes, and thank you, if you need to hear it. I appreciate it you didn't sit in the chair with Kenny."

"Well, Mindy wanted to, but I talked her out of it rather quickly."

Mindy nodded her head in agreement, still in a bit of shock and not fully comprehending the conversation between Sam and Wade.

"Oh, Wade. You have some animals to recover."

"Do what?"

"Yeah, whoever dragged Kenny's body in broke the lock on the gate and left the gate open a bit."

"Man, that's just great," Wade said, shaking his head in sarcasm. "Why is it that animals only go one way when there is a gate open? None of them ever come in. They always go out."

"Seems like it, doesn't it?"

"Yeah, could you tell how many got out?"

"From what I saw, it was at least one red stag and two

blackbucks, probably bucks since the tracks had dew drops and were the same size."

"Sam, you have more experience than I do with escaped animals. What do I have to do?"

"First, recover the animals, either alive or dead. It's your choice. Then you have to file a report with the state describing what happened, how you dealt with it and what you'll do to prevent it."

"Let's see. I can recover the animals. They won't go very far, I'm guessing. I can tell the state what happened and what I did in response. It's the last requirement I'm struggling with."

Sam grinned. "Do you mean how you'll prevent this? Put up a sign that says dead people can't trespass or you're going to shoot them again."

Even Mindy could not refrain from giggling.

"What else did you guys find outside the gate, Sam?"

"The usual. We found the tire tracks from the vehicle and footprints from Kenny and another guy. No cigarette butts or anything we can get DNA from. No hotel keys dropped by mistake. No rental car receipts or anything else that's going to make this easy to solve. But we found one thing in Kenny's pocket that will need some explaining."

Wade's eyes arched. "What's that, Sam?"

"It's a piece of paper that says '*one hour*' and has your name scribbled beside it."

4 SATURDAY MORNING
EVERGREEN PLANTATION

Wade gripped the steering wheel of the ATV so tight his fingers hurt on the way back to pick up Bruce and Mandy. Mindy was almost a puddle, molded as close to Wade's side as possible. Neither said anything on the trip between the stands. Halfway between the stands, Wade's mouth fell open when he saw Bruce and Mandy walking toward them along the ATV trail.

He pulled up alongside the father and daughter.

"I'm so sorry, Wade." Bruce began. Then he saw Mindy still cowering beside Wade and turned to Mandy. "You were right, Honey. Something is wrong."

Mandy leapt to Mindy's side of the vehicle and the twins hugged and communicated in a telepathic sense beyond the capability of humans that are not twins to understand.

"Bruce, what happened to you guys? Is everything okay?"

"Yeah, only it seems Mandy sensed something was wrong with Mindy right before daylight. I kept telling her she was okay, and you were with her, but she wouldn't listen. We didn't shoot anything because she kept insisting that we find Mindy because Mindy was in a stressful situation. I tried hard to talk her out of it, Wade. But when you guys were late picking us up, I gave in and we started looking for you guys. I wasn't sure which way to go, but Mandy said she felt like you were in this direction."

"Wow!" Wade eyed the twins closely. He had heard of the extrasensory ability of twins to feel each other's stress levels and pain, but he had not believed it until now.

I'll never question it again! This is amazing!

Wade explained the morning events to Bruce and Mandy, although Mandy was barely listening. He omitted the part about the piece of paper being found in Kenny's pocket with his name on it.

"No wonder Mandy went crazy in the stand. She kept squirming in the seat and standing in the blind. Somehow she knew Mindy was in peril, although she wasn't really in peril, but she was stressed to the max, I bet."

"That would be a safe bet, Bruce. We'll have to get her some counseling, I'm afraid. She's pretty shook up."

"I'm okay, Detective Ranger."

The voice behind Wade startled him and made him jump in his seat. Mindy was speaking as coherently as he had ever heard her.

"Mandy and I decided we must accept this as a part of life and to make the best of it."

The twins looked at each other and put their arms around the other one. Mindy continued. "I lost my focus for a little while, but Mandy helped me regain it. Now we can help you."

"Unbelievable, but great. I mean, from just a few minutes ago until now, the transformation is unbelievable."

Then he stopped and frowned.

"This doesn't mean you plan to be a part of the investigation, does it? You don't have any authority to help."

"We've got just as much authority as you do, Detective Ranger. You're not in the FBI anymore, and the appointment as a Federal Investigator was for Rachel's case only. So we have just as much right to investigate as you do." Mindy's jaw clenched in her determination.

"Do you remember that you were kidnapped in that case and if I hadn't figured out who had you, there's no telling what would have happened. Besides, I'm still officially listed as a Federal Investigator."

Mandy responded, "We knew you were coming. Besides, we would have figured out how to deal with him, eventually."

I hate arguing with the twins. They come from right field, left field, the cornfield and the Field of Dreams all at the same time. How can I win this one? Probably can't. The next best thing to do is pretend to go along with them and keep them busy on side issues far away from the main investigation.

"All right, but you have to do exactly as I tell you. You only communicate through me and not directly with Sam. If she gets a hint you're helping me, she will skin all of us alive and throw us in the Pearl River for the turtles. Can you agree to that?"

Both twins nodded, but were looking at the ground when they did.

"Ladies, I need your assurance. I don't want to impede Sam's investigation and I don't want you getting in the way of it either."

The twins mumbled to each other in voices so low Wade could not discern the words. Mindy spoke for the pair of them.

"We agree, Wade. We won't impede Sam's investigation."

"And you will do exactly as I say if you help me?"

"Yes, we will."

"Good luck, Wade. You'll need it with these two helping you." Bruce laughed.

The quartet rode in silence back to the Lodge. While Bruce, the twins and the rest of the hunters and guides ate a hearty breakfast, Wade was on the phone with the Mississippi Department of Wildlife. He burst into the dining room and motioned for the girls to follow him. When they arrived in his office, he pulled out three rifles.

"These are dart guns, ladies. I never knew why they had more than one of these before, but now I do. I talked to the Department of Wildlife and told them what happened. They suggested we dart the animals that escaped. If, and only if, we can't dart them, then we need to eliminate them."

"Is that a fancy way of saying if we can't take them alive, then we shoot them?"

"That's what it is. We'll take some corn down by the gate they escaped from and pour it out on the ground. Normally, hunting directly over corn is illegal in Mississippi, but we've got permission to use it in this case. My bet is that the two Blackbucks and the Stag will travel along the fence, trying to get back to familiar ground. When they reach the corn, they'll recognize the gate and linger there long enough eating corn for us to get a shot at them."

"Won't they run off when we hit them with a dart?"

"Probably will, but I've planned for that. I'm loading the darts with a heavier dose of cocktail than usual."

Mindy interrupted. "We might have some of that cocktail for ourselves."

"It's not that kind of cocktail. This is a combination of two drugs, Xylazine and Telozol. It'll knock them out, especially with the dosages I'm putting in the darts. This cocktail is more like a super-sized dose of GHB. You know, the date drug."

Both girls' heads bobbed up and down, fully aware of the effects of GHB.

"I've heard of girls whose drinks have been spiked with that stuff. But from what I've heard, it has different effects on different girls." Mandy shook her head and ran her hands through her strawberry-blonde hair.

"You're right, Mandy. How much someone weighs, the amount of GHB used, the amount of alcohol consumed prior to being drugged, the girl's immune system and who knows what else all cause the effects to vary. The same is true with animals. They all react differently."

"What if they run off?"

"We've experienced some bucks that were all keyed up during the rut that ran off after being darted. Between the adrenaline and the built-up testosterone levels, it took a while for the drugs to take effect. Some of them went quite a way."

"How did you find them?"

"We've got these." Wade held up some of the longest darts the twins had ever seen. "In this end, we put the cocktail. In the other end is a transmitter. It sends out a signal that we can track with this receiver."

He held up an antenna attached to a set of headphones.

"We can get a reading on their location from several hundred yards. Hopefully, the dart will stay in the animal until he or she succumbs to the drug."

"Where do we aim?"

"Some folks like to shoot them in the neck to get the

cocktail in the bloodstream quickly. I prefer shooting them in their big butts. It's a bigger target with a bigger tolerance to prevent something bad happening. These darts are being propelled by a .22 caliber shell. They can cause a lot of damage if they hit in the wrong place on an animal. I've seen what they do when they hit a spinal cord or if an animal gets gut-shot with a dart. It's not a pretty picture, so let's make sure of our shots."

"Okay, the butt it is. Do you want us to shoot the stag or the blackbucks first?"

"Why don't you two try for the blackbucks and I'll try for the stag? Okay?"

The twins nodded in agreement.

"Wade, one more thing."

"What is it, Mindy?"

"Suppose we're successful and we get the animals back alive. What happens if a hunter shoots them? Won't the drugs still be in the animals make them dangerous to eat?"

"Excellent question, Mindy. If we get them alive, we'll put them in a side pen to recover. The retention time for this cocktail is about thirty days, but we'll leave them in the side pens for around two months just to make sure all the drugs are out of their systems before we put them back in the hunting area."

"Man, you've thought of everything, haven't you?"

"Not everything. I don't know how I'll solve a murder case with Sam on one side of it and you two on the other side."

5 SATURDAY AFTERNOON
EVERGREEN PLANTATION

WADE HAD SECOND THOUGHTS ABOUT INVOLVING THE twins in the capture of the animals that escaped through the open gate. They were inexperienced and unpredictable. He could only guess how they would react to being on the ground twenty feet from a red stag that could easily kill them. Regardless, he invited them and now all three of them were sitting behind a huge fallen tree on the other side of the logging road from the gate. Wade poured out four buckets of corn on the ground in front of them, much more than he normally thought necessary. He figured the first chance would be the best chance to get the animals, so a little extra corn couldn't hurt.

They sat behind the log for about thirty minutes without seeing any animals when Mindy squirmed. Wade motioned for her to be quiet, but she continued to squirm. Suddenly, she jumped up and began taking off her pants.

"I'm sitting on an ant bed," she whispered, but not too quietly.

Sure enough, Wade saw the ants crawling up her bare legs after she removed her pants.

"I don't blame you. They're everywhere!" he exclaimed as he started helping Mandy brush the ants off of Mindy. When he reached her panties, he hesitated.

Mindy looked at him, and then Mandy laughed and pulled down her sister's underwear. Wade turned his back to Mindy, wanting to help her but not wanting to embarrass her.

"You've already seen me naked, Wade. Now get these damn ants off me!"

Wade again started helping Mandy pick the ants off her half-naked sister.

"There aren't that many ants on my butt, Wade. You can quit pinching me now."

Wade stopped picking ants and stepped back, stammering in an unintelligible mumble.

"I'm just kidding you. Get them off of me. I don't care where you have to pick them. Just get them off of me."

After only a few minutes, they removed all the ants from her body and Mindy stood there in between them.

"Are you going to let me have my clothes back now, Wade? Or am I going to stand here naked beside the road for the rest of the day?"

Turning a little red in the face, Wade extended his arms holding Mindy's pants.

"I was going to turn them inside out and get the rest of the ants off them before you put them back on."

"You really can't take a joke, can you? I was just kidding. I know you are trying to help."

"Why don't you girls go through the clothes and make sure you get all the ants? I'll be right back. Don't put these back on until I get back."

Wade handed the pants to Mindy and hurriedly walked

back toward the ATV parked a few hundred yards from the log.

When he returned, he held a small jar in his hands. He noticed that Mindy had put her panties back on, but not her pants.

"This is a balm we use for the animals for cuts and abrasions. It's loaded with aloe and will help with the stings and the pains. Just rub in on every bite you can find. It's heavy duty, so it shouldn't take too long to take effect."

Mandy laughed.

"They aren't hard to find. She's swelling up every place one of them bit her. Why don't you let me put that on, unless you really want to rub it in real deep?" Mandy didn't wait for an answer and held her hand out to take the lotion from Wade.

Wade pulled out another small container.

"What's that?"

"It's gas that I siphoned from the ATV. I'm going to pour it on that ant mound so we have no more trouble with them."

"Won't the Stag and the blackbuck smell it?"

"Mandy, as much as we've moved around and with the balm, they'll know we're here or at least that we've been around. I'm hoping they want a little corn more than they want to get away from us, at least for a minute or two until we can put a dart in them."

Wade marveled at the unabashed manner of Mindy as she held her arms above her head as Mandy rubbed the balm all over her body. Mandy didn't bother finding the welts of the bites, but applied the lotion in large doses everywhere, even inside Mindy's panties.

"Enjoying the show, Detective Ranger?" Mindy was laughing.

"I was just wondering if it was working. We've used it on whitetails, elk, blackbuck, fallow and axis, but they all have one thing in common; none of them can tell us if it really helped or not."

"It helps. I may have to get me some of that stuff. And you're right. It is heavy duty. It didn't take long at all to take the sting away."

"Good, now you can get dressed before your dad or Sam shows up wondering what we're doing."

"They'd probably both have a few questions for sure."

Wade turned his back toward Mindy.

"Don't you think it's a little late for that, Wade?"

"Maybe, but at least when you guys tell Sam, I can tell her I wasn't watching."

Both twins giggled.

Wade doused the ant nest with gas and then laid a piece of tarp over it. When he finished, Mindy had her clothes back on and was ready to resume their quest for the animals.

"Sorry, Wade. But I didn't know what else to do."

"There wasn't much else to do, Mindy. But I'd prefer if we kept this between us three, if you know what I mean."

"We understand, Wade. Sam might not see the humor in it like we did."

Wade just nodded.

The trio settled behind the log, waiting for the surrounding woods to become quiet. Even the wind came to a halt. Suddenly, the red stag appeared at the gate, seemingly out of nowhere. He stared directly at Wade and took a step in his direction. There was no doubt in Wade's mind that the stag knew he was there.

The stag took another step toward the log and then turned sideways and began eating the corn strewn on the ground. Wade slowly raised the dart gun and aimed right at the old stag's rear end.

I can't miss at this distance. Breath in. Breath out. Squeeze the trigger. Don't jerk it.

Wade heard the distinct '*thwack*' of the dart hitting the body of the stag before he realized he had fired the shot. Through the scope on the dart gun, he could only see a small fragment of the side of the animal, but he heard and then felt the reaction of the irate beast. In two steps and less than two seconds, the stag was soaring over the log that Wade and the twins crouched behind.

Wade instinctively rolled under the edge of the only cover available to him and pulled Mindy under the log with him. She grabbed Mandy and dragged her under the log. The stag, meanwhile, only ran ten yards past the log and turned around.

Wade's body froze in anticipation of another charge from the European version of the North American elk.

Why did I leave the rifle in the ATV? Wow, that was careless. Do we have time to jump to the other side of this log? This pistol is just gonna piss him off more than he already is, but it's all I have. I hope the twins will be okay while he's mauling me.

Wade pulled his pistol while keeping his eyes on the now still animal. When the stag lowered his head and antlers down until the horns were only about six inches from the ground, Wade aimed for the back of his spine. He heard, 'thwack, thwack' and saw two darts sticking out of the big stag's neck. The old bull raised his head and turned it slightly toward the twins, as if surprised by this sudden attack that he did not expect. He turned toward Mandy at the other end of the log from Wade, but his hind legs weren't getting clear messages from his brain. One or two teetering steps toward the trio were the best he could do before all four of his legs gave way and he crumbled to the ground. His antler tip fell on Wade's boot.

"Goodness gracious! You girls just saved my life!"

"I just peed all over myself!" Mandy exclaimed.

"I wish that was all I did on myself!" Mindy yelled in an equally loud voice.

"Damn, that was too close. I've never had one react like that before." Sweat poured down Wade's forehead and the back of his shirt was soaked. He had not realized how much the fear had gripped his body and then he was even more amazed at the twins' ability to react so quickly in that situation. He pulled his wedged boot from underneath the antlers and tried to stand on unsteady legs. Only the support of his hand on the log kept him from falling. He opted to sit on the fallen tree to prevent further embarrassment.

When Wade shifted his gaze from the stag to the twins, he noticed they weren't doing much better than him. Mindy collapsed against the log, still staring at the stag. Mandy closed her eyes with her head resting on the log.

"I want to tell you guys how grateful I am. That was amazing. What made you do that? Thank you once again."

"You're welcome, Wade. We didn't have time to think. We just reacted. I hope he's okay."

"He'll be fine," Wade assured Mindy, although he wasn't so sure himself. He had never hit one of his animals with six cc's of cocktail, four of them directly in the bloodstream. He had no idea if the stag would make it or not.

"There's some toilet paper in the glove compartment of the ATV if you really need it."

"I do."

"Me, too."

The twins raced up the logging road toward the ATV, leaving Wade alone with the old stag. He pulled out a towel he had anticipated using under much calmer circumstances and wrapped it around the stag's head, blindfolding him. Then he pulled two cotton balls out of his pocket and stuffed one in each ear of the bull, stifling his sense of hearing. Wade knew the stag was still aware of the movement around him, and muffling some of his sensory abilities would help keep him calm until they could call the other guides to bring the tractor with the front-end loader to move him to a holding pen.

"Now you behave while I get these darts out of you." Wade reached the two in his neck with ease and gently pulled them out. He had to fight the brush to get the one out of his hip.

When he finished, he looked at the old stag with admiration.

"I'm going to call you 'Marine'. You didn't care what the odds were. You were going to charge ahead, regardless. Yes, Sir. You will be known as 'Marine' from now on around here."

Wade dabbed a generous portion of balm on the two wounds in the neck and the one in the bull's hip. The creamy yellow lotion helped clot the blood still oozing down the beast's neck.

This will make you feel better, Marine. Who knows? One day you may forgive me for doing this to you. I'll promise you this. I won't let any hunter I'm sitting with take a shot at you. It's up to you to avoid the rest of them.

Wade reloaded all three dart guns while leaning against the log, watching the old stag only inches from him. The clatter of the return of the twins made him glance in that direction. They stopped in the middle of the old logging road and froze, looking toward the gate. Wade's gaze followed theirs to focus on the two blackbucks munching on the corn, unaware of the rest of the world.

Knowing that the bucks had an eyesight magnification over ten times that of humans, Wade waited until both were facing the other direction before bringing one rifle to his shoulder. He saw the dart hit the intended target right in the rump. The buck skipped twice and continued to feed, barely raising his head. Wade put the empty rifle down and picked up another one. He sighted on the second buck and gently squeezed the trigger.

The second buck took two big kangaroo hops to the edge of the woods. The first buck faltered and stagger, eventually succumbing to the cocktail mix and crumpling in a pile. The second buck unsteadily walked over to the first buck and sniffed him. When he got no response, the second buck prodded the first one with his horns. Within seconds, the buck fell directly on top of the first one.

The twins waited for a few seconds and then raced down the hill. Wade put his finger up to his lips and motioned for them to come behind the log with him. He handed them each a towel and some cotton balls and showed them how he had blindfolded the stag and stuffed the balls inside his ears. He motioned for them to do the same with the blackbucks.

When the twins finished with the blackbucks, Wade phoned the Lodge and asked for someone to bring the tractor down to pick up the animals. The trio then sat on the log and watched the sedated bucks and the stag.

"Been an eventful day, hasn't it?"

"No, getting married, having a baby and getting divorced on the same day would be an eventful day. This one was WAY beyond that!" Mindy wasn't pulling any punches.

"Maybe we should change our slogan to 'Come experience the most fun you can have with your clothes on' or something like that." Wade was grinning.

"Except I didn't keep mine on all day, if you remember."

"We'll have to change that to read, 'Come enjoy the experience of a lifetime, with or without your clothes'."

"That should get you more business, I'd think. Only I wouldn't mention the dead body in the stand when you're doing all of that advertising."

"That might put a little damper on the excitement."

Mandy joined the conversation.

"You could say something like 'You'll never match the thrills you will discover at the Evergreen Plantation' and that would be the absolute truth. I doubt if any of the other ranches have dead bodies in their stands."

"I hope they don't."

"If you let us, we'll find out who put him there."

"We don't even know why he was put there. We could have gone weeks without someone hunting that stand. The wind has to be right, the hunter has to walk a good way off the trail to get to it and the timing has to be right. Come to think of it, nobody should have known Mindy and I would hunt that stand this morning. I didn't decide on it until I walked out and checked the wind after I got up this morning. There is no way somebody beat us to the stand and stuffed Kenny in there after I decided we would hunt there."

Wade ran his hand through his hair.

"How in the world would you go about finding out who put him there?"

"He's a City Councilman. Everybody down at City

Hall talks about the latest news, and this will far and away become the latest news. Don't you remember last time? All we have to do is show a little skin to the computer nerds and we'll get whatever we want."

Mindy winked at Mandy. "Works with you anyway. But I have to show more than a LITTLE skin, it seems."

Wade's complexion turned red.

"I didn't ask you to get naked. You could have let those ants eat you up, you know."

"But how do I know you didn't sit me on that ant hill on purpose?"

Wade looked away and then at the ground.

"I guess you'll just have to trust me on that one."

Mindy scooted right next to Wade on the log and put her arm around him.

"I trust you Wade. Otherwise, you wouldn't have seen any skin today or any other day."

"Thank you, Mindy. I hear the tractor coming."

6 SUNDAY MORNING
EVERGREEN

"Sam, I don't get it."

"Get what, Wade?"

"Everything. How did whoever put Kenny in the stand know we would hunt there? Why did Kenny have my name written on a note in his pocket?"

Wade took another sip from his cup of Community Coffee at the Evergreen Café. He had instructed the guides where to put the hunters before leaving the Evergreen Plantation to meet Sam for a late breakfast. As the unofficial gathering place in the city, the restaurant was astir with activity and rumors.

"How well did you know Kenny?"

We interviewed him in the Rachel Chastain case, but, if I remember correctly, he had an ironclad alibi."

"That's right. He was out of town. Off in Atlanta or Memphis or something like that when she was killed."

"Was he part of that project that everyone kept so secret?"

"He was at one meeting at least, but I don't know how

in-depth that meeting was and even if they discussed the project at that one."

"I still wish I knew what that was all about, Sam."

"Me, too. Even if it turned out not having anything to do with Rachel's death, I wanted to find out why everyone was scared to mention it."

"I'm trying to remember if we ever talked with Kenny after that first interview."

"I don't believe we did. We had a whole list of likely suspects, and we needed no more." Sam laughed. "And none of our suspects turned out to be the killer. No one will ever confuse us with Sherlock and Watson, I'm afraid."

"Didn't we find out if he was especially close to Rachel? Did Kenny have relations with her?"

"He said he had a brief relationship with her. None of them knew about each other, so he could have had an ongoing relationship with her and no one would have ever known, except the killer. And he's not talking."

"Back to my original question. Why did they put Kenny's body in that hunting stand with my name on a note in his pocket?"

"When did you decide that you and Mindy were going there?"

"Not until yesterday morning. I got up like I usually do and got a cup of coffee. Then I went outside to drink my coffee and check the weather. Yesterday morning was cool and damp, so the bucks would move late into mid morning. The wind was blowing out of the northwest, and I positioned the hunters so the deer wouldn't smell them on the stands if they took their normal paths from feeding areas to bedding areas. That stand was perfect for the weather."

"Who did you tell?"

"Nobody, not even Bruce. I had some second thoughts

on the way to the stand about switching, but went with the one I chose."

The waitress refilled their coffee cups. Her smile strained and there was no joy in her eyes.

"Would you like to order now?"

Sam answered for both of them.

"We'll just have the usual."

Wade didn't know what the '*usual*' breakfast was for Sam at the Evergreen Café, but didn't particularly care this morning. He handed his menu back to the waitress without opening it.

"Nobody could have known you would take Mindy to that stand. What is the likelihood that you would have assigned one of the other guides to the stand?"

"Given the conditions, probably ten to fifteen percent. But how many people even know it exists? We don't exactly publish our stand locations in the Evergreen Weekly."

Wade rubbed his temples in exasperation.

"I hadn't thought of that. Connie and I grew up out there taking care of the place, but most of the folks in Evergreen have never been out there. They wouldn't have any idea how to get to any of the stands, much less one like that one. It isn't on one of the main ATV trails."

April, the owner of the café, appeared at their table side.

"Wade, Sam," she nodded.

"Good morning, April. Looks like business is still good."

"Better than ever, Sam. It's amazing how good business is when we take the trouble to cook fresh food instead of all the frozen garbage."

"Great. You've done a good job since taking over, April. Congratulations."

"Couldn't have done it without your help, Sam. That's why I wanted to tell you something."

"What is it, April?"

"Sam, you know how it is with waitresses. Most people think we're part of the furniture and don't pay us any mind when they're talking. It's as if we're not even there."

Sam nodded, feeling a little guilty for not acknowledging their waitress this morning.

"Wade, I overheard some people talking, but I'm not sure if it means anything at all."

Wade was all ears and leaned toward April. As she was about to continue, their waitress appeared with a tray of food. Wade discovered the "*usual*" meant two biscuits, two strips of bacon, two sausage patties, two slices of ham, three eggs sunny side up and a dollop of grits covered in butter.

After distributing the food along with glasses of orange juice, the waitress disappeared back into the kitchen. April had also vanished.

"I wonder what that was all about."

"I don't know, Wade. We'll find out, eventually."

They picked at their food, not overly hungry after their brief discussion with April. The sausage, bacon, and ham were fresh, and the biscuits were straight out of the oven. On a normal day, Wade would have devoured them. But today, he was more interested in finishing the conversation with April. He picked at his food and occasionally glanced at the kitchen doors.

After what seemed like an eternity, Wade noticed April stick her head out of the kitchen and carefully scan the entire room. Satisfied with what she saw, she again took a position next to their table.

"Wade, I overheard Kenny and a lady talking last week. I didn't hear the entire conversation. I would have been too obvious if I stayed by their table all the time, but I mingled with the folks next to Kenny's table to hear some things."

"Who was she, April?"

"Never seen the lady before or since. It's been so long since I've seen Kenny that I almost didn't recognize him without his suit. All of this may just be a coincidence, Wade."

"No problem. I appreciate you trying to help. What did you hear?"

"I heard a bit here and a bit there, but from putting it all together somebody wants to take the Plantation from you."

"Do what?"

April quickly looked around the room, but none of the remaining patrons looked up at Wade's tone.

"That's what I heard, Wade. Somebody wants your property, and Kenny was looking at ways to get it from you. Something about a tax lien on the books that nobody knows about."

"But I paid my taxes at the end of the year just like everybody else. I've only had the place for less than a year, so I couldn't be far behind on any of them."

April frowned. "This would have been from before you owned the place. It would have been from a long time ago."

"How could I have title to the place if there's a tax problem with it?"

"Did you do a title search when you got it?"

"Under the circumstances, the government owned it before me and I assumed the title was clear."

"I can't stay here talking with you, but I'd look into it if I were you."

April disappeared into the kitchen.

Wade shook his head.

"How could they transfer a property to me if they didn't have a clear title?"

Sam took a sip of tea. "It happens all the time.

Unfortunately, it sometimes involves our department when the disputes get out of hand. Property lines and title disputes are fairly common."

"I can't believe this!"

"We can get it straight, Wade."

"How?"

"Two ways that I can think of. Get a title company or real estate attorney to do a title search first. That'll tell you if there are any liens against the property. Next, have it surveyed. Once you get it surveyed, you could put the results in the local paper and give public notice. Then anyone that would dispute the boundaries has ninety days to file a claim."

"Seems like a tremendous expense for nothing to me. I either own the Plantation or I don't."

Sam shook her head.

"Only if life were that simple, Wade."

"To get it surveyed, we're probably talking about fifty to a hundred grand. I don't have that kind of money."

"It might cost you more if you don't. I had an uncle that bought a cabin on two hundred acres next to a seven acre pond. The guy that had it before him had owned it for twenty-two years. My uncle got sick and put it up for sale. The new buyer had the property surveyed and found out the property line ran right across the pond and through the middle of the cabin. Since it had been less than thirty years, my uncle had to buy out the true owner of the rest of the property before he could re-sell it. He had to overpay for the land under question in a circumstance like that."

Wade wiped his mouth with the napkin. "Nothing is simple, is it, Sam?"

"You said you didn't have that kind of money. The Plantation is worth several times that, isn't it?"

He nodded.

"Sure. The land alone is worth way more than that. The Lodge is worth more than that. The animals are worth more than that. But that doesn't mean I have enough cash in the bank to pay for it. Do you know how much cash it takes to run a place like the Plantation? The feed, vet bills, maintenance and repair on the buildings and the equipment, property taxes, catering expenses, guides and all the rest?"

He paused.

"Of course you do. You own a place just like it. The difference is that you have established your place, and it has a positive cash flow. The Plantation suffered, shall we say, under the previous management and I haven't had enough time to build up enough clients to keep it cash-flow positive."

"I didn't realize you were in a predicament. You never mentioned it to me and I'm your fiancée. We're supposed to share our problems."

"It's not your problem yet. If I couldn't get it up to speed before we got married, I was going to tell you. I don't want there to be any surprises when we get married."

"It is my problem because I love you. Whatever your problem is it's mine too."

He shook his head. "Not yet, Sam."

"Wade, like you said, our ranch is well established. We make enough off of Ol' Mose, our breeder buck, to support all of our operations. When you throw in the other bucks, the does and the semen, we do pretty well. I can write a check for you today."

"Sam, do you know how bad I would feel taking a check from you?"

"I promise you. I wouldn't even notice it. We haven't

discussed my finances at all. So now is as good of a time as ever."

Wade lowered his voice. "Sam, I'm not marrying your checkbook. I love you, not your money."

"I know that, Wade. But you told me where you were financially. It's only fair that I tell you where I'm at, so there aren't any surprises."

"Okay, but I'm still not taking any of your money."

Sam's voice rose.

"You're as stubborn as a jackass, Wade Dalton. When I tell you I wouldn't miss the money at all, I wouldn't. I am a multi-let's say I am very well off financially. When Daddy set up the deer breeding business, he kept fifty percent and gave Connie and me twenty-five percent each. He set it up, so he pays for all the expenses out of his fifty percent. That means that Connie and I each get to keep twenty-five percent of all the revenue with no expenses subtracted. Do you know how much our deer breeding operations generate every year?"

"Based on the limited knowledge I have, it's several million dollars per year."

"You're right. Several million. I take one hundred thousand from that revenue plus the salary from my job, and that's what I spend every year. The rest goes into tax-exempt municipal bonds, and I make about five percent tax free from those every year."

"Sam, from what you're telling me, you're rich! I mean, way rich! Why didn't you tell me before?"

"It's not something I ever talk about. I don't really have any expenses. I live with Daddy at the ranch so I don't have any electricity bills, water bills, insurance bills or any of that stuff. The county furnishes me a car and a telephone and I can use one of our farm trucks if I need to for personal use so I don't even buy my gasoline. So I guess you could say I'm financially sound."

'That might be the understatement of the year."

"Let's put it this way, Wade. Once we're married, neither you nor I, or any of our children will have to worry about having enough."

"Sam, I knew you were doing okay, but I never dreamed you did that well." Wade paused. "But I'm still not gonna take your money. We aren't married yet."

"Men! You guys have two things that make life complicated. Your egos and your dicks. And I'm not sure which one is worse!"

Sam slammed her napkin on the table and abruptly rose and strode toward the exit door.

I messed that up. Was it my ego or my dick? Does it matter?

Wade motioned for the waitress and made the sign of a check mark with his hand. She came over to the table with the check in one hand and a pot of coffee in the other. Wade nodded when she presented the coffee to him.

"Do you know who the best real estate attorney is in town?"

"There's only one that I know of that specializes in real estate. That would be Collier Templet over on Court Street."

"Collier Templet on Court?"

"Yeah, not far from City Hall and the Courthouse. Now it's spelled, t-e-m-p-l-e-t, but it's pronounce like 'Tom Play'. Sometimes people from out of town don't know that."

I wonder how long I have to live in Evergreen to not be an out-of-towner.

"I know that name." Wade rubbed the side of his head. "That's right. He handled the paperwork for the transfer of the Plantation. I talked with his assistant a lot more than him. Seems like a nice enough guy."

"But he's not open today, with it being Sunday and all. You might try to catch him in the morning."

"Thanks, I'll do that."

Wade sipped on the hot coffee while he pondered the situation. His eyes were staring down at the floor when a gorgeous set of legs appeared in their view. Raising his eyes slowly, they focused on an hour-glass figure and a creamy complexion under a perfectly groomed head of blonde hair.

7 SUNDAY MORNING
EVERGREEN

"May I sit?"

Wade fumbled out of his chair and pulled out a chair for the lady.

"I'm sorry. I was kinda thinking about something."

"I saw her leave, and she didn't look too happy."

"You can say that again."

"I assume you're Mr. Dalton, Wade Dalton."

"Yes, I am."

"I'm Victoria Engle. My friends call me Vicki."

"Hello, Vicki."

"Wade, I represent a firm in Jackson. One of our clients asked me to contact you."

"Okay—"

"I know this is unusual, but this is an unusual situation for us."

"Uh, that is a fact."

"I'll get straight to the point. Our client would like to know if you'd be willing to sell the Evergreen Plantation."

Wade looked at her quizzically, his eyebrows arched.

"Why?"

Victoria coughed. "He'd like to buy it."

"Why?"

"Wade, we don't get involved with our clients' motives. We're a private firm. People come to us when they want to buy or sell something, either a business or a home or some land. This client came to us wanting to buy some land."

"He wanted to buy some land, or he wanted to buy the Evergreen Plantation?"

"I'm not at liberty to discuss everything our clients may tell us. I'm sure you understand our role and the confidence our clients place in us. They want to know whatever they discuss will be held in the strictest of confidence. Now, having said all of that, I didn't hear a 'No' from you."

"Did you hear there was a dead body found on my property yesterday?"

"I came in last night and I heard about that. I'm afraid there aren't many secrets in a town like Evergreen."

"You're right."

Wades eyebrows wrinkled. "Vicki, did you say you're from Jackson?"

"That's right."

"Where is your client from?"

She shifted uncomfortably in her chair. "Again, our client has asked that all information about him remain confidential at this point. I'm sure you understand."

"I don't understand. Why would they not want to say who they are?"

"Because word would get around and they would get bombarded with folks that have a couple of acres here and a couple of acres there for sale. That is not the market our client is in, so hence the anonymity."

"So how do I know this offer is legit?"

"If we come to an agreement on the price, I'm

authorized to arrange a flight for you tomorrow to Houston to meet with us. At the meeting, we'll have an Intent to Purchase form ready for your signature and a certified check in the amount equal to five percent of the purchase price. That deposit will be yours to keep no matter if we close the deal or not."

"Are you kidding?"

Victoria smiled. "My client is serious."

"I want to make sure I understand you, Vicki. Your client wants to buy the Evergreen Plantation. He wants to remain anonymous for reasons unknown. But he's willing to put up five percent of the purchase price with a certified check, and if anything goes wrong with the deal, I get to keep the five percent."

She nodded. "That is correct."

Wade leaned back in his chair. "So how much is your client willing to pay for the privilege of owning the Evergreen Plantation?"

"I have been authorized to offer you twenty million dollars."

Wade's mouth fell open, stunned at the words he heard.

"Vicki, how familiar are you with the local real estate market?"

"Not too familiar. Why?"

"My guess is that you know the offer is way over any appraisal that will come with the land."

"My client is not worried about appraisals. It's a cash offer. No financing is involved. No appraisal will be required or performed. However, time is of the essence with the offer. It's only good for two days. If we don't have an answer within the next two days, they will withdraw the offer."

Why are they offering me twenty million dollars? It isn't

worth half that much. Maybe a little more than half. It seems odd that a day after a dead body is found on the property, somebody wants to buy it. This 'somebody' doesn't want me to know his identity. Something really smells bad about this deal. The only way to find out what is wrong with it is to play along.

"Let's say I'm interested, but not ready to commit, Vicki. Where do we go from there?"

"Let me check. It will only take a minute or two. Will you excuse me?" Vicki rose from her chair.

Wade half-stood and plopped back down in his chair, bewilderment written on his face. The waitress appeared at his table-side with a full pot of coffee.

Vicki returned to the table.

"Okay, here's the plan. We'll send a plane over to pick you up in the morning at seven sharp. To keep on schedule, we'll use the private airstrip on the east side of Evergreen. Do you know where that is?"

"I'm familiar with it."

"Good, we'll have the plane there waiting for you. We'll take you to Houston and have a limo pick you up at the airport. The limo will take you to a hotel right outside the airport premises. When you get there, go to the front desk and ask to be taken to the Evergreen conference. They'll make sure you get to the right place."

"What paperwork do I need to bring, Vicki?"

Vicki was not prepared for this question. She stammered and stuttered before saying, "Don't worry about bringing any, Wade. My clients have everything they need to meet with you."

"Okay. What—?"

"Why don't you wait until tomorrow morning to ask your questions. My clients are much more qualified and informed about this situation. Normally, I'd be in a better position to answer all of your questions, but this is a unique situation."

A line of sweat formed at the top of Vicki's head.

"No problem. Tell your clients I'll be happy to meet with them tomorrow."

"Good. Don't be late."

Vicki almost ran to the front door of the restaurant.

April suddenly appeared at Wade's table.

"Wade, I wasn't trying to eavesdrop, but there's something about that lady that bothers me. She's the one that met with Kenny the other day and she paid in cash. Most people use a debit card or a credit card. But more than that, she would barely talk to me. I mean, I tried to make small-talk and she wouldn't say hardly anything."

"I appreciate it, April. I'll be careful."

"One more thing, Wade."

"What is it?"

"She told you she was from Houston, didn't she?"

Wade shook his head. "She said she was from Jackson..

"Then why is she driving a car with private Louisiana plates on it?"

There was one diner who knew why Vicki had Louisiana plates.

8 SUNDAY MORNING
EVERGREEN

THE MURDERER SAT ONLY THREE TABLES FROM WADE, holding a newspaper in front of his face. No one paid attention. The news of the discovery of Kenny Thigpen's body had the residents of Evergreen buzzing like a beehive. Everyone had a story about the dead man. Some were good. Others not.

The killer slumped in his chair. The body should not have been discovered for months. A high game-proof fence surrounded over three thousand acres that made up the Plantation. With the few hunters booking outings, the murderer assumed the remote stand would not be visited this soon.

It was not the Plantation that the man wanted. But he had to go through the owner of the Plantation to get what he desired. Desire with a continuous roaring fire that seared his soul. If the body had been discovered in six months or a year. Wade would have had a hard time explaining why his name was in a dead man's pocket and hidden in his remote deer stand.

However, Wade had witnesses for last night. With no

doubt about the timing of the death, the ex-FBI agent had an ironclad alibi. How could things have gone so wrong?

He could only catch bits and pieces of the conversation between Wade and Sam. As soon as he heard about the cash flow issues at the Plantation, an idea formed. A man with those kinds of problems usually made poor short-term decisions. A quick phone call and the alternative plan emerged. The woman did not like it. He did not tell her the entire plan. Only that he needed to get Wade out of town for the next couple of days.

A few minutes later, Vicki Engle entered the Evergreen Café.

Then he listened to Vicki make the proposal. When Wade agreed, the killer wanted to yell out and bang the table. The plan, formed in a minute, had a chance of working.

Then he heard Pearl's brief conversation with the owner of the Plantation. Vicki had become a loose end. But first things first. He had a lot to do before morning.

9 SUNDAY AFTERNOON
EVERGREEN PLANTATION

"Welcome back."

Wade raised his eyebrows when he found Mindy waiting for him at the Lodge.

"Did your sister forget to take you with her?"

"No, silly. I didn't go out hunting this morning. I can't go out hunting without my own special guide."

"May I ask why not or is that a secret?"

"No secret, Detective Ranger. The other guides might try to take advantage of a naïve young girl like me." Mindy said with a sly grin.

"Young, yes. Naïve, not a chance. I might have to pay them combat pay to spend an afternoon in the stand with you."

"You don't have to worry about that. I sent them all home. I told them you were the only guide for me so they might as well go see their girlfriends before they go see their wives."

"I bet that went over real well."

"It did. They told me to make sure you don't get into any trouble, though. Not sure by what they meant by that."

Again, she had a sly little grin.

"And what would Sam say about you and I being out here by ourselves?"

Mindy looked serious now.

"She knows I'm all talk and you're all walk, so she wouldn't be concerned in the least."

"Huh?"

"She knows I talk about sex all the time, but do nothing. She also knows you never talk about it and you only do something about it with her. So she isn't worried about me or Mandy. She doesn't take us seriously."

"I'm not so sure about that, Mindy."

"I am. Otherwise, would she let us play in your lake naked while you watched us? I don't think so. Especially if she thought you might try to do something. She's got you right where she wants you."

"If that's so, why are we not speaking to each other?"

Mindy looked up, surprised. "Uh oh. Did you guys have a fight?"

"She left me in the restaurant a little while ago without speaking."

"What did you guys fight about?"

"The only thing couples ever fight about, I guess. At least one of the top two, anyway."

"That'd be sex and money. Since you two are too shy to be talking about sex at a restaurant, I'm gonna guess it was about money."

"You're not as naïve as you would lead people to believe."

"Why does she need money? She's got a great job and from what I understand, their ranch is doing well. So why would she hit you up for money?"

"That's just it. She didn't hit me up for money."

"Then I really don't understand."

"She tried to give me money. Or loan me some money. The Plantation doesn't have a lot of clients, so our cash flow is limited. She offered to help until the cash flow improves."

"I didn't know that. I thought you were doing great here."

"We're doing okay. It takes a lot of cash to run a place like this and right now I don't have it."

"From what I'm gathering, you turned her offer down."

"What else could I do?"

Mindy slapped her forehead. "Duh! How about letting her help you?"

"That didn't seem appropriate."

A deep furrow crossed Mindy's forehead.

"Are sex and money the only things you guys think about all the time?"

Wade looked at her as though she could see right through his heart.

"That's what she said. Only she was a little more blunt about it."

"I don't blame her. I would have walked out myself."

"Why? I don't understand women."

"That's why I would have walked out. Guys just don't get it."

Wade shook his head and paced to the bay window overlooking the lake. He stared at the lake for a long time.

Mindy walked up beside him and put her arm around his waist.

"Girls love a man because they love him, not his job or his money and certainly not for sex. Guys think money will be the reason girls love them, but in most cases that just isn't true. Sure, almost all women want financial security, and some will take that over love. But what a woman genuinely wants is romance."

"I still don't see what that has to do with me refusing to take her money."

Mindy laughed and moved over to the window next to him.

"Because she saw an opportunity to help the man she loves. That man is so stubborn and egotistical that he's worried that she would think less of him if he accepted money from her. She wants to help because she loves you. You are refusing because of what she might think and she's trying her best to show you what she thinks by giving you the money. It's really not that complicated."

Wade shook his head.

"Sounds pretty complicated to me. No matter what I do, I'm sponging off my fiancée or I'm a stubborn jackass. Not much upside either way, is there?"

"Not as long as you have the idea that you need to be in control all the time, like most typical men."

Wade began pacing back and forth.

"So what do I do?"

"Take a dozen roses and go over there with your hat in your hand, or maybe in this case with your dick in your hand and apologize to begin with. Then thank her for her offer and accept it, even if it's a temporary loan. Pay it back as soon as possible with interest, and then you can feel good about not sponging off of her. Both of you will come out ahead."

"You 're smart for a naïve young lady."

"Before, you called me a girl. Have I graduated to being a lady now?"

"I guess you could say you have, at least in my opinion."

"Now nobody is gonna chase me around." Mindy

sighed. None of you guys get excited about having sex with a 'lady' as much as you do with a 'girl'. I thought I had a couple more years before that happened."

Wade grinned broadly.

"You don't have to worry about that. You and your sister are gonna drive guys crazy for quite a while, probably until you're old maids. I have no doubts about that."

Mindy looked relieved. "So do you still think I'm sexy?" The corners of her mouth turned up.

Wade just shook his head and started for the kitchen to get a cup of coffee. Just as he reached the door to the kitchen, he turned back toward her. "You are."

The brightest smile he'd ever seen covered her face.

He left her in the den of the Lodge, looking out over the lake. When he returned, he held two cups of coffee, one for each of them. "I'm going to have to apologize to you. I won't be able to take you out hunting in the morning."

"Why not?" Disappointment was evident as her body sagged slightly.

"It's a bit of a long story, but the gist of it is that someone has offered to buy the Plantation and I'm gonna fly over to Houston to meet with them in the morning. I haven't even told Sam yet."

Mindy put her hand to her mouth. "You're not gonna sell this place, are you?"

"I don't know. They made an offer I have to consider."

"Whatever it is, it's not worth it. There aren't many places like this in the whole world."

"I just told you about the cash flow problems."

"Yeah, but those are only temporary. If you sell the Plantation, that will be permanent."

He nodded. "I know. That's what bothers me among some other things."

"What other things?"

"The lady that made the offer for one. She just appeared out of nowhere. She didn't have a business card. She told me she was an agent from Mississippi, but she was driving a car with a Louisiana license plate and she wouldn't identify her clients. It all sounds a little fishy."

"Why didn't you tell Sam?"

"She'd already left the restaurant and I guess my pride wouldn't let me call her after that."

"Men," Mindy sighed, shaking her head.

Wade looked at the floor, knowing what he said confirmed everything Sam and Mindy had already told him about the faults of a man's pride. Now he dreaded calling Sam and admitting that she was right, but what choice did he have?

"I think I'll wait to tell Sam."

"I agree. Don't tell her yet."

"Those guys will want an answer tomorrow."

"So what? Didn't you say they offered you a bunch of money?"

"Way more than it's worth."

"Then they'll wait for an answer if they want it that bad. I don't know how much money you're talking about, but if they're willing to pay more than it's worth, then they'll be willing to give you a couple of days to get back to them."

"They said they were in a hurry and couldn't wait."

"And when guys are trying to get me to take my clothes off, they tell me a bunch of lies too."

Wade laughed. "I bet."

"You wouldn't believe some lines guys have used on both Mandy and me. Sometimes they will use them on both of us at the same time."

"Some guys will say almost anything to get what they want."

"One line I remember because he changed it when he tried it on Mandy. He asked both of us, 'Do you like chicken?' I answered, 'yes' and Mandy answered, 'no' when he used it on her later. I'd already told her he used it on me."

"So how is '*Do you like chicken?*' a pickup line?"

"When I said, '*yes*' he said '*Me, too. Let's have sex*' and when Mandy said '*no*', he said, '*Me either. Let's have sex.*'"

"I assume it didn't work with either of you."

"No, but it was unique. At least I remember it."

Wade looked at Mindy and laughed. He picked up the coffee cups and returned them to the kitchen. When he returned to the den, Mindy was leaning back in one of the huge leather recliners. He sat in one of the over-sized rocking chairs across from her.

"I've been thinking," the twin said.

"And—?"

"You shouldn't tell Sam about the offer until after you meet with these guys and see if they're legit."

"I'm not sure that's fair to Sam."

"Okay, let's say you tell her. What's gonna be her reaction?"

"We'll probably rehash the conversation that we had this morning. She'll insist on loaning or giving me the money I need to keep operating, and then she'll get more irate when I refuse to take it. I'll try to explain this situation to her, even though I don't understand it myself."

Mindy nodded. "Exactly what I was thinking."

"I'm gonna start calling you '*Dear Mindy*'. So what's your advice?"

"Wait until you know what you're talking about. I know

that's tough on you, being a man and all. But put that big ol' ego aside and listen to a female."

"I'm all ears."

"Right, if only it were that easy. If you go to her now, she's gonna ask you a bunch of questions you don't have answers for. Most of what you'll be telling her is pure conjecture on your part. You don't know who these people are or why they want the Plantation. If you wait until tomorrow afternoon, at least you'll have some facts and maybe, just maybe, you can convince her you are considering all the facts and are weighing them carefully. Then you can tell her you're gonna make an informed, intelligent decision."

Wade ran his hands through his hair. He had never dreamed one of the twins could be this mature.

"I see what you're saying. That may be the best approach. I can go over there in the morning and get some answers before I tell Sam anything."

"Not exactly."

"Huh?"

"*We* are going over there. There's a lot better chance that nothing nefarious will happen if there's two of us. If you go by yourself, all they have to do is trot out a big-booby girl and you'll sign anything. If I go with you, they'll wait on the girl and you won't sign anything or I'll break a finger or two."

"Mindy, I can't let you go with me. These guys could be dangerous. I don't know them at all, and I mean that literally."

"So be a Boy Scout and go prepared for anything. If we're going through private airports, then you can carry anything you want to be comfortable, even your pistol."

Wade had to lean back in the rocking chair and consider

what Mindy said. Her thought process seemed logical to him, and the last thing he was expecting from a twin was a mature logical discussion. He glanced at her with a newly acquired admiration. There was only one little problem that Mindy had not addressed.

"And what will Sam say when she finds out that I flew to Houston with you instead of her?"

"Do we have to lead men by their hands all the time, Wade? There are some things you don't tell your fiancée for her own good. This is one of those things."

"But what if she finds out?"

"Did she find out you were squeezing my boob the first time we sat in the stand together?"

"Wait a minute. I wasn't squeezing your boob. You were asleep and twisting and turned up against me until that happened accidentally."

"An accident for over thirty minutes, Wade? That's more unbelievable than '*Do you like chicken?*' is."

"But you were asleep. At least I thought you were asleep. I didn't want to disturb you."

"I know. It's always the pregnant girl's fault."

Wade stopped rocking. "We didn't—"

"I know, Wade. I'm just using that as an analogy. You guys always blame the girl for anything. Anyway, I'm just kidding, but I'm serious about Sam not finding out about that situation. Mandy is the only one I've told and we've kept it a secret since that day."

"But there isn't any secret to keep."

"So did you tell Sam about it?"

Wade had been staring directly at Mindy and now looked sheepishly away.

"No, I didn't tell her."

"Nor I. I won't tell her about Houston either. In fact, I

won't tell anyone, including Mandy. That's how much I care about going with you to make sure you're doing the right thing here."

Wade was impressed. He rose from his rocker, walked over to her recliner and kissed her on top of her head. "Thank you."

"Wade, can I ask you one question?"

"Sure."

Mindy grinned. "Do you like chicken?"

Wade laughed and turned to go down the hall. Halfway to his bedroom, he turned back toward Mindy.

"I've got to go to bed." After a brief pause, he added, "Alone."

10 MONDAY MORNING
EVERGREEN PLANTATION

WADE HAD NOT REALIZED HOW DRAINING THE LAST couple of days had been. After getting into bed, he didn't stir until his alarm clock rang out, waking him from a deep sleep. The first thing he noticed were two small arms around him and two small breasts protruding into his back. Startled, he virtually leapt out of bed.

"What are you doing in my bed, Mindy?"

Mindy rubbed her sleepy eyes and sat up.

"Sleeping. At least I was. I need another couple of hours if you don't mind."

"I mind. You can't keep sleeping in my bed. Last time, you and Mandy did this, and I told you then that you couldn't."

"Wade, relax. Nothing happened last time with me and Mandy, and nothing happened last night with me and you."

"So why are you in my bed?"

"Because I wasn't comfortable sleeping alone in this big ol' lodge. I came down here, and you were already asleep. I just climbed in and went to sleep with you."

"But you don't have on any pajamas! You've only got a tee shirt and—"

"We told you last time. Neither of us sleep with pajamas on. Never have."

"What would Sam think if she came in and found us in bed together and you with no pajamas, Mindy?"

"I hadn't really thought about that, Wade."

Wade shook his head in disbelief as he pulled his pants on. He thought Mindy displayed maturity beyond her years during their conversation the previous evening. Now he wondered if she hadn't reverted to a nine-year-old in need of attention. She reminded him of the young elk calf he saw that had become separated on the opposite side of the lake from its mother. The little calf wanted so badly to be with its mother that it kept calling and kept calling. The mother cow elk stood on the opposite shore, waiting for the calf to cross. Finally, the little calf started swimming across the lake. About half way across, the calf changed its mind and swam back to the shore where it had come from.

To Wade, Mindy was a lot like that little calf. She wanted to be a woman, but she was afraid to leave the comfort zone of being a girl. Being a girl meant she didn't have to consider the consequences of her actions. But she also didn't have the freedom of being a woman. Wade felt sorry for her.

"Mindy, I didn't mean to yell at you like that. But you surprised me when I woke up and you were here. The first thing I thought of was Sam and what her reaction would be. She's the most important person in the world to me and I don't want to do anything that'd risk losing her. Do you understand?"

"I understand. Sometimes, we don't see how things look to other people."

"Right now, I'm looking at your boobs through that flimsy tee shirt. Even though I can appreciate the view, you probably should put on a shirt or a top or something. Otherwise, I might get the wrong impression."

Wade laughed, hoping he wasn't too hard on Mindy.

"I don't know. It depends."

"Depends on what, Mindy?"

"Do you like chicken?" Mindy giggled as she turned her back to Wade and got dressed.

Wade eased out of the bedroom and brewed some Community Coffee.

"Welcome, I was only expecting one passenger this morning."

"We had some last-minute changes in our plans. I'm Wade, and this is Mindy."

"No problem. I'm Mike and I'll be your pilot today. We'll be traveling in a Cessna 206 with a few modifications. The engine has over three hundred horsepower, the wings are extended by an additional eighteen inches, and it can comfortably seat six passengers and plenty of luggage."

Wade laughed.

"We brought two backpacks with us just in case that three hundred horsepower engine quits on us. You don't have a backup for it on board, do you?"

The pilot chuckled. "We have about everything else. If anything happens, it has three emergency exits; here, here and here. Grab a parachute by the exit, strap it on and jump. Pull the cord on the parachute and float to the ground. The parachutes are the quick-disconnect types, so if you land in water, unbuckle the disconnect in the middle of your chest and get out from under the parachute as quickly as possible."

"Anything else?"

"Do either of you smoke?"

Both Wade and Mindy shook their heads.

"Good, there's a no-smoking policy on board. If a fire breaks out, there's a fire extinguisher and a fire ax by each exit. But don't be a hero. Get the heck out of there and let me deal with it."

"Where do we sit?"

"Pick a seat on each side of the plane. That'll help balance us out and make it a little smoother flight."

"How was your trip from Houston this morning?"

"I'm not from Houston. I'm in Jackson. They chartered me yesterday to pick one passenger up this morning in Evergreen and fly him to Houston. They told me to wait at the airport until you got back and bring you back to Evergreen this afternoon."

"I thought they were sending someone from Houston. My mistake."

"No problem."

Wade and Mindy sat across from each other in the back seats closest to the emergency door on the side of the plane. They stowed their backpacks under the seats in front of them. Wade looked around, assuring himself the parachutes were within easy reach. He kept drumming his fingers on the chair arm, and his feet couldn't get comfortable in the space between the seats.

"What's wrong?" Mindy asked.

"Something isn't right, but I can't put my finger on it." Wade kept looking around. "Maybe you should get off before we leave."

"Nope, I'm staying with you, Wade."

Wade frowned. "I don't have a good feeling about this, Mindy."

"You don't want to sell the Plantation. That's what you don't have a good feeling about."

He rested his head on the back of the seat.

"You might be right. I don't have a warm fuzzy about that."

"If you get paid as much as you think for the Plantation, you won't need a warm fuzzy. You'll be able to buy or rent as many as you need."

Wade laughed. "You're right. Maybe I'm being paranoid over nothing."

The powerful Cessna easily lifted off the short runway at the private airport. Wade was surprised at the smoothness of the ride and relaxed. Mindy looked out of the window next to her seat.

"Look, there's my house. See it. I've never seen it from the air before. It looks so small from up here." The excitement evident in the tone of her voice made Wade smile.

"Hey guys." The captain poked his head out of the door of the cockpit. "Take-off was fine. We should arrive in Houston in less than an hour. Sit back, relax and enjoy the flight. I'll let you know when we get close."

Wade kept watching the ground below them through his little window. The bright morning sun rose behind them as though it was trailing the Cessna to keep tabs on it. The brilliance of the eastern sky soon enveloped the entire vista, and Wade could discern the edges of the Gulf of Mexico. The plane traveled almost due west, parallel to Interstate 10. The route looked like it'd continue a tad north of the interstate, but the road number would change to Interstate 12 between Slidell and Baton Rouge.

Interstate 10 dipped down to New Orleans and merged back with Interstate 12 in Baton Rouge, just east of the Mississippi River.

"Can you name the towns we're passing, Mindy?"

"Let's see. We passed Slidell, so we should be over Covington and Mandeville now and Hammond coming up in a few minutes."

"Trey Yuen is in Mandeville."

"Chinese, I'm guessing."

"The best Chinese restaurant in Louisiana, but it isn't your normal Chinese food. They use a lot of the Cajun spices and have a mixture of traditional Chinese dishes with a fresh Louisiana seafood as the base."

"I've had some Chinese dishes with shrimp before, but I don't know where the shrimp came from."

"We'll have to go there sometime. Maybe you and Mandy can join Sam and I for a Saturday night."

"Are you gonna help us order? I mean those Louisiana seafood dishes."

"Absolutely! We'll get some of the best ones like Spicy Alligator, Tong Cho Crawfish, Alligator with Fresh Mushrooms Szechuan and Crawfish in a Spicy Lobster Sauce and we can all pass them around and taste each one."

"That sounds like a plan to me. In Evergreen, we just go to the five-dollar Chinese lunch buffet. I usually get the chicken-on-a-stick and egg rolls."

"Sam and I eat there too, but we're talking about a different level of food at Trey Yuen. It's like comparing a fast-food hamburger to a Filet Mignon from Ruth's Chris."

"Now you're talking my language."

"I normally prefer buffalo or axis over beef, but Ruth's has customized ovens that get the steaks unbelievably tender. When I hear the expression '*melts in your mouth*' the first thing that comes to my mind is a filet from Ruth's Chris."

"Hmm! Don't you love those"

"They do a good job, all right. I think it's amazing what the dreams of one lady can become."

"That's awesome. My dreams might turn into something one day."

"What do you dream about doing, Mindy?"

'You're just going to laugh at me if I tell you."

"I've done a lot of despicable things in my life, but I've never laughed at another person's dreams."

"Okay, but only if you promise you won't laugh."

"I promise."

"I want to be a missionary in Ghana."

Wade stammered. "A what?"

"You promised you wouldn't laugh."

"I'm not laughing. But you surprised me. Of all the things I imagined you would want to be, I never even thought of being a missionary as one you'd pick. And in Africa. Why a missionary and why Ghana?"

"We have some friends that are missionaries there. They're doing wonderful things. Most of the remote villages in Ghana don't have fresh drinking water and the entire village will bathe, wash clothes, and drink from the same water where the cows take a dump. Then the kids get infected by a parasite called a Guinea worm. It's like a thin long worm that keeps growing and growing inside their bodies until it gets too big and then either kills them or maims them. Those things can grow three feet or more inside the body. Then it tries to get out through the legs or the feet. The pain is unbearable and the kids put their feet in the water for relief. The worm will come out in the water and breed in the same water. One worm can have over a million eggs. It's gross. Our friends drill fresh-water wells for an entire village. Their efforts have reduced the number of guinea worm cases dramatically. Once the village trusts them, they're able to bring modern medicine, education, and the gospel to them. I'd like to make a difference in people's lives like that one day."

"That makes what I'm doing feel real small in comparison."

"Not really. You can impact more people at the Plantation than you've ever dreamed of helping. Open it up for kids, especially handicapped kids, to come out there in the summer and help feed the little deer. Or let handicapped hunters go there for a big discount or even free."

"You know, an outfit called me and wanted to do something like that. I just put them off. Now I'm kinda ashamed of myself."

"As you should. Why don't you do it?"

"I don't know. I was just getting started and to put it bluntly, I'm a little uncomfortable around the handicapped."

"You shouldn't be, Wade. They're people just like us. They have dreams just like us. They want to make a difference in this world just like us."

Wade dropped his gaze to the floor.

"When you put it like that, I'm ashamed. Maybe I can find his number and call him for this year. I know he's from somewhere down near Springfield. Shouldn't be hard to find him."

"You're forgetting one thing."

"What's that?"

"You're on your way to Houston to sell the Plantation.

How are you going to do that and host handicapped hunts at the Plantation if you don't own it anymore?"

"You're right. I don't want to sell the Plantation. You've made up my mind for me. It doesn't matter how much they offer, I'm gonna keep the Plantation. I want to use it to make a difference in people's lives, and I can't do that if I don't own it."

"So why are we on this puddle jumper going to Houston then?"

"We're not. Keep your seat and I'm gonna tell the pilot to turn this thing around and take us back to Evergreen."

"Hurry, I haven't had my chicken yet, today."

Wade laughed as he got out of his seat. He glanced out of the window while he was getting to his feet and saw the plane was flying at a considerably lower altitude than before. He had been so engaged in the conversation with Mindy that he hadn't noticed the change before. Using the luggage compartments to steady himself, Wade shuffled up the aisle to the cockpit. When he reached the end of the aisle, he stuck his head inside to talk to the pilot.

"Hey Captain, I've changed my—"

12 MONDAY MORNING

ON THE PLANE

HIS BRAIN QUIT SENDING WORDS TO HIS MOUTH AS HE tried to comprehend the scene before him. His mouth was still moving, but nothing coherent was being uttered. Eyes widening, they absorbed the images and sent them to a clogged pathway lacking the ability to receive and process them. Slowly, his mind transmitted commands to his motor skills. His hands, moving in slow motion, checked the pilot's neck for a pulse. Confirming his fears, there was no beat. To make sure his mind wasn't playing games, he felt for a pulse on the pilot's limp wrist with the same result.

Now, with his brain almost fully functional again, his legs and feet accepted the orders and complied. Wade whirled from the cockpit and almost ran down the aisle. His voice still wasn't normal, slightly animated but under control.

"Mindy, grab a parachute and strap it on! Then grab your day pack! We're gonna jump!."

Mindy's hazel eyes widened. "Why? What's going on" She was already moving even as she asked questions.

"The pilot looks like he had a heart attack or something.

He's dead and the plane's on autopilot. We're descending at a good clip. Hurry!"

Mindy was moving at warp speed, her parachute already strapped on and hugging her backpack to her chest. She hurried to the exit door with Wade only a second or two behind her. He paused only long enough to snatch a small fire hatchet off the wall by the exit.

"Have you ever done this before?"

"If you mean killing myself by jumping out of a plane, this is the first time." Mindy still had a sense of humor. "How about you?"

"Nope, but there's no time like the present." His eyes stared at hers for two or three seconds before he lowered his gaze to find the release mechanism for the exit. To his surprise, the door opened fairly easily after he triggered the release.

Mindy turned and looked at him with her feet on the edge of the plane, nothing but the bright sky in front of her. She leaned over and kissed him on his lips before suddenly disappearing out of the plane. Wade heard a faint, "Geronimo" as she quickly faded from his sight.

Wade followed, with no bravado, leaping as far out into the sky as he could to clear his body from the flight of the small plane. With his heart pounding, he yanked on the primary pull cord of the parachute. Relief swept through his body as the parachute blossomed, jolting his body upward and slowing his rate of descent. His next thought was to look behind him and a large grin crossed his face when he spotted Mindy's broad open parachute not too far below him. He clung to his own day pack and hoped that Mindy was doing the same when he saw the terrain where were about to land.

He thought about trying to steer his chute closer to

Mindy's, but his unfamiliarity with skydiving prevented him from taking the chance of becoming entangled in her chute. Looking down, the treetops drew closer and closer until he could discern the swampland beneath them. While still suspended far above the treetops by his parachute, Wade turned in a circle, trying unsuccessfully to spot a town nearby. Then he narrowed his visual search closer, hoping to spot a hunting camp or boathouse, but no signs of civilization were apparent within his limited perimeter.

Wade heard, rather than saw Mindy crash into the large water oaks running down a ridge between the sloughs of the swamp. He pulled on the cords of his chute, slowing its descent and redirecting it slightly toward a small opening in the water oaks close to where he spotted Mindy's chute dangling from some limbs. Relaxing his body and bending his knees, he half-rolled when he contacted the soft earth. Wasting no time, he tossed his day pack aside and unbuckled his chute before sprinting in the direction he had last seen Mindy.

He ran less than fifty yards before he heard his name being yelled in the dark swamp. Glancing toward the direction of the voice, he saw nothing. Then he looked up and found Mindy suspended in midair, the cords of her chute tangled in one of the huge water oaks. She was hanging not more than fifteen feet above the ground, enticingly close but so far from safety.

"Looks like you have a problem, Mindy," he said, slightly amused at her predicament. The smiled quickly faded when he saw the tears streaming down her face.

Why do I feel like I need to pop off all the time? She's scared and I'm making fun of the situation. I've got to be the biggest jerk in the world right now.

"I think I broke my ankle, Wade."

She's hurt, not scared. I thought I couldn't feel any worse.

"Hold on. Let's figure out how to get you down from there without doing any more damage."

"Why don't I just unbuckle this stupid chute and you catch me?"

"We could do that, but we might hurt you more if I don't catch you."

"I just want to get down."

He could sense the panic growing in her voice.

"Relax. I know you're in pain. I'm gonna get you outta that tree without making it more serious. It won't take long. I promise."

Wade surveyed the immediate vicinity. The trunk of the old tree was way too big for him to get his arms around it and shinny up. There was no way to straddle its immense girth with his knees. There were several limbs directly above Mindy that would support his weight.

No wonder she hit her ankle trying to get through all of those.

Looking around, he formulated a plan with the assets at his disposal.

"Hold on! I'll be right back."

"Hurry. Please hurry." Mindy cried.

He raced back to his chute and grabbed the day pack that he had tossed aside. Pulling out the little fire ax that he had snatched from the plane, he sprinted back to Mindy, being extra careful not to trip over one of the many fallen logs. Reaching the spot directly beneath Mindy, Wade reconsidered his plan one more time before concluding it would be the best short-term solution.

"You're will be all right. This shouldn't take long at all."

Wade stepped only about a dozen feet from the base of

the old water oak. Turning his head from side to side, he picked out a young white oak that would work. Wade knew how much the local wildlife population depended on the sweet tasting acorns of the white oaks that provided much of the protein and nutrition they needed to survive the winter conditions. He reluctantly passed the young white oak and picked a young pine tree growing on the ridge. He reasoned that the soft pine would be easier to chop, and it'd grow back much quicker than the sturdier oak. Wade hacked a dozen quick strokes with the ax near the base of the small pine, and it was ready to fall. He pushed the trunk so that the top of the pine fell against the limb above Mindy. He stepped back to observe the angle the fallen tree made and decided the make-shift ladder would have to do.

"I'll get above you using this pine tree. If something happens, unbuckle your chute and drop to the ground. I don't expect anything bad to happen, but you never know."

"Okay, Wade. But please hurry. My ankle is killing me."

Wade climbed up the soft pine with no problem for the first half of the ascent. Then he regretted his decision not to cut the young oak tree as the pine buckled under his weight. Gingerly, he inched his way until he could barely reach the oak limb above Mindy. Placing both feet on a pine extrusions, he leapt as high as he could and grabbed the oak. Despite aching arms, he pulled himself up on the limb.

"Whew. Let's not do that again." He sighed.

"Didn't your mother ever teach you to never leave a girl hanging?"

"I think she had something else in mind when she said it. I don't believe she meant it literally."

"Well, this is about as literal as it'll get. Now get me down from here."

Wade straddled the limb above Mary and inched his way out to a point almost directly above her.

"I'm gonna try to untangle some of this cord and lower you to the ground. If it lets loose too quickly, just bounce the best you can to protect your ankle."

"Bounce the best I can. Is that the best advice you can give me? I have to get stranded in the middle of nowhere with someone that tells me to bounce the best I can. This isn't going to be a good day."

Wade laughed. "It probably isn't going to be a great day. Now get ready."

He got his knees up on the limb and stretched as far as he could to reach the entanglement. Some snarled cords were several feet above him and beyond his reach, even if he could stand on the limb.

"I'm gonna have to cut some of these cords. Hold on."

"Where do you think I'm going? It's not like I have a big choice in the matter."

"I guess you don't, at least right now. I'm gonna get you down without hurting your ankle any further if I can. But it won't be easy."

Wade dug his utility knife from his pocket and began cutting the cords above his head. Every time he cut one, he could see Mindy sag toward the swampy ground. When he had all but the last two cut, he wound the others around the limb and sat on them.

"Okay, brace yourself. Try to roll when you hit the ground if I can't hold you."

"Bounce. Brace myself. Roll. You're not very consistent with your advice, are you?"

"I guess not. I've never been in a situation like this one. Are you ready?"

73

"Still not sure what I'm supposed to be doing to get ready, so I'm as ready as I'm going to get."

Wade shook his head and shrugged his shoulders. He looked up at the last two cords and switched the knife from his right hand to his left. He grabbed the cords with his right hand and slashed at them with the knife. The cords held with about three quarters of the breadth cut. Wade took a deep breath and slashed one more time with the knife in his left hand. Immediately, Mindy's weight jerked against the awkward position that Wade's hold with his right hand. She fell almost a foot before the strands that Wade was sitting on held her above the ground, expanding and contracting like a bungee cord.

"We've got the bounce out of the way. Can you get me down now?"

"Should be able to."

Wade wrapped the remaining two cords once around the limb and then scooted back and undid the cords he had been sitting on. He undid them until they also were looped only once around the limb. He let out a couple of inches of cord at a time, slowly lowering Mindy until she was on the ground."

"Don't stand. Let yourself go all the way."

"The last time I let myself go all the way, I thought I was gonna get pregnant. Are you proposing?"

13 MONDAY MORNING

ATCHAFALAYA BASIN

WADE LAUGHED. "No, YOU KNOW WHAT I MEAN. LET your whole body go to the ground."

He finished lowering Mindy the last few inches and backed up toward the water oak's tree trunk. He swung his leg over the limb and onto the little pine tree. Supporting the entire weight of his body with only his arms, he placed both feet on the lowest limb he could reach. Letting go of the oak limb, Wade shinnied down the little pine in record time and raced over to Mindy.

"He started unbuckling her chute frame. "Are you okay?"

She looked down at her leg with tears rolling down her cheeks. "I bounced, braced and rolled, but my ankle is killing me." She glanced up at Wade. "Thanks for getting me out of that mess."

"No problem. Let's see what's going on with your ankle."

Wade lifted her shoe and rested it on a log. Removing her shoe and sock, he rolled her pants leg up, feeling her foot, ankle and shin on all sides. He ran his hands several times over the entire length of her foot and ankle, applying pressure at several points. He could see the ankle was already swelling in contrast to her slim legs. A deep purplish hue set in right above the ankle.

"I don't think there is anything broken. You won't be able to move around very well for a few days, though. That's a bad sprain or tear. What did you hit?"

"I hit a little bird on the way down." Mindy shook her head. "What did I hit? I hit the damn tree. I musta hit every damn limb on that tree. I felt like one of those pinballs bonging around up there."

Wade laughed and glanced up toward the path Mindy took through the limbs of the old water oak, with the chute still hanging two thirds of the way down it.

"I'll give you this much. You turned that live oak from a city street into an interstate. No red lights, side streets or anything to slow anyone down at the top of it. Just big old limbs left for the squirrels to race on."

"I hope they appreciate it more than I do right now. What do we do next, Doctor?"

"With your foot in the condition it's in, we aren't gonna walk out of this bog. Even as small as you are, I can't carry you out. Some of this ground is boggy, some of it is like quicksand, and there's a lot of sloughs and bayous between us and where we want to go. There's no way you could make it through those."

"I can try, Wade. We can't be that far from civilization."

"It wouldn't be much use trying, Mindy. We're in the Atchafalaya Basin, somewhere north of Morgan City and south of Krotz Springs if I had to guess. But the basin is bigger than the state of Rhode Island and has a lot meaner and more dangerous critters. To try to walk out of here in your condition would be pure suicide."

"What the hell are we gonna do? As much as I like you, I don't want to spend the rest of my life here with you."

"I'm trying to make sure we have a life. You're gonna have to trust me."

"Why don't we call someone and let them know where we are?"

"If you remember, I said this swamp is bigger than Rhode Island. No one has decided it makes good business sense to put a cell tower in the middle of it for the critters to call their loved ones. But give it a try. Your service may reach farther than mine."

Mindy unsnapped her cell phone from her waistline and tried to get a tone. She tried to reach the Internet and failed. Then she bawled. The heaves came from deep within her, not an occasional tear running down her cheek, but a soulful mourning.

After a few minutes, the sobbing turned to mere tears. "If we can't walk out and we can't call out, how are we gonna get out? Do you think someone will come looking for us?"

"That's what I've been thinking about for the last few minutes. I'm sorry if I wasn't more positive, but you're old enough to understand the reality of the situation. Do you remember when I said something was odd about the situation at the private airport?"

"Yes, I remember you saying that."

"I couldn't put my finger on it, but now I know what was bothering me."

"What was it, Wade?"

"No one was inside the private airport. No one was logging us in and showing the rest of the world that we got on this plane this morning. I'd be willing to bet that my truck is no longer at the airport and there's no record of that plane stopping in Evergreen."

"So you don't think it is an accident that our pilot had an apparent heart attack?"

"I don't think it was an accident. Now I believe someone tried to murder me. I don't believe they're after you because no one knows you're with me unless you told Mandy."

"I was going to text her from the plane, but didn't get around to it until it was too late."

"I didn't tell Sam either. It was too early when we left, and I meant to call her when we knew some facts."

"Wade, no one has ever tried to kill me before. This doesn't feel good."

"If it makes you feel any better, I don't think they were trying to kill you this time either. Whoever it is, and I don't have a clue who that might be, is trying to kill me."

"Have you made anyone mad lately?"

"Other than Sam, you mean?" Wade laughed at his own joke. "Nope. How can I make anyone mad unless I forget to feed the animals at the Plantation? They get mad at me, but none have tried to kill me. Maybe that stag you and Mandy darted, but he got a peaceful nap out of the deal."

"Who is your beneficiary in your will?"

"I don't have a will yet. The estate attorney in town and I still have to get together to decide on everything."

"So who gets the Plantation if you die?"

"Next of kin, I guess. I really don't know how that works in Mississippi. I have some cousins over in Tyler in east Texas, but they have a different last name. I've got one cousin in Morgan City. I'm not sure how they would track them down."

"Especially if they aren't trying real hard."

"We're gonna have a while to think about it and sort it out. We aren't going anywhere soon. Let me look at your ankle again. I have some stretch bandages and some aspirins in my pack. I'll run get it and be right back."

Wade trotted back to the site where he landed and picked up his pack. Then he heard an eerie shriek from underneath the old water oak.

"Wade! Wade! Wade!"

"I'm coming, Mindy." Wade sprinted toward the shrill voice. He slowed down as he neared Mindy, seeing nothing but pure fright in her broadened eyes.

"What is it?"

Mindy, afraid to move any part of her body, nodded to the ground between her feet. Wade's heart raced when he recognized the threat.

14 MONDAY MORNING
ATCHAFALAYA BASIN

"Okay, Miss Mindy. Be real, real still. Breathe as slowly and as shallow as you can."

Wade laid the pack on the ground and picked up a forked stick lying next to it. He continued to hold the ax in his right hand.

"What we've got Miss Mindy is a water moccasin, better known in these parts as a cottonmouth. We're gonna make friends with this one. Just stay frozen for a bit while I ease up on him."

Wade took two gingerly steps toward Mindy and the snake. The cottonmouth curled up in between Mindy's warm legs.

"Snakes are cold-blooded and he's only looking for a warm place to take a nap."

Wade continued to get into position. Once there, at Mandy's feet he eased the stick between her legs along the ground. When the stick got within two inches of the snake, the cottonmouth started coiling, getting in a position to strike. Wade plunged the stick underneath the snake and flicked it out from between Mindy's legs in one motion. The snake landed three feet from Mindy. Wade lunged toward it, jabbing the small fork right behind its head. With the head pinned, Wade lifted the ax high above his head and struck the cottonmouth right behind the stick, severing its head.

Wade looked down at his trembling hands and noticed for the first time that beads of sweat were pouring off his temples. His shirt was completely soaked. When he looked at Mindy, he saw her lips trembling, but nothing was coming out of her mouth. She kept staring at the spot between her legs where the snake had been.

Wade leaned over and hugged her. Then he sat beside her.

"Don't worry, Mindy. He's not gonna bother you anymore."

"But what about his friends?"

Wade laughed gently.

"We'll take care of them if they visit us."

Mindy sat up and squeezed Wade. "Thank you for saving my life."

"You're welcome, but I don't think I did. That snake would have moved along eventually if nobody bothered him."

"I was gonna bother him. He was about to get peed on."

Wade grinned. "I'm not sure how he would have reacted to that."

"Have I ever told you I totally, and I mean totally hate snakes. I mean, really hate them."

"No, but you're gonna get your revenge on this one. We're gonna have him for brunch."

"Do what?"

"Eat him for brunch. I've got a few MRE's in my pack,

but we're gonna need to supplement those with some of God's bounty around here."

"When pigs fly. I don't know what an MRE is, but it doesn't sound too appetizing and I know that I'm not eating any snakes. You need to go kill a cheeseburger with fries or a pepperoni pizza with extra cheese. I'd even settle for some fried chicken, but nothing named cottonmouth or moccasin."

"What are you gonna eat?"

Mindy looked around for her pack.

"When you said pack for the day, I thought you meant food in case we got hungry on the way over or on the way back, so I packed some for both of us for the trip. I've got three or four sandwiches and I'd much prefer them over a dead reptile."

"Okay, I'll get you a sandwich. That'll take your mind off the snake and your ankle."

"Damn, I hadn't even thought of my ankle since I saw the snake."

"Amazing how our priorities change in life depending on what we're facing, isn't it?"

Wade dug for a sandwich in her backpack, noting how heavy it was for a day trip. He looked into it and saw several more sandwiches, soda pops, water, cookies and candy. There were even some bags of potato chips.

"I see you brought along all your survival needs with you. Planning on staying a while?"

"At least I'm not gonna be eating snake, if that's what you mean."

Wade pulled out a sandwich that looked like either tuna or chicken salad.

"Here, eat this one before it spoils. Do you have any others with mayo on them?"

"Yes."

"You can have them for a late lunch. Take one of these soda pops, but save the can for later. We'll need it to boil water."

"How in the hell are we going to boil water in a soda can? It won't hold enough to boil."

"We've got to make do with what we have, Mindy. We don't have all the appliances and cookware that we have at the lodge. Out here, everything is recycled until it's useless."

Wade handed Mindy the sandwich and soda pop. "While you eat this, I'll fix something up to keep you off the ground. That'll keep his friends from bothering you or at least make it more difficult. It'll also help keep the ticks and red bugs off that little butt of yours."

Wade sized up the materials he had to work with in the immediate vicinity. After a few minutes of contemplation, he climbed back up the pine tree to the water oak limb and edged out on the limb, this time walking out on it holding on to the limbs above. With the cords cut part of the way, he worked the chute loose from the remaining branches and watched it flutter to the ground. He scurried back down the little pine and started re-arranging the parachute. Twenty minutes later, he had a hammock stretched between two water oaks.

"Let's try that and see if it will hold you."

Mindy licked her fingers to get the last taste of the sandwich and finished the soda pop.

"No problem, but you're gonna have to help me."

"Let me know if it hurts."

He gently lifted Mindy and gingerly placed her in the make-shift hammock.

"This isn't bad. I could get used to it."

Wade had a wry grin on his face.

"At the Atchafalaya Resort, we do our best to please our guests and make sure they're as comfortable as possible, even those that complain about our exquisite menu."

He adjusted one end of the hammock, raising it slightly. Grabbing her pack, he tied it on the end of the hammock, easily within her reach.

"That'll keep the critters around here out of it."

"And just what critters do you have at the Atchafalaya Resort?"

"Only the friendly kind, Ma'am. Only the friendly kind."

"Like the one you're going to have for brunch?"

"Sometimes, even the friendliest of our critters forget that they shouldn't bother the guests. Then we have to gently remind them."

"Wade, what kind of these friendly fellows might decide they want to share a room with me?"

"You've already been greeted by a cottonmouth, one of the most aggressive and venomous snakes in the world. There are tons of them around. We also have Eastern diamondback rattlesnakes, alligators, black bears, bobcats and a slew of spiders. The alligators and bears were almost killed off by excessive hunting, but they're making a comeback now. For the non-lethal pests, we have raccoons, squirrels, garter snakes, water snakes, rat snakes, and plenty of rats that love to get into packs and eat up your food. That's why you don't want to leave it on the ground."

"Great. Now, I feel safer." The sarcasm in her voice was unmistakable.

Wade pulled out some lotion from his pack.

"This will help the pain and the discomfort. It's also good for itching after I put the bandage on."

He applied the lotion and then placed a stretch bandage

taut around her ankle and up a little on her shin. He put her sock back on her foot on top of the bandage.

"A little compression will help keep the swelling down some. We'll leave the shoe off for now. You aren't going anywhere soon. Do you want me to take the other one off?"

Mindy nodded.

Wade searched in his bag and found the mosquito spray. After liberally spraying Mindy, he applied some to himself.

"See, we have everything at the Atchafalaya Resort."

"Aah, Paradise. And how long are we going to spend together in Paradise?"

Wade handed her some pain pills out of his pack.

"Take two of these and call me in the morning."

"Okay, Doc. But you're avoiding my question. How long will we be here like this?"

"Be a good patient and swallow those pills. They may make you a tad drowsy, but at least they'll ease your pain some. A quick nap wouldn't hurt you at all right now."

"Hah. You just want to sedate me so you can ravage my body and I won't be able to resist. I know your kind."

Wade laughed. "Ravaging your body isn't in my top ten right now. It may get there after a month or two out here, but it isn't right now."

"A month or two? Is that how long you expect us to be in this godforsaken place?"

"A little while ago, you were calling it a resort."

"That's when I assumed we might be here for a day or so, not a month or two."

"Relax, I don't think it'll be that long. We should be able to get out this weekend. Now, take those pills."

"Are you sure you're not a horny old man trying to take advantage of a young girl like me?"

"Mindy, there's not a man alive that's going to take advantage of you or your sister. You guys stay way ahead of us; way ahead."

He left to retrieve his own chute from the drop area. When he checked on Mindy, she was sound asleep, gently breathing in a regular rhythm. Worried that the pills might have been too much for her petite body, he checked her wrist for a pulse rate. He then placed two fingers against her throat to confirm the regularity of the pulse.

Mindy's eyes flickered. "See, I told you all you wanted to do was molest me in my sleep." She closed her eyes with a smile on her lips.

Wade shook his head, grinning.

This is going to be an interesting time in the Atchafalaya Basin with this young lady. I wonder what Sam is thinking right now.

15 MONDAY NOON
EVERGREEN

"Where could they be?" Sam asked for the hundredth time.

"Relax, Sam. That boyfriend of yours knows how to take care of himself wherever he is and whatever situation he's in. He'll be fine." Gus said with an overstated confidence.

"Gus, it's not like Wade not to call. It's not like him to leave, to go anywhere without telling me where he's going and when he'll be back. It's not like him to leave his truck in the middle of the National Forest. It's not like Mindy to go anywhere or do anything without telling Mandy. Those two are so close. They tell each other everything. I don't or can't understand the bond between them, but Mandy doesn't have a clue where they are."

"I can't argue with you. We'll just have to wait and see if we can recover anything from Wade's truck that'll give us a hint about what is happening."

"Why was it out there on that gravel road in the middle of nowhere? There was no key in the ignition, according to the people that found it. Do you think he and Mindy went for a stroll through the woods and got lost?"

"That doesn't sound like Wade. We won't know until we find them."

Sam continued pacing back and forth, while Gus more or less meandered around the huge conference table in the center of the room. Gus looked down at the floor and then up to the ceiling as if looking for answers anywhere in the room.

"Do you think we'll find them, Gus? Do you really believe we'll find them alive?"

"Yes, I do. But I don't think they're up there in the National Forest. That truck was moved up there without a key. Somebody jimmied the ignition and drove it up there and abandoned it. We've got to find out the who and the why and then we'll know."

"Gus, over half of the population is traipsing around the woods up there. If Wade and Mindy left anything up there, somebody's gonna find it. There's no way Wade would have panicked if the truck broke down and tried to cut through the woods, especially if Mindy is with him. He would have stayed on the road all the way back to town."

One of the Evergreen deputies eased the door open and stepped in.

"Sam, I don't want to bother you, but we have some information, and I'm not sure if it's related to the case or not."

"What is it, Jeremy?"

"Sam, a farmer that lives by the old airport reported that a plane landed and took off early this morning. He doesn't have a clue about the make or model, just that one landed and then left a few minutes later."

"Is that unusual, Jeremy? Isn't the airport still open? Didn't it transfer to a private company or something?"

"Normally, it wouldn't be, Sam, but the private company that bought it shuts it down on Mondays through Wednesdays. It's mostly open for the weekend pilots. Sometimes a pilot will use it on the other days, but it's unusual. Anyway, I don't know if or how it fits into anything here, but I thought I'd let you know."

"Okay, Jeremy. Check with the owners to see who might have used it and follow up with whatever logs or records they keep out there. Try to track it down if for no other reason to see if they saw anything unusual this morning. Wade doesn't know how to fly a plane. We'll have to ask Bruce or Mandy if Mindy has taken any flying lessons."

"Will do, Sam?"

"Thanks, Jeremy."

The deputy remained for a second or two in the doorway on the way out.

"Is there anything else, Jeremy?"

"It's just that we know what you're going through, me and the other deputies. We wanted to let you know we're gonna stay on this no matter how long it takes and we're not gonna charge you any overtime to do it. We wanted to let you know that."

Sam walked over to Jeremy, stood on her tip-toes and hugged him tightly, planting a long kiss on his cheek. Jeremy, red-faced because he'd never been kissed by a sheriff before, stumbled out of the conference room.

Gus's phone rang and Sam only half-way listened to one side of the conversation. Gus punched the button to end the call and turned to Sam.

"They've checked with the bus station, train station, the

other airport and even some taxi cab companies. Nobody has seen them and no one's bought a ticket using either of their names."

"Okay, let's look at the other end of where that small plane would have gone. Have someone check the private airports in New Orleans, Baton Rouge, Natchez, Jackson, and Biloxi. It should have landed in one of those if it landed here searching for fuel and didn't find any."

"Hey, that's thinking. I could see that happening."

"I appreciate it, Gus. It still doesn't feel right though. Biloxi is only thirty miles from here on a straight line. He should have made it there, and if Wade and Mindy were on a plane anywhere in the United States, they still could call us."

Gus shrugged. "You're right." He started meandering around the table again.

"Gus, can I ask you a direct question?"

"Sure. What is it?"

"Do you think there is any kind of relationship between Wade and Mindy? You know, the romantic type."

Gus laughed. "My goodness, Girl. Of all the world of possibilities out there, that's the last one I could imagine. When the bug bit that boy when he saw you, there ain't the chance of a fly in a roomful of bullfrogs he's gonna have eyes for anyone but you. He's so smitten by you he'll never do anything to hurt you. I don't know much about women. You know that since I've been married four times now. But I know something about men. Some of us tend to wander, and some don't. Wade is part of the 'don't' crowd."

"Thanks. I believe in Wade, but I needed to hear it from someone else. I hope you'll keep this between us."

"Girl, you have so many secrets of mine you've never told. I believe I can keep this one."

"We need to go back to square one. We're not any closer to finding them than we were this morning."

"Okay, the last time you spoke to him was at the café yesterday. You said you got into an argument with him. What was that about?"

"I don't even remember the specifics, Gus. Something about money and men being pig-headed and stubborn."

"So you think he's stubborn, huh?"

"Aren't all men?"

"Some more than others. Did I ever tell you about the time I bought that mule from Roy McMullen?"

"Not that I remember, Gus."

"I paid Roy four hundred dollars for that old jackass. When I got him home and took him out to the field to plow, he just stood there. I yelled and screamed, but that old jackass just stood there. Finally, I got tired of it and got my cattle prod. That's one of them things like we use today, just not as much of a jolt as one of these Tasers. Well, I stuck in right on his rump and let him have it, the full load. He turned his big head around and looked at me and then he just laid down. Wouldn't move a muscle. So I hit him with another jolt. He just laid there like a baby in a crib. For the next week, every time that mule saw me coming, he'd just lay down in the field. I was married to my second wife then. It might have been my third or the girlfriend between the two, but that don't really matter. Anyway, whoever I was with didn't want to keep feeding that jackass if he wasn't working. Told me she already had one of those around the house and didn't need another one. At that time in my life, I was trying to please the women in my life, so I took him back to Roy. Roy told me he didn't have any use for a mule that wouldn't plow, but he'd take him back for free. I knew I couldn't take him back home with me, so I let Roy have him. I went on into town and went to the bank and got four hundred dollars out so I wouldn't have to admit to my wife what I'd done. On the way back home, I had to pass Roy's farm, and there in the middle of his field, Roy was plowing up a storm with that old mule. I jerked my pickup off the road and went up to the fence. Roy saw me over there and ambled over, bringing the mule with him. He asked me if everything was okay and I told him that old jackass didn't plow a square inch for me. He said maybe I was using the wrong approach. I told him I'd yelled and screamed and beat that jackass and even used a cattle prod on him. He smiled and told me that was great news. Of course, I didn't think it was so great and told him so, using some of the same cuss words I'd used on the mule. Roy just stood there grinning. When I asked him what he was so happy about, he told me he'd already made over a thousand dollars selling that mule and getting him back for free. I was flabbergasted. 'How do you get him to plow when nobody else can' I asked him? 'It's not hard' he told me. He pulled a little box of sugar cubes out of his pocket and went up to that mule and gave him a couple. That mule almost drug him out to that field and started plowing. You see, Sam. I used the wrong approach with the mule."

Sam was laughing despite the situation. "What in the world does that have to do with Wade?"

"Sam, Wade's a fine young man, but he's not that much different from all other men when it comes to taking advice from women."

"Huh?"

"We're all jackasses when a woman tries to drive us in one direction. You have to give us a little sugar and we'll bust through walls for you. Just don't try to drive us over the bridge. We're just like that jackass; we're gonna lay down on you. Maybe if you'd tried to use a sugar cube on Wade, you'd know where he is right now."

"As if I didn't feel bad enough. Was that supposed to make me feel better?"

"Nope, but it made you quit worrying, if only for a minute or two."

Jeremy stuck his head back inside the room.

"Keeping you up to date, Sam. They found a plane that crashed in the Gulf of Mexico a few miles south of Morgan City. The initial reports are that divers found only one body in the cockpit, but the plane is under water, so it might take a few days to get it pulled out."

"Thanks, Jeremy. Check with Houma and Morgan City to make sure it didn't drop Wade and Mindy off at either of those."

Jeremy pulled his head back outside the conference room.

"Gus, that didn't get us very far. Even if the plane that crashed is the one that stopped in Evergreen, Wade and Mindy weren't on it. So much for that lead."

"We'll get one, Sam. It's been less than twenty-four hours. They might be at a big poker game on one of those boats for all we know."

"Thanks, Gus. I mean it. Thanks for everything."

"No problem. You've done more for me in the past."

"What do you think they're doing right now?"

A knock on the door interrupted the conversation.

"Hey, Sam. They said I could find you back here."

Sam glanced up at the physically fit man in the expensive suit.

"We're sorta busy, Collier. Can it wait?"

Collier Templet entered the conference room.

"If it's about Wade and the missing girl, that's what I came by for."

Sam looked at him, surprise written on her face.

"Do what?"

"It's not much, but I figured you'd take any information right now."

"You're right. What do you have?"

"I was having breakfast, actually brunch, at the Evergreen Cafe. The waitress told me about the rumors that Wade and the girl were missing."

"And?"

"She told me that Wade had mentioned my name and told her he was gonna meet with me this morning."

"What about?"

"She didn't know exactly, but said it had something to do with the transfer of the Plantation."

"You handled the transfer of the Plantation for him, didn't you?"

The dapper man nodded.

"I was working on behalf of the Agency, but I only supervised the process. My assistant met with him to sign all the papers most times."

"Did your assistant note any problems?"

"Only once. Her boyfriend came in while Wade was making a pass at her. He yelled and cursed, but Ann calmed him down."

"What is Ann's last name?"

"Clement. Ann Clement," Collier said.

"And the boyfriend's" Sam asked.

"Andy. He played football. Big fellow."

"Could he lug Kenny's body more than a hundred yards?"

Collier chuckled. "With one hand."

16 MONDAY AFTERNOON
ATCHAFALAYA BASIN

"What's that god-awful smell?" Mindy gagged, attempting to rise out of her hammock.

"Roasted cottonmouth over an open flame. We serve it only to the finest of our clients at the Atchafalaya Resort. Mansurs on the Boulevard may be the best restaurant that serves Redfish on a Plank that the entire world loves, but they don't have Cottonmouth on a Stick."

Mindy sniffed the air again. "I don't believe you're gonna have to be too worried about them stealing your recipe. Redfish smells and tastes good and yours, let's say I'm not able to get past the smell. It's like a mixture of rotting fish and sour milk."

"Yeah, but with a dash of salt it becomes an exotic delicacy."

Mindy laughed. "Only if you like to see your finest clients barfing all over themselves."

"Are you sure you don't want any?"

"No thanks. Looks like all bones to me."

Wade took a bite of the elongated meal.

"Not bad."

He took another small bite.

"Especially if you like rotten eggs soaked in fish oil. Leaves a tad of an after-taste in the roof of your mouth, but it's a meal."

Mindy turned up her nose.

"I'll stick with my sandwiches for now. Unless you ate them while I was asleep."

"I've been working on some other things and cooking Mr. Cottonmouth here. How many sandwiches did you bring?"

"Four. I thought you might get hungry on the flight back from Houston this afternoon. You might as well eat one instead of that thing. They've all got mayonnaise on them and will spoil overnight."

"If you put it that way, I guess I'd rather eat one than see it spoil. I can save this elegant cuisine for later."

"Or feed it to the turtles. I'd rather have turtle soup than that thing."

"Not a bad idea, Mindy. I prefer a little sherry with mine, but we might make it edible."

Wade retrieved a couple of sandwiches from Mindy's pack, handing one to her with a soda pop.

"May I serve you our entrée de jour, Ma'am? It's our gourmet ham and pure American processed cheese served between two baked slices of our wheat and yeast combo? Most of the mere common establishments in the neighborhood call it a ham and cheese sandwich, but here at the Atchafalaya Resort, we like to make the descriptions a tad more elaborate. We also charge more for the creativity."

"Why, thank you, Sir. It is exquisite. Please add five percent to your tip."

"Thank you, Ma'am. We don't get a lot of big tippers out here."

Mindy took two of bites of her sandwich.

"Hmm. This really is good."

"Don't forget to save room for desert, Ma'am. We have a specialty today."

"And that would be?"

"Cottonmouth pie, Ma'am. It's been one of our favorites since we opened."

Mindy crinkled her nose. "Ugh. You know how to ruin an appetite, don't you?"

"I assure you, Ma'am. It's the best Cottonmouth Pie in the world."

She looked around. "I don't see a lot of customers standing in line to get some."

"This is Monday, our slowest day of the week. Wait til Friday night. You won't be able to find a seat."

The smile briefly left Mindy's face. "Do you really think we'll be here that long, Wade? We'll starve to death, die of thirs,t or go crazy way before then."

"We won't starve to death before the weekend, that much I know. You've got enough food in your backpack to last that long, and I expect we'll be able to add to it with the abundance of nutritious food out here. They don't call Louisiana 'Sportsman's Paradise' for nothing. We won't die of thirst. There is plenty of water and I'll figure out a way to catch some rainwater. I also have some water purification tablets in my pack so we won't get sick on it."

"You make it sound like we'll be stranded for a long time."

Wade walked over to the side of Mindy's hammock and clasped one of her petite hands in the middle of both of his.

"I honestly don't know how long we'll be here. It's won't be easy. The uncertainty is the toughest part of it all. Not knowing is worse than knowing some times. But think of

Mandy, Bruce, and Sam. They don't have a clue where we are or what we're doing. They don't know if we're dead or alive. I'd rather be here than in their shoes right now. If our roles were reversed and Sam was missing, I'd be bonkers right now. We need to keep ourselves busy so we don't go crazy."

"How am I going to stay busy when I'm laid up in this hammock?"

"We've got plenty to do and I'll need your help. The first thing we need is to weave together some palmetto leaves. We need to intertwine them into a waterproof covering for a lean-to type of hut I'm going to build over your bed here."

"How are you going to do that?"

"Cut some of those water oak saplings and lean them against the limb at a forty-five degree angle against the limb above you on both sides. That'll give us the sides to the hut. Then we'll layer the palmetto leaves from bottom to top, creating a waterproof roof. It may not seem important now, but when one of those all-night storms comes rolling in, we'll appreciate having a dry place to get under."

"Were you an architect in your career?"

He laughed. "I graduated in common sense. We need the basics: water, food and shelter in that order. We've already figured out that we can get the first two. Now, we need to start on the third. Everything else is lagniappe."

Wade didn't have to wander very far from the campsite to find a large stand of palmetto plants, their large leaves in the shape of a hand with long protruding fingers. The stems were long and skinny, making Wade wonder how they supported such long leaves. He chopped down two dozen, and then split the stems down the middle, leaving about half the leaf on each side.

After hauling his bundles of leaves back to the side of Mindy's hammock, he showed her how to interweave the fingers of the leaves to make the tops water resistant if not waterproof. While she worked on that chore, Wade cut down a couple of dozen saplings and stripped the limbs from the trunks of the young trees. He leaned them against the limb above Mindy, adjusting the length of each one with his ax. When he finished cutting and adjusting the side of the hut, he lashed the saplings together with some parachute cords.

He tested the strength of the lean-to by climbing to the top. There was no give in it assuring Wade it would hold up in the weather. Then he began the slow process of layering the interwoven palmetto leaves from the ground to the top of the structure. He ran out of leaves several times and had to replenish the pile that Mindy was working with. He probably used too many leaves, but he wanted to make sure they'd be protected from any storm. Using some twine from his pack, he tied off the skinny stems to the leaning saplings to ensure there wouldn't be any slippage during a high wind.

When he finished one side of the hut, he stepped back to survey his work in progress. He was pleased with their work so far, but was surprised that the sun was on the verge of disappearing over the western horizon. He hadn't realize how much time they had spent on this simple chore. "We'll have to finish this side of it tomorrow. I don't want to wander off in the swamp at night and I don't want to use up the flashlight battery. We might need it if we walk out of here."

"Not sure I like how that sounds. But I agree with you. I'm so tired, I could go to sleep for a week."

"You did great today. You're not real good at steering a

parachute, though. You might want to work on that if you plan to do this often."

"I didn't plan to do it today. But at least we're alive and have a chance. I wish I could get out of this hammock and closer to the fire."

"Your wish is my command, Ma'am."

Wade gently lifted Mindy out of her hammock and placed her on the ground next to the small fire.

"This fire will keep the mosquitoes, ticks, red bugs, spiders and snakes away."

"Then we need to move it underneath my bed." Mindy laughed.

"Actually, that's not a bad idea. Maybe not directly underneath your bed, but at least underneath our little shelter. We don't want Roasted Mindy in the morning."

"Yeah, I always said I wanted to be hot, but not that hot."

Her giggles made Wade feel better.

"You don't have to worry about that. You and Mandy could seduce the paint off a bowling ball if you wanted to."

"So why doesn't it work on you, Wade?"

"I have too much to lose. Sam is so special to me that fifteen or twenty minutes of pleasure could never replace what I would risk."

"Fifteen or twenty minutes? Aren't you bragging or exaggerating a little?" Mindy laughed.

"Okay, just a little. How about five to ten minutes of pleasure?"

"Hmm. Most of the guys I know are more like bottle rockets with a short fuse. And after they blast off, they're about as useful as a used bottle rocket."

Wade laughed out loud. "Hadn't really thought of it like that. Not bad though."

"Wade, what are we going to do out here without TV, without music, without computers or even cell phones that work?"

"We're gonna stay busy. We have to complete the other side of our hut and make it completely waterproof before a storm sneaks up on us. I've got to figure out a way to catch the rainwater. I'd rather drink that than the water out of the slough. We also need to feed ourselves for a couple of days. I have some MREs, but not enough to last forever."

What exactly is an MRE again?"

"Stands for Meals Ready to Eat. The army used to serve them, but now they've gone commercial. Not great, but good if you're hungry."

"Let me guess. They come in Cottonmouth and Alligator flavors."

Wade grinned. "No, I believe the ones I have are Pasta Alfredo with Chicken and the others are some type of lasagna. Just add boiling water directly in the pouch and stir. Let it sit for ten minutes and Presto, you have a meal."

"Pasta Alfredo and lasagna don't sound too bad."

"There may be some other flavors in there. I wasn't paying too much attention when I bought them. You know, it's kind of like buying insurance. The only time you really read the fine print is if you need it. I was hoping never to need the MRE's."

"Beats the hell out of what you tried to get me to eat for lunch."

"I'll admit they should hopefully taste better than that. They aren't supposed to replace a filet from Ruth's Chris, but they should help get us through the week."

"Oh, my. Ruth's Chris filet. Can we make reservations for tomorrow night?"

"And miss the full adventure of the Atchafalaya Resort?"

"Oh yeah, the pleasures of the Atchafalaya basin. How silly of me."

Wade picked up a log and threw it on the fire, sending sparks flying, illuminating the immediate area around the fire. The flickering flames chased away the chill of the damp swamp surrounding the campsite.

They sat in silence by the fire, each alone in their own thoughts. Despite the confidence he displayed for Mindy, he had plenty of misgivings about spending several days alone in the swamp with her.

"I think I'll build that fire under your bed. Not only will it keep the critters away, it'll keep the nighttime chill from bothering you. Remind me to get that space blanket out of my pack and put over you tonight."

"How about you?"

"It won't take long for me to put up my chute as a hammock beside yours, if you don't mind the company."

"When my assistant made the reservations here at the Atchafalaya Resort, the clerk assured her I'd have a single room. But since you went out of your way to serve the Cottonmouth Pie, I guess the least I can do is share my room with you."

Wade carried a log that was burning on one end and placed it just outside of the make-shift hut. He gathered plenty of the fallen timber surrounding the camp and placed it beside the new fire site. After revving the fire up, he placed some green limbs over the top, knowing they would burn slowly through the night. He then placed green palmetto leaves on top of the pile a few at a time, never enough to smother the fire.

"What are you putting those on there for? Won't it make it smoke up the place?"

"That's the idea, anyway. We should get a lot of smoke out of them, but only for a little while. That'll clear out all those critters we were talking about and send a signal to the others to stay away. If we don't do this, we'll have those pesky little fellows climbing all over us all night. Makes it hard to get a good night of sleep."

"I'm glad I brought along Wilderness Jim for my companion on this merry adventure."

"Wait until you see me wrestle some of those alligators in that slough behind you before you pass out too many accolades. Those type of critters get just as hungry as me and you and they're a lot bigger than we are."

"Hadn't really thought about that. But they wouldn't want me though. I wouldn't be much more than an appetizer for them. On the other hand, a big strapping hunk of meat like you would make them a fine meal."

"I don't know whether or not to take that as a compliment." Wade grinned. "But speaking of food, I'll get the other sandwich out of your bag and split it with you if you're hungry."

"For some reason, I'm having trouble getting full."

Wade was surprised to find two sandwiches remaining in her pack.

"You must have made five sandwiches instead of four. We can finish them if you like."

"Sounds good. I don't remember what all I put in there."

"You still have plenty of food and lots of drinks left, but I don't see any more sandwiches."

17 MONDAY AFTERNOON
EVERGREEN

"Gus, I know they're okay, but I wish I knew where they are." Sam continued pacing up and down the conference room, unable to sit comfortably for any length of time. The dark bags under her swollen eyes told more about her than any words could have expressed. She had tried to keep up a confident exterior throughout the day, but as the hours wore down, she became more and more withdrawn. "He would have called me if he could. Why hasn't he called?"

"Have some confidence in him, Girl. He will get to a place where he can contact you. I don't know where he's at, but I still believe he's okay. It's been less than a day. For anyone but Wade, we wouldn't even have started an investigation yet."

"I know. We usually make people wait twenty-four hours. Now I know how they feel and I'll never make them wait a full day again."

"We don't even know if Mindy is with him. She might be off playing with a new boyfriend for all we know."

"C'mon, Gus. Even you don't believe that. They're together. Of that, I'm sure."

"Wade can take care of both of them."

"For Mindy's sake, I hope so. I'm not sure she's capable of ordering a hamburger by herself."

"Don't be catty. They're just friends; unusual friends, I admit. But they're just friends." Gus didn't know if he was trying to convince Sam or himself.

"I'm the Sheriff and I feel so useless right now."

"We've turned over every rock and stuck our hand in every stinking hole in this county. We've rousted every two-bit hustler and threatened to take them and their families to jail. But nobody knows anything. If any of that scum had any idea of something bad happening to Wade, we would have known it by now."

"So, where do we go from here?"

Gus meandered around with his hand on his grizzled chin. Suddenly, his eyes widened.

"Sam, a long time ago when I attended Evergreen High School, we had a teacher named Mrs. Kornsby. We called her 'Witch Kornsby' behind her back, but we were real careful not to let her overhear us. She was one of the meanest old ladies I've ever met in my life."

"Is this going to be another long story, Gus?"

"Why? You got something better to do?"

"Not really." Sam plopped down in one of the conference room chairs.

"Anyway, as I was saying before I was so rudely interrupted, we had Mrs. Kornsby for a teacher and nobody liked her. She taught math and seemed to enjoy failing students. She taught the old-fashioned math, not the kind they have today with all the computers and gadgets that take away people's ability to think for themselves. You know, that's what is wrong with these young kids today. They don't have to think for themselves. They just punch a button on a computer or a car and everything is done for them."

"Gus, please."

"Okay. Did I mention that she taught math? Ah, I thought so. Well, you see; Mrs. Kornsby—I never knew her first name, but I guess that ain't that important. Anyway, Mrs. Kornsby used to give us problems that we had to figure out instead of just throwing a bunch of formulae and numbers at us. She loved to give us word problems, and she always taught us we had to pick out the right formula to fit the problem. I remember one of them was about a girl named Susie. Susie met a boy she didn't like, but he asked for her phone number. Susie didn't want to give it to him, but she gave him a formula to figure it out."

"Gus, please, please, please."

"Mighty testy, aren't we? That's the problem with you youngsters. No patience at all."

"Are we going to get to the end of this story?"

"Keep your shirt on. Mrs. Kornsby taught me one thing. Toward the end of the school year, she gave us a one-question test that was worth as much to our final grade as all the other full-length tests combined. We fretted all week about how long this one question would be and how many formulas we'd need to solve it. Finally, that Friday came and sure enough, there was only one question on the test."

"And?"

"The question was 'When you get the final test, what is the first thing you need to do to solve each problem correctly?' You know, I was the only one in the entire class that got the answer right. There were only six kids in the entire class, but I was the only one to get it right. All the others had answers like 'Apply the right equation' or 'Put the right numbers in the correct formula' and things like that."

"And your brilliant answer was?"

"Read the damn problem. You can't figure out how to solve a problem unless you know what the problem is. We've got to figure out what the problem is here before we can solve it."

"I don't know. We know exactly what the problem is. Wade and Mindy are missing and we don't have a clue why they're missing or where they are. Seems simple to me."

"You hit it at the end of that statement, Sam. We don't know why they are missing. That's what we need to figure out. Then we'll know where they are."

Sam's pacing intensified. "And how do we find out why they are missing?"

"Go back and read the problem."

Sam clinched her fists. "Gus, you're talking in circles. I'm not getting what you're saying."

"Two days ago they found a body in one of Wade's hunting stands on his property. Wade's name was written on a piece of paper inside one pocket. Mindy was with him when they discovered the body. In fact, she was the one that found the body. Correct?"

Sam nodded her head, but her fists remained clinched.

"Do you really think it is a coincidence that Wade and Mindy disappeared this morning? Those two events have to be connected."

"But how?"

"I don't know. That's why we have to go back and read the problem."

"Okay, I'm willing, but where do we go to read the problem?"

18 MONDAY AFTERNOON
EVERGREEN

GUS RAPPED SHARPLY ON THE DOOR OF THE DECEASED Councilman, Kenny Thigpen. An elderly lady answered the door.

"Hello, Eve. Is Reba in? We'd like a few minutes with her if she's up to it."

"Let me check. This whole thing is just terrible on her. Why don't ya'll come in while I check on Reba?"

Eve left Gus and Sam alone in the tidy parlor and disappeared into a bedroom. Gus whispered in Sam's ear, "That's Reba's mama."

A few minutes later, a disheveled slim lady emerged from the bedroom, wiping her eyes with a tissue.

"Hello, Gus. Hello, Sheriff. I know we've met, but I don't remember where."

"That's okay, Ms. Thigpen. We met at one of the Mayor's office parties. Please, call me Sam."

"Okay, Sam. And call me, Reba. I knew your father fairly well from some public functions, but he rarely brought you and your sister to them."

"He thought it was better for us to spend time with the

animals out at the Plantation. My dad would get a little frustrated with the nuances of politics, I'm afraid."

"Come on in and have a seat. I apologize about the mess everything is in. You know, with everyone coming in and out— "

Sam saw no mess, but responded anyway.

"That's okay, Reba. We understand and know this is under terrible circumstances. We're also aware that my deputies have already spoken to you."

"They came by Saturday to let me know about Kenny."

Gus plopped down on the brown couch, and Sam took a seat in one of the rocking chairs. Reba sat in an overstuffed leather seat across from them. No one sat in the recliner next to the reading lamp.

"Reba, we're not gonna take much of your time. I tried to come by Saturday night, but the ladies told me you weren't up to talking just yet."

"That was my sister and my neighbor. I apologize, but everything was such a shock to me. I was in a daze. I still can't believe it happened."

Reba wiped a few more tears from the corners of her eyes. There was no mascara left to on her lashes to run.

"Reba, did Kenny know Wade? Wade helped me investigate the murder of Rachel Thomas, the intern at City Hall."

"He'd met him because of the investigation. I thought both of you interviewed Kenny together. At least that's what he told me. I've heard that Wade is missing along with another young lady, Sam. Is it true that he's your fiancée?"

"Yes, it's true. We're trying to find out if there's any connection between the two incidents."

"I don't know, Sam."

"What was Kenny doing out at the Plantation early

Saturday morning? Did he tell you why he was going out there?"

"I only know what I told your deputies. Kenny got a phone call late Friday night or I guess it was actually early Saturday morning. He said something about Wade and got up and dressed. I asked him what was going on and he said he had to meet someone, but he didn't tell me who or why. He said it wouldn't take long and for me to go back to sleep. That's the last thing he ever said to me."

The tears that had come so frequently for Reba since Saturday reappeared, flowing freely down her face. Sam had trouble holding back her own tears and took out a tissue from her pocket and began dabbing her own eyes. When she glanced at Gus, his old grizzled face wrinkled, and one or two tears formed. Gus shifted uneasily in the rocking chair and looked around the small den.

"Reba, I know this is hard, but do you know of any connection between Kenny and Wade other than the murder investigation?"

"I don't know. I wasn't involved in Kenny's business dealings very much. He rarely spoke about the things he did at work."

"Tell me what he did again. Some sort of adviser, wasn't he?"

"He was a business adviser. He helped businesses grow, buy up other companies, or get their own ready to sell. Maybe Wade talked to Kenny about the Plantation."

"Wade said nothing to me about it, Reba. But he might not have told me everything. Men sometimes don't like to tell us about all the stuff going on in their lives."

"Ain't that the truth?"

"Did Kenny go out of town for business very much?"

"Not for a long time. Then he started going out a lot. Mostly to Biloxi for meetings and conferences."

"Did that continue after the murders at City Hall?"

"No, he almost never went out of town after that."

Reba slumped noticeably in her overstuffed chair.

"Did Kenny ever mention Ann Clement?"

"Isn't that the girl that works for Collier Templet?"

Sam nodded.

"We know her. She's a nice girl, beautiful."

"Have you met her boyfriend"

"Kenny did. He was disappointed when Andy didn't stay at Southern Miss. Kenny thought he could have been the best player since Brett Favre, but Andy left."

"What did Kenny think of Andy?"

"As a player," Reba wiped another tear, "he thought Andy was great. But he said the kid has anger-management issues. He has a hard time handling stress. Why are you asking these questions about Andy? Do you think he killed Kenny?"

"His name came up, but we have no reason to suspect him." Sam replied.

"Wouldn't surprise me. Kenny said he broke another player's arm when the thought the kid was hitting on his girlfriend."

"We won't take up much more of your time. Can I ask you for one more favor?"

"Sure, Sam."

"Can we get a key to Kenny's office? He might have some records down there that'll shed some light on some of this."

Reba hesitated, then nodded. "If you think it'll help?"

"I hope so. I want to find out what happened to Kenny

and find out if there is a connection between that and Wade and Mindy."

"I hope you find them, Sam. I never got to tell Kenny 'Goodbye'. I just went back to sleep Saturday morning."

"I know the funeral is in the morning and I'm gonna try to make it. Can we come back tomorrow afternoon?"

"Yeah, sure. I can't guarantee I'll be in any better condition then, but let me get that key for you now just in case."

Sam and Gus left Reba's with the key in their pocket, but very few answered questions.

19 MONDAY AFTERNOON
EVERGREEN

"WHAT ARE WE LOOKING FOR?"

Sam and Gus searched the small two-room office of Kenny Thigpen, the now deceased City Councilman. He shared it with his assistant, Traci Long. Gus, hearing the question from Sam, glanced up from the pile of papers stacked in front of him.

"Any connection between Kenny and the Plantation, or Kenny and Wade, or anything that will give us a direction to go in."

"It'd be a lot easier if there were a big arrow that said 'Start Here'. His office looks like yours."

"I don't have an assistant like he does. When are you going to put one of those in the budget?"

"Then I wouldn't get any work out of you and we'd be dealing with lawsuits all the time for harassment."

Gus chuckled. "Depends on who you hire."

Sam shrugged and continued digging through the filing cabinets.

"Sam, I thought of a great idea."

Sam arched her eyebrows.

"Why don't you hire the Thomas twins? We could get two for one."

Sam was wiping sweat from her brow. "I'm sure you'd like that. They'd harass you more than you could harass them. For an old pervert like you, that'd be heaven, which is why it'll never happen."

"Here we go." Gus pulled out a series of manila folders from one of the ragged cardboard boxes.

"What is it?"

"They're labeled '*Expense Reports*'. If I know Kenny, he wrote off his trips with Rachel as business expenses. There may be something in here about the mysterious project that nobody will talk about."

Gus threw half of the folders on the desk toward Sam and kept the other half in his lap. Sam quickly shuffled through her stack and suddenly froze on one.

"This one is labeled '*Pics*'. Hope it's what I think it is."

The first few pictures were of Kenny and Reba with other city officials and their significant others. Sam recognized images of the officials that were now deceased: Mayor Ed Moore, City Councilman Bill Brogan, Purchasing Manager Frank Davis and Intern Rachel Chastain. Included in the other photographs were Bruce Thomas and John Grimes. There were a couple of group photographs of the city officials without their mates at some sites that Sam did not recognize.

"I don't know where these were taken." She handed them to Gus as she looked through them.

Gus held one in his hand for a while. "This one is in Jackson. I recognize the hotel. I took one of my married dates up there. It's well known for its discretion in those matters."

"Think they were there for a conference?"

Gus shook his head. "The conferences these guys went on usually were for the type of job they held at City Hall. You know, Frank went to Civil Purchasing conferences, Bruce goes to City Management conferences and so on. They wouldn't usually go to a conference as a group."

"Then why would they all show up in Jackson at the same time?"

"Let's see. This photograph is stamped *June 13* from two years ago. Let's look at the corresponding expense report and see if it gives us a clue."

"Aha, here it is." Sam sighed after twenty minutes of searching. "It says *'Fact-Finding Trip; Jackson–The Big Project'*. It doesn't say what "The Big Project" is, but the city manager approved the expense report, so it must have been legit."

"Don't tell me we're back to that again. Didn't you and Wade ask everybody in town about the project during the murder investigation and got nowhere?"

"That's the only time I've ever heard of a secret being kept in Evergreen. But not a single person would or could tell us what it was all about."

"If you and Wade still don't know what the big project is, then how can his disappearance be tied to it? That doesn't make any sense. You can't tie things to people unless they at least know what it is."

"You're right, Gus."

"Whoa! Did I hear someone tell me that Ol' Gus is right about something? Be still my achy break heart. I've got to make a note of this."

He pulled an imaginary notepad out of his pocket and wrote an imaginary note with an imaginary pen.

"There. That documents it. I was right about something."

He put away his imaginary notepad back into his pocket.

"Okay, wise guy. You don't need a hammer to drive home your point. Let's keep looking."

Sam pulled out another yellow envelope that had '*Pics*' written on the outside. She peeked inside and shuddered, holding the envelope at arms-length until Gus took it. He peeked inside the envelope and whistled.

"Our murder victim in the last case, if I'm not mistaken."

"Yeah, in positions only a contortionist should be able to make."

"Well, she didn't have any clothes on to restrict her."

"Nope. Not a stitch."

"This explains the business conferences Kenny attended in Biloxi. If I had to guess, most of the business was monkey business and it was all with Rachel. No wonder Kenny didn't tell Reba more about his business trips." Gus was still looking at the pictures in the envelope.

"Gus, put those filthy things away."

He grinned. "But they may be evidence, Sam. I need to examine the evidence, don't I?"

"I guess so. Just don't tell me about them unless you find something in there that'll help me find Wade and Mindy. And quit drooling. It's not professional."

Sam kept looking while Gus focused on the photographs of Rachel. In the next envelope she opened, her heart sank. She handed the envelope to Gus.

Gus took one look inside and whistled, shaking his head.

"Those would be of me, I suppose."

20 MONDAY AFTERNOON
EVERGREEN

THE VOICE IN THE DOORWAY TO THE INNER OFFICE startled both Sam and Gus. Sam stood erect immediately and Gus closed the clasp on the envelope.

"Traci, we didn't hear you come in. Reba gave us permission to look through Kenny's office and loaned us a key."

"I didn't expect anyone to come by until after the funeral. I wanted to find those pictures and get rid of them before anyone else found out about them. Can I have them?"

"I'm sorry, Traci. We can't let you have them until we figure out if they're somehow a part of Kenny's murder."

"There's no way they had anything to do with that, Sam. These were between Kenny and me and nobody else."

"Tell me about them. How did Kenny come into possession of them?"

"He took them."

"You were okay with him doing that?"

"No, of course not!" Traci sat down in one of the office chairs. She closed her eyes and put her hands over them for several seconds. When she removed her hands, her eyes were red, and her face contorted to one side.

"I have bills just like everyone else, Sam. I'm not proud of what I did. I couldn't see any other way."

"Go on."

"I got a notice that they were going to cut off my electricity before payday. I came into Kenny's office and asked for an advance on my check. The business wasn't doing good, and he didn't have a lot of spare change lying around. But he told me that if I would show him some skin, he'd advance me the money. I thought about it and somehow reasoned with myself that I wouldn't be showing him much. So I pulled up my skirt until he could see some leg. He gave me the advance."

Traci paused and glanced around the room as if to make sure no one else had slipped in to overhear the conversation. She looked back directly at Sam, virtually ignoring Gus.

"That meant the next check was reduced by the amount he'd advanced me, and I never seemed to catch up after that. The next time I came in, he wanted to see more cleavage. The next time I had to unbutton my top completely."

Traci paused for a long time.

"I'm not sure when it crossed the line or even if there was a line, but eventually I was doing a striptease on his desk and he was taking pictures. I never meant for it to go that far, Sam. I just didn't want them to cut my electricity and my phone off. The way he made it sound, he'd be the only one that would ever see those pictures, so there was no actual harm."

Sam nodded.

"Does anyone else know about them, Traci?"

Traci started crying and her voice was much softer.

"God, I hope not. I truly hope not."

Sam noticed the ring on Traci's finger. "Engaged?"

"For three months."

"Have you set a date yet?"

"No, but we're close. If he finds out about the pictures—"

"Relax, Traci. We're not gonna tell him. I can't legally give them to you right now. I have to keep them."

"But you know how it works in a town like Evergreen. You've seen them and Gus has seen them." Her face flushed when she glanced at Gus. "Now every deputy at the station will see them and tell everyone they know."

"No one at the station will see them, Traci."

Traci looked up, her eyes wide in disbelief.

"The law, as I understand it, provides that I can put any evidence in a lock box until I can transport it to the evidence locker at the station. It just so happens that I have a lockbox in my trunk and I'm not going to the Sheriff's office tonight, so for safe keeping I'm gonna put the lockbox in my safe at our ranch. The only ones with the combination to the safe are my dad, my sister and me and they don't have a key to the lock box. I don't know how long it may be before I get around to getting it to the station, but if we need it for whatever reason, I'll have maintained custody throughout the process. I believe we can stay legal and preserve your integrity at the same time."

"What about you, Mr. Gus? Are you willing to keep my secret, at least for now?" Traci looked expectantly at Gus.

"Young Lady, I've done a lot of vile things in my life and a lot I'd like to do over again, but I've never betrayed the trust of a young lady engaged to another man. I never will." Gus set his chin and looked directly at Traci.

"I believe you, Mr. Gus."

"Traci, tell me about your fiancée."

"Rick Morgan. He's the most wonderful guy in the world. He treats me like a queen and gets along with my parents. He's everything I've ever wanted in a man."

"Nice. Where does he work?"

"He's teaching science and coaching the football team at the junior high. He's talking to the head coach at the high school about moving over there and becoming an assistant coach."

"Did he play at Evergreen?"

"He was a captain on the team six or seven years ago. Then he played at Mississippi Junior College for a couple of years before getting his degree at Ole Miss. He's perfect for me, Sam."

"Sounds like he's a good guy. You said a few minutes ago that he didn't know about the pictures. What would he do if he found out?"

Traci's eyes narrowed, and she lost a little color in her face.

"He'd probably beat the crap out of Kenny and then he'd break up with me."

Traci's mouth opened a little, but no words came out.

"What is it, Traci?"

"You don't think Rick had anything to do with Kenny's death, do you? Rick wouldn't do that. He's not that kind of person."

"Most of us aren't until someone hurts the person we love, Traci. Then we become different people. Or we become who we really are, but disguise it until something drastic happens."

"Not him, Sam. He is the sweetest guy in the world."

"Do you know where he was late last Friday night?"

"He was with me until around eleven. We went to the

pizza place and had the buffet. Then we rented a movie and went to my apartment and watched it. He must have left between eleven and twelve."

"So you guys aren't living together?"

"I have an apartment even though I can barely afford it. My apartment is the only way we can have some real privacy. Rick still lives with his parents, even though he could afford to move out. He's a little tight."

"Did ya'll talk on the phone, text each other or email each other after he left?"

"I usually send him a text every night right before I go to bed. I'm sure I sent one last Friday night, but I'd have to check my text log to make sure. Hold on."

Traci started furiously hitting buttons on her cell phone.

"Look, here it is. I just said, 'Nite, C U tomorrow.' I don't show a return text, which isn't that unusual. Sometimes he sends one back and sometimes he doesn't."

"Okay, that shows you texted him around midnight. You were at your apartment when you did that, correct?"

"That's correct, although I guess there's nobody that can verify that. I don't usually invite a bunch of people over to watch me sleep."

"I know, Traci. But don't get upset. We have to find out where everybody was and rule as many people out as possible before narrowing the list of suspects down."

"Am I a suspect, Sam?"

"At least not now, Traci. I believe you've been open and honest with your answers. I know how embarrassing this might be for you. Let's switch topics for a few minutes. Tell us about Kenny."

Traci stared out of the window before turning back to face Sam.

"Kenny was two different people. He had a public side

and a private side. The public side of him was outgoing, professional, and likable. The private side of him was kind of sad. He would get withdrawn and pessimistic, at least until the last year or so."

"What happened in the last year to change him?"

"I'm guessing now, Sam. I probably shouldn't do that, but you asked."

"What do you believe changed him?"

"I think he found another girlfriend, Sam."

"You say another. Do you mean another one besides you and what you guys did here in the office? Maybe I misunderstood you before."

"Oh, no. We weren't boyfriend and girlfriend or anything. We never had sex, Sam. He just liked to look."

"Okay, so when you said 'another', you meant he had previous girlfriends?"

"Only one that I know of, Sam. He somehow got involved with Rachel Chastain before they murdered her in the woods. But that didn't last long. She was—uh, how can I say this? She was more high maintenance than he could afford is the most polite way I know to put it."

"Was he still seeing Rachel at the time of her death?"

"I don't believe so. The only reason I say that is for a little while, maybe for three months, he asked me to do what I was doing, you know performing for him more and more. He started paying me extra to do more, but we never had a physical relationship. I thought for a while he was going to make me have sex with him, but he never did. He hinted at it a time or two, but never asked me outright to do it with him. Then it became less and less frequent. He started taking more trips again and seemed to have a lot more money."

"Wait, you're saying Kenny started getting more money after Rachel died than he had before?"

"Yeah." Traci rubbed her fingers through her hair. "Although I never really made a correlation between those two things before. The last few months, he had a lot of money and I don't know where it came from. The business here sure wasn't getting that much better."

"Do you think Reba knew about Rachel or this other affair, if there was another?"

"I don't see her that much. She only stops by here now and then. She calls once or twice a day, but when Kenny was out with Rachel, I'd tell her he was at City Hall and didn't want to be disturbed down there."

"So you knew about what he was doing with Rachel even when it was happening?"

"One day he was out and called in and asked me to get a file off his desk. When I got in here to get it, there was another file on top of it. It was open and showed him and Rachel together, and I mean together."

"That was careless of him."

"But he wasn't a careless man. I believe he wanted me to see it. He wanted me to know, for some reason I can't fathom, that he and Rachel were doing it and he had pictures to prove it."

"So who is, or was the newest girl in his life?"

"I really don't know, Sam. For a while, back right after Rachel was killed, those two Thomas twins showed up here a few times and flirted with Kenny, but I don't think anything happened there. They're too young, even for Kenny."

"Do you have Rick's number handy? We'll need to verify everything with him. Except for the pictures, Traci. We won't bring them up."

Traci punched in the access code for her cell and gave Rick's number to Sam.

"Traci, do you know of anyone that might have a reason to want to hurt or kill Kenny?"

"About half of his clients."

"Why?"

"Kenny's clients, or at least most of them, lost money on Kenny's advice. He wasn't very good at what he did."

"So how did he stay in business?"

"People are buying and selling businesses all the time. Most of them should never be in business. They don't have a clue what it takes to run one, how much money it takes to run one and how to promote their businesses. They figure that if they open the doors, people will come. You know, like in the movie. But in real life it doesn't work that way."

"Traci, you're talking to someone that's run and is running a small business. I know about the pitfalls. Where was Kenny going wrong?"

"The biggest thing he'd do is underestimate the amount of working capital the clients needed to go into business. He'd tell them if they had three months working capital, then they had too much. That's just not true."

"Give us an example."

"Okay, if you were going to open the Cates's Café, for instance. Kenny looks in the book and comes out with a figure for inventory, first month's rent, equipment and insurance. Let's say it's a small café, and the number came out to seventy thousand dollars. He'd add twenty thousand as a guess for what the restaurant would need over the next three months and tell you that you need ninety thousand to open the restaurant."

"Sounds reasonable." Gus interjected.

"It's not even close, Mr. Gus.

"What's missing?"

A lot. Deposit for the rent, dead time when there's no revenue coming in, but there's still expenses, training time and costs for new employees, uniforms, spoilage, employee theft and I could go on and on. The employee theft is out the wazoo, before you open and after you open. They see food and don't think anything about eating some or taking it home. Same thing with the drinks. Most people don't know they'll have to run the water lines, gas lines and electrical lines differently and all of that costs they will have to bear before they get any revenue. They forget that it takes money to advertise. One guy told me that a business either has to advertise its grand opening or it'll soon be advertising it's *going-out-of-business* sale. From what I've seen, I believe it takes between four hundred thousand to one million dollars to open a nice restaurant and ensure it'll stay open long enough to survive. It depends on the location, size and style of the restaurant. Some extravagant ones will cost more."

"Holy Jehoshaphat." Gus was rubbing his forehead. "I never thought of all of that."

Traci hesitated before replying. "Most people don't. They want to get into business. They were depending on Kenny to get them into one they could afford. Eighty to ninety percent of them didn't last two years. And the banks are hesitant to loan any business money if the track record is less than two years."

"You know your stuff, Girl. I'm impressed." Gus said with a sign of admiration in his voice.

"Thanks, Mr. Gus. I tried to tell Kenny, but he was set in his ways. He said most businesses were gonna fail anyway, so why not make money off their inability to survive? Inevitably, they'd come back to him in a year or two and he'd get to resell the business to someone else."

"Does Reba know anything about running this business?"

Traci shook her head.

"I guess this business will fail along with all the rest. I'm not sure what I'm gonna do. There aren't a lot of jobs out there in this economy."

Sam looked around the office.

"Why don't you take this one over? I'm not sure how much it's worth, but with Kenny gone, I wouldn't think it'd be much. Or you could start your own."

Traci dropped her gaze to the desk. "I can't afford to start my own, Sam. Remember, the upfront costs are considerably higher than most people estimate and I'm having trouble paying my rent."

Sam pulled her cell out and after checking her notes taken previously during the day, punched in a number.

"Reba, Sam here. Sorry to bother you, but I have a question that needs an answer."

After a brief pause, "Are you planning on keeping Kenny's business running?"

"Okay, instead of closing down and getting nothing but headaches, how much would you take for the assets? Not a stock buy-out, but the phone number and the records, mostly."

"I see. Let me see if I can help you."

"No problem, Reba. I'll get back to you after everything settles down."

Sam ended her cell call and turned to Traci. "Reba will sell the phone number and records for ten thousand. Is that a good price?"

Traci laughed. "It's a steal for somebody that can afford it."

"How about operating expenses? How much are they a

month?"

"For everything except Kenny's pay, it runs about six thousand a month. That includes my salary and health benefits. That was one thing I appreciated, the health benefits."

Sam reached into her pocket and retrieved her checkbook.

"Here's a check for one hundred and twelve thousand; ten thousand for Reba and one year of working capital and money for an assistant. Can you draw up the paperwork?"

"Sure, Sam. Why do you want to buy this business?"

"I'm not buying it. We are. I get fifty-one percent for funding it and you get forty-nine percent for running it. Any excess money you make above your expenses will be put into the bank for a buy-out fund. When the fund equals my investment, you can buy me out of my half with that money. Is that agreeable with you?"

Tears well up in Traci's wide eyes, even as a huge grin spread across her face.

"Sam, I don't know what to say. I'm at a loss for words, but thank you, thank you, thank you."

"Don't thank me until you see how hard it is to run a business."

"Why are you doing this? You don't even know me that well."

Sam shook her head.

"I can't really explain it, Traci. Maybe part of it is the emotions I'm feeling with Wade missing. Part of it is the abuse I've found out about right here in Evergreen. Maybe I just don't want you to have to dance on another boss's desk to get your paycheck you've already earned. Whatever the reason, I know it's the right thing to do."

"But what if I fail, Sam?"

"Then I want you to look me in my eyes and tell me you did the very best you could do. I don't think the two things are compatible. If you do your best, you won't fail."

Traci walked over to Sam and gave her the tightest hug she could give. Even old Gus was daubing his eyes with a big grin.

"I'm not gonna fail you, Sam. I won't fail us."

"I know, Traci. Look, we'd better get on with the investigation. Can you either fax or email me a list of Kenny's clients that may have been dissatisfied with his work? Also, if you find something that would tell us who his newest girlfriend might be, let us know."

"Thank you again, Sam. I'll get that list to you."

Gus and Sam reached her car before either said anything.

"We'd better find Wade soon or you're gonna go broke."

"I know, Gus. I don't think I've ever done anything that impulsive in my entire life. But it sure felt good inside to do it."

"It may feel good inside, Sam, but I'm not sure it was good business."

"I know it wasn't. Heck, it wasn't even close to being a good business decision. Maybe I'm trying to bribe God. You know, if I do enough good things, then He'll return Wade to me safe and sound."

"I don't go to church as much as you do, Sam and I don't pretend I'm at all religious, but from what I remember when I attended, He don't work that way."

"I know that, Gus, but I've got to try everything and I mean everything to get Wade back. What's next on our list?"

"We can either interview Rick or Mandy. Whichever you like."

21 MONDAY AFTERNOON
EVERGREEN

"Mandy, thanks for taking the time to see us. I know this has to be tough on you and Bruce."

Mandy stroked her long strawberry blonde hair. "I can barely concentrate on anything. Ya'll come on in."

Gus sat in the brown leather recliner while Mandy and Sam sat on the sofa together.

Sam leaned forward. "I know the feeling. I want you to know we're doing everything we can to find your sister and Wade. We'll find them. Somehow, I just know we'll find them safe."

"I know you are. I went up to the National Forest with all of those volunteers this afternoon, traipsing around in the woods, but she isn't there. I knew after I was there for fifteen minutes that we were looking in the wrong place." Mandy looked away.

"How did you know?"

Mandy raised her head. "There are some things that can't be explained about twins. I know you and Connie are as close as sisters can be, but there's nothing like a bond between sisters that share the exact genes. Not the genes from the same parents, but the one fertilized egg that split and made us both. We can sense each other if we're in the same room or miles apart. I know a lot of folks think that's nonsense, but they don't have a twin sister."

"Tell me what you're sensing." Sam sat on the edge of the sofa.

Mandy clasped both hands together.

"Just what I said, Sam. They aren't in the National Forest. At least Mindy's not. I can't speak for Wade, but I assume they're together. I can only say for sure she's not in the forest or anywhere close to it. Daddy is still up there looking with everyone else, but it's a waste of time. He feels like he should be there with the volunteers since they're out there giving up their time to look for them."

"Anything else?"

"She's alive. I know that. She went through some turmoil earlier during the day, but now she's calmed down. I get the feeling that someone's watching over her, which I can only assume is Wade."

"Can you tell if she's with Wade all the time or just part of the time? Do you get a sense that they're stuck somewhere together?"

"That's what I'm sensing. But again, my senses only come from Mindy, not from who's with her. Now and then, I get a sense of increased stress, so they might not be together all the time, but for the most part, I think they're together."

Sam could not help but smile.

"That's the best news I've had all day. That means there's a great chance both of them are still alive and together. Thank you for sharing that. You mentioned you could sense Mindy in the same room or a long way apart. Do you get a sense that you're a long way from her?"

Mandy paused.

"I hadn't really thought about it. I was just glad I could sense her and know that she was alive and safe. Now that you've brought it up, my sense is that she isn't close to Evergreen at all. Otherwise, I believe I would've gotten a stronger vibe from her when I was with the volunteers this afternoon in the forest. I didn't get that sense of being physically close to her, so I guess that means she's a long way off, if you believe in my vibes from her."

Sam smiled the more Mandy talked, and her eyes cleared for the first time since Wade's truck was found in the National Forest. "I'm sure glad we came by to see you, Mandy. You'll never know how much this means to me. I believe in your connection to Mindy."

Mandy leaned back in her chair.

"Most people think these vibes or senses between twins are poppycock. But Mindy and I learned a long time ago they're real and get stronger. Or maybe we just learned how to better interpret them. I'm not sure which is the case, but we have more faith in them now than ever before."

Sam put her two hands together and pointed them at Mandy.

"Thanks for sharing yours with us. I've never considered the bond, if you will, between twins. I've heard that sometimes twins can feel each other's pain, but I never thought about it above that. You know, the feeling of being close or safe or happy. That's unfamiliar territory for me."

Mandy fiddled with her hair before answering.

"I don't know about other twins. I can only tell you about Mindy and me, nothing else."

"I have a huge favor to ask of you, but I don't want to get you in trouble or put you in danger."

"If it helps us find Mindy and Wade, all you have to do is ask."

"Several people from City Hall, including Kenny and your dad, took a trip to Jackson last year and we think Wade and Mindy's disappearance may be connected to something or someone on that trip. We could get subpoenas for the records at City Hall, but that may take several days if not weeks to get through. We want to know who went, where they stayed and why they went to Jackson. We were hoping you could help us find out about that trip, off the record."

"Was Rachel with them?"

"Yes, and all the guys that were connected to her. The ones that were murdered last year all went on that trip. If we go to the city, they'll probably want to keep the expense reports and any resulting reports sealed under the circumstances."

Mandy quit playing with her hair. "Did you say Daddy was with them?"

"He was."

"Hold on." Mandy punched a speed-dial button on her cell phone. "Hello, Daddy?" She rose and walked out of the room into the backyard.

Gus leaned over to Sam and whispered, "Do you really believe all that gobbledygook about one twin being able to feel the other one's pain even when they can't see each other?"

"I've never considered it before, Gus. But the important thing to me right now is that Mandy believes in it and she has no doubt that Mindy is alive and safe."

"You're dancing around the question. I asked if you believed in it, not if Mandy believes in it."

"I didn't dance around your question. I answered as truthfully as I can."

"If you danced any more, we'd have to get you one of those tutus and a pair of slippers. Do you really believe in it?"

"I have to believe in it. That's all I have to hang onto right now."

"Because if she's right, then Wade is safe. Is that what you mean?"

Sam closed her eyes and nodded. "That's probably part of it." She opened her eyes and looked at Gus. "Okay, that's a big part of it. I have to believe Wade is safe, Gus. I don't want to lose him now. What Mandy is saying gives me the hope I need to keep moving forward."

Gus didn't say anything, but leaned back in his chair.

"Gus, you don't believe in this, do you? The sensory stuff?"

"I think we're looking at it from the perspective each of us have on this investigation. You know, the old chicken and pig thing for breakfast."

"Chicken and pig thing?"

"It's an old saying and I'm not sure who came up with it. Both the chicken and the pig are committed to breakfast. The chicken is committed to giving us eggs for breakfast and the pig is committed to being breakfast. Whole different perspective. I'm the chicken and you're the pig in this investigation and all of this ESP stuff. I want to believe, but you have to believe."

"Gus, I didn't know you were a philosopher."

"Only when I'm sober, Dear. Only when I'm sober. Speaking of that, can we get a drink around here somewhere?"

Sam laughed and shook her head. He then heard Mandy re-enter through the back door.

"Daddy will meet with us tomorrow morning as early as you want to. He doesn't want to leave the volunteers up at the Forest right now."

22 MONDAY NIGHT
ATCHAFALAYA BASIN

WADE BRUSHED THE REMAINDER OF THE FIRE TO THE center of the circle.

"C'mon, it's time for little girls to get into bed."

Mindy's hazel eyes reflected in the moonlight. "Are you making a proposal, Sailor?"

Wade stomped out a few embers near the edge.

"I'm proposing that you get in your hammock and I get in my hammock and we get enough rest to have the energy to do everything we need to do tomorrow to get ready for the rest of the week."

"Party pooper."

"Maybe so, but you'll thank me tomorrow."

Mindy grinned.

"Only if the room service around here serves me a western omelet and a frosty glass of orange juice before I have to get up."

Wade gave her a mock salute.

"Sorry, Ma'am. We're a little short of western omelets unless I can find some turtle or alligator eggs in the morning. We may be short of orange juice. We've been having trouble with our food supplier lately."

She shook her finger at him.

"That's not going to help you keep that one-star rating you got so far. I'd hate to see you slip to no stars. Bad for business."

"I agree, Ma'am. I'm certain we can find some cottonmouth omelet, only without the omelet part of it."

"No thanks. I just remembered omelets aren't on my diet." Mindy quit grinning. "Wade, do you really think we'll be here until the weekend? Why the weekend?"

Wade poked at the dying embers with a stick.

"Hunters. The Basin is one of the best hunting areas in North America. There's more deer and hogs in here than most places on earth. It's also in the middle of the flyway for ducks and geese, not to mention the rabbits, squirrels, alligators and other varmints people like to hunt around here."

"So why will it take a week?"

"The hunters come in on weekends, mostly. Some of the Basin is closed off except for the weekends, and in other areas, that's just when most of the hunters come out."

Mindy's prior grin turned into a frown.

"That leaves us with surviving until Friday afternoon or Saturday morning, then."

"That's my guess, Mindy. But we're more prepared than most folks. We have plenty of food and shelter. I'm gonna work tomorrow on a fresh water supply that isn't as muddy as the slough water."

"Wade?"

He looked directly at her. "Yes?"

"Remind me never to complain there's nothing on the

six hundred channels of TV again. Seems like that's not so important anymore."

He laughed.

"I agree with you there. Sometimes, it takes something like this to get our priorities in order. This qualifies as one of those times, I suppose."

Wade walked over to Mindy and gently picked her up. Cautiously, he carried her to the make-shift hammock and placed her in the middle, trying to not further injure her swollen ankle. He placed the space blanket over her petite body. "This will help keep the dampness off of you tonight. It'll also help with the mosquitoes, though I think sometimes they can get through steel doors. If nothing else, it'll help you feel safer."

She grabbed his hand. "My, you are chivalrous. Sam is a lucky girl."

Wade took his hand off hers and turned away. "I don't think she felt that way yesterday. I wish I hadn't said the things I did or acted the way I did. If only I could go back and undo it, I would."

"Relax, Wade. You couldn't help it. You're a male."

Wade chuckled and crawled up to his chute. As he spread out on it, he was pleasantly surprised at the comfort it afforded under these circumstances. He was also surprised at how tired he'd become. Even with all the difficulties surrounding them, he fell into a deep sleep.

Clickety-click. Clickety-click. Clickety-click.

The unmistakable sound of claws embedding in the trunk of the old water oak raised the hackles on the back of Wade's neck, immediately awakening him from a deep sleep. The pupils of his eyes widened to gather in the little light from the moon as they strained to get a glimpse of the source of the sound. His focus went up the tree to the ground below in the early morning haze from the deep swamp. A dense fog swept over the bog, adding to the unease and prickling his senses.

Clickety-click. Clickety-click. Clickety-click.

Wade was awake enough now to determine the animal was descending the other side of the water oak. Looking straight at the oak only inches from his head, he saw out of the corner of his eye a fleeting shadow cross on the ground between the make-shift hut he'd constructed and the dying embers from the fire a few feet away. Wade strained to see or hear anything else, but there were no more sounds or sights to tell him more about the identity of the animal. He glanced over at Mindy and was relieved to see the measured breathing that indicated she wasn't awake. Wade spent the rest of the predawn hours with his eyes wide open and his hand on his revolver.

23 MONDAY NIGHT
EVERGREEN

Sam listened on the phone as Rick explained his relationship with Traci.

"Did you know Kenny very well?"

"No, Ma'am. I met him a few times when I visited Traci at work, but I can't say that I really knew him, Sheriff."

"What did you think of him?"

The young man paused before answering. "Just what Traci told me."

"What did she tell you, Rick?"

There was a long silence. "Didn't you talk to her this afternoon?"

"Yes, but I'd rather hear from you what she said about Kenny."

Rick stuttered when answering the question. "She told me he was a nice enough boss. That he had a few quirks, but overall he was a nice guy."

"What quirks did she mention?"

Another long silence. "I'd really prefer if you asked Traci directly about Mr. Thigpen."

"She may have told you something that she didn't tell

us. We need to cover all of our bases. We have a murder that we need to solve. I'm asking for your help."

"Okay, what was the question again?"

"What quirks did she mention?"

"Oh, some silly things like try to look up her dress or down her shirt." He paused. "You know, the things a teenager would do rather than a grown man. She said he wasn't very mature in that area."

"Do you think she felt safe working for Kenny?"

"I didn't mean to imply that he was dangerous or anything like that. He was just immature. I think Traci could handle Kenny pretty easily."

"So she never told you if he tried to go any further than looking up her skirt or down her shirt? Is that what I understand?"

"Yes, Ma'am. I'm sure she would have told me if anything else happened. She and I have a close relationship." The youngster spoke with more confidence. "I guess we should if we're going to get married, huh?"

Sam stared at the lock box containing the packet of pictures of Traci in various stages of undress in Kenny's office. She shook her head and continued.

"Did you ever meet Kenny outside of his office?"

"Only one time that I remember, Sheriff. He invited Traci to a luncheon at City Hall, and Traci asked him if I could come along. He agreed, and we both went down there. All the local politicians were there."

"Anything happen there that would make you think Kenny was in any danger?"

"Not really." Another long pause. "Mr. Thigpen got into an animated discussion with another girl there. You know, the one killed up in the forest. Rachel."

"Were you able to hear what they were talking about?"

"Just bits and pieces. Something about not enough time, a big project and a meeting in Jackson. I wish I could be more helpful, but I wasn't trying to listen to them. I kinda got distracted."

"How so, Rick?"

"Do you really have to know that?"

"Yes."

The confidence dissipated.

"There's two twins that went to the luncheon. Me and Traci and Rachel were the only ones there around the same age as them, so I was just looking at them, you know. Traci thought maybe I was looking too close and wasn't paying enough attention to her. That's one of the few times we've ever gotten into a fight."

"Would that be the Thomas twins, Mindy and Mandy?"

"That's right." Rick chuckled. "Duh. One of them is missing with your boyfriend, isn't she?"

"That's correct."

"It's a small world."

"We're just about finished. Has Traci ever told you of anyone that was angry enough or had any reason to harm Kenny?"

Sam could hear Rick inhale deeply on the other end of the line.

"I want to make sure I answer this accurately, Sheriff. She told me of a bunch of folks that had a reason to be mad at him. But she never told me anyone was mad at him or tried to do him any harm."

"I appreciate you being honest, Rick. One more question."

"Yes'm."

"Where were you late Friday night and early Saturday

morning?"

"Hmm. I know I was with Traci. We're together just about every night." Rick breathed a little harder into the phone. "Oh yeah, last Friday night we got a pizza and rented a movie. We watched the movie at her apartment. I don't remember exactly when it was over, but I returned it to the kiosk after we watched it. I usually forget if I don't return them as soon as we're finished and end up having to pay extra for them. I don't like that."

"What then, Rick?"

"Uh, I went home."

"Can your parents verify this?"

A long pause. "They were asleep when I got here."

"So they can't verify the time you arrived back at your house?"

"No, Ma'am, I guess not."

"Okay, that's all the questions I have for now, Rick. I'll see you guys at the funeral tomorrow."

24 TUESDAY MORNING
ATCHAFALAYA BASIN

Wade eased out of his chute as soon as the predawn light was bright enough for him to see without using his flashlight. He tried not to disturb Mindy and was relieved when he glanced at her horizontal body in her chute and her small chest expanding and contracting in a rhythmic pattern. He hoped that she had slept peacefully through the entire night.

As soon as his feet touched the ground, he immediately searched for signs of the animal that had been in the same tree as he and Mindy. The soft bog held all the clues from the night before, and after only two steps, he found what he was looking for. Suddenly, the temperature in the foggy swamp seemed to drop dramatically, bringing a chill across Wade's entire body, causing him to shiver.

That's one helluva cat! Look at that paw print. It's as big as my hand, even bigger. That's no bobcat. He must've been sitting in the water oak above us all day yesterday watching everything we did. He could've attacked Mindy any number of times in her condition and she wouldn't have had a chance. I'm not sure I would've had a chance if he'd attacked me. I wonder why he stayed up there all day and most of the night before coming down.

Wade nervously walked back to the water oak and examined the branches above the make-shift hut on the opposite side of the tree. He found what he was looking for about twenty feet above his hammock. A half-eaten whitetail fawn wedged in a fork of the water oak, guaranteeing the big cat a good meal without the fear of scavengers on the ground stealing it before it could return.

It has to be a jaguar. Only a swamp jaguar is big enough to carry a deer that high. But there's only been a few sightings of a black cat on a few game cameras that I've heard about. Can we be the unluckiest people alive to land in a tree that one of the few jaguars in the entire Atchafalaya Basin has stored his next meal? Apparently so. Hell, his next meal may me Mindy or me. He could carry either of us to the top of the tree with no trouble at all.

Wade walked around the tree and back several times, alternating his gaze from high in the branches to the foggy area immediately surrounding their camp, which Wade now knew was much less safe than he had previously thought.

What do we do now? We can't move. Mindy's ankle won't allow her to go anywhere soon. Even if I try to carry us, the big cat can track us a lot quicker than we could slog through this mess and go a lot further than we can. He still has a meal left in the very tree our hut is next to and we're in his territory now—his territory! That doesn't sound good.

Wade spent the next hour weighing their options before coming to a conclusion. He retrieved the small hatchet and chopped down a lot of small saplings. By the time Mindy woke up, he'd gathered enough to fully encapsulate the make-shift hut.

"Good morning, Princess. I trust you had a good night's sleep in our most luxurious suite."

Mindy laughed. "Most luxurious suite, huh? I'd hate to see the economy suites. It wasn't too bad. You might have the maintenance staff adjust the air conditioner a tad. It got a little chilly late in the night."

"Sorry, Ma'am. I'll have the staff inspect it immediately."

"Oh, yeah. One more thing."

Wade looked up expectantly. "Yes?"

Mindy forced a smile.

"You might ask the critters to get their own suite. They make too much noise when they party at all hours of the morning. Bad manners of their part, if you ask me."

Wade stared at her, his mouth agape. "You heard him?"

"Yes. And I know you did. You quit snoring as soon as he started coming down the tree and you never went back to sleep. At least that stopped your snoring, though. Don't get me wrong. I'm not complaining, just commenting."

Wade shook his head. "I didn't think you were awake."

Mindy grinned. "You never learn, do you?"

"I guess not. Anyway, we need to make some adjustments to our cozy living quarters if we want to be safe."

"What do we need to do?" Mindy pushed her legs over the edge of her make-shift bed.

Wade pointed at her.

"You need to sit by the fire and keep it going about twice as high as we had it before. I don't think we'll have much to worry about next to the fire during the daylight hours. Big cats usually like to hunt in the darkness where they have an advantage over their prey."

"Is that why he stayed in the tree yesterday? He didn't want to kill us during daytime?"

Wade rubbed his hand through his hair.

"I'm not sure. That was probably some of it. Part of it was that he had a fresh kill and had already eaten when you came crashing through his tree. Fortunately for us, they like to take long naps after eating just like house cats. Can you imagine how surprised he was when you arrived in his world and woke him up? You ended up below him, so he probably felt trapped until nightfall. He's never seen anything like that before and was just as confused as we were."

"So why are you so concerned? If he wants to eat and sleep, then he should leave us alone. He's already got a meal ready for him in the top of the tree, so he doesn't need any more. Why would he bother us?"

Wade chuckled.

"Would you rather have a fresh steak or a day-old steak? Look at it from the cat's perspective. You're a lot slower and easier to catch than a deer. You aren't as tough to get to as a turtle or an armadillo, and you have a lot more meat on your bones than a rabbit or a mouse. He can pack you right beside the little fawn up there in about thirty seconds, and then he'll have meals for the rest of the week."

Mindy glanced down at her body. "So I'm the perfect meal, huh?"

"Pretty much so."

"Funny. I've never thought of myself that way. I'm not sure I enjoy thinking of myself being part of the food chain and not at the top of it."

"Remember, it's not how we think out here in this swamp. It's how that big cat thinks. He's not overly concerned with making any new friends. His only goal in life is to survive. We're in his territory now."

Mindy lookcd at all the small saplings Wade cut down.

"What are we gonna do with those? Do you know how hard it is for a girl to get her beauty rest when you keep whacking every tree you find out here?"

"Sorry about your beauty sleep. I was hoping you could rest, but I wanted to get an early start. I'm gonna lash these together so that our entire structure is surrounded and try to make it harder for the cat to get in. We'll interweave more palmetto leaves and leave us a small gate to get in and out of. "

"Do you really think that will keep the cat out if he really wants to get us?"

"Nope." Wade patted his revolver. "But long enough for me to let him know he doesn't have reservations in the Presidential Suite."

"I take that to mean you're gonna sleep with that pistol in your hand again all night."

"You saw that too, huh? You don't miss much, do you?" Wade looked intently at her and then smiled.

"Nope. But don't tell anyone. I like it when they underestimate me and think I'm just an irresponsible kid. Makes it a lot easier, if you know what I mean?"

Wade nodded.

"I guess I've underestimated you and Mandy a time or two. Let me get some extra firewood and I'll set you next to it. Then, if you don't mind, start weaving more of those palmetto leaves together. I'll start adding those extra poles to the ends and tie them off."

She shifted in the chute. "What about breakfast? Room service didn't answer when I called down this morning."

"If that cat comes back before we're finished, we may be breakfast instead of having breakfast."

Wade strode over to Mindy's hammock and examined her ankle, again feeling and poking all around it and up her shin.

"Get that smile off your face, Sailor. I need you to be alert in case that cat comes back, not focusing on how my legs feel to you." Mindy grinned.

Wade continued to press her flesh. "Just checking for any more swelling or red lines that would indicate a blood clot. I don't see any, so I think you're going to be fine."

He lifted her from the hammock and placed her next to the big blaze from the extra logs he put on the fire. She wove the palmetto leaves with a purpose, working much faster than she had the day before. Wade lashed the poles, making any entrance for the cat much more difficult than the day before.

A few hours later, he stepped back and observed a much more secure hut with no noticeable gaps in the exterior. He liked what he saw. "It's not perfect, but it'll do. You did a great job on those leaves. We'll give that old cat fits if he visits us tonight."

"I hate to complain about the room service, but can we please get some breakfast now?"

Wade smiled.

"I believe we missed the breakfast serving, but maybe we can open a spot for you at the brunch seating. Will that be okay, Ma'am?"

"I don't care if you call it breakfast, brunch, lunch, dinner or supper. I need something to eat!"

Wade pulled a bag of chips and a soda from her pack and handed it to her.

"Eat this until I can find something in our pantry."

He pointed and turned in a full circle, indicating their entire surroundings.

"I'll go check it out. Care for anything in particular?"

"Cheeseburger, extra mayo with fries and a cherry soda." She hesitated. "And one of those fruit pies would be great."

Wade laughed.

"I'll see what I can do."

He carefully slogged to a nearby patch of young water oaks, his gaze continuously shifting from the oaks to the ominous swamp around him. Using the hatchet, he chopped down a young oak and sharpened the end to a honed point. He tossed his newly fashioned spear until he became accustomed to its flight. Wade felt comfortable hitting anything within ten yards.

He returned to the camp.

"I won't be long, Mindy. Don't go anywhere and don't answer the door to strangers. You know how they can be in this neighborhood."

Wade had a wry grin on his face until he handed her his revolver.

"If you see the old Kitty Kat, use this on him. It holds six shots and you need to use all six. I won't be that far and I should be able to get back by the time you finish him."

She grabbed his arm.

"You just make damn sure you make it back here safe. I don't want to spend the rest of the week out here alone."

Wade hesitated.

"That wouldn't exactly be my first choice either, Mindy. I promise; I'll return. Hey, General Patton said that, didn't he? And he returned."

Wade looked out again at the swamp.

"So will I."

He took her hand off his arm and disappeared into the depths of the swamp. Wade wasn't sure what he was after, but he knew that Louisiana, particularly the Atchafalaya Basin, was host to a plethora of wildlife. He just needed to find some that was edible and easy to take. Crossing over a few small sloughs on some fallen logs, he trailed down a higher ridge that wasn't as boggy as the rest of the swamp. He checked his surroundings often to see if the big cat was near and re-orient himself to prevent losing his way back to camp. All the cypress sloughs looked the same. He marked some trees with a slash from his hatchet, not deep enough to do any permanent damage, but overt enough to see in the daylight. He reached a small pool of water where two sloughs merged into one and sat on one of the old cypress stumps next to it.

At first he saw nothing. After more than a half-hour sitting on the stump, the swamp life returned to normal, and he started seeing much more movement in the area around him. A small cottonmouth swam right next to his boots and eyed him suspiciously. The little snake decided whatever this blob was, it couldn't eat it. Wade decided the snake he had tasted the day before was enough cottonmouth to last him for a while. He might change his mind if he and Mindy could find nothing else, but was in no hurry to try it again.

Another thirty minutes of sitting produced nothing except a sore butt. Then he heard a noise similar to a baby's whine. The noise drew closer and closer until he discerned the brown outline of a large swamp rat, at least that's what he called them.

The nutria was ambling straight for Wade. He was aware they weren't real fast on dry land, but were excellent swimmers and could stay submerged under water for five minutes or more. When the large rat-looking blob was within two feet from the stump, Wade lunged the spear straight through his side into the ground on the other side, pinning the rodent to the ground. He inhaled and exhaled deeply, realizing he had hardly breathed since spotting the animal. Avoiding the webbed claws of the struggling prey, he dispatched the nutria with one swift stroke of the hatchet.

Withdrawing the spear from the dead body, Wade felt a twinge of remorse, but it didn't last long. Nature would replace the nutria several times over in the next few months, and Mindy needed something to eat today. After eviscerating the nutria, Wade retraced his steps back to the camp, bringing only the carcass, the heart and the liver with him.

"Hi, Honey. I'm home." He said in a voice loud enough for Mindy to hear before she could see him or accidentally mistake him for one of the swamp critters. He didn't want a pistol pointed at him when he entered the clearing.

Mindy turned from the fire.

"Hold on, Dear. I was just taking the pecan pie out of the oven. That doesn't look like a cheeseburger and fries you're carrying."

"They were out of buns. Can you believe that? Actually, they were out of cheese, burger patties and fries. Poor management if you're asking me."

Mindy wrinkled her nose.

"It doesn't look like fried chicken. It's definitely not a pepperoni pizza. And it's not General Tso's Chinese crawfish. So what the hell is it?"

"You're so close, Ma'am. We have spared no expense to prepare for you one of our more exotic menu items that you can find only here at the Atchafalaya Resort. You won't find this delicacy at any of those want-to-be establishments that keep popping up everywhere."

"All kidding aside, what is it? It looks like a coon or an over-sized squirrel."

"Ma'am, because we know you're gonna be a repeat customer, we're not gonna bore you with the standard fare of coon and squirrel. We've imported a nutria from the wilds of South America for your dining pleasure today that we'll roast over an open flame at your table side. I don't think you'll find that kind of service anywhere else in the world." He paused. "At least not within walking distance."

She laughed.

"Do you know anything about them?"

"They have spread quickly over the swamps and marshes of south Louisiana. An adult nutria can weigh up to twenty pounds and will eat a third of its body weight every day, destroying the environment other animals require to survive. The females can have two or three litters of five or more babies each year, creating a population explosion. We're doing the swamp a favor by taking this one."

"If you insist. I prefer mine lightly battered in cornmeal and deep fried, sprinkled with a dash of Cajun seasonings and served over a bed of rice pilaf with some Cajun boiled corn on the side."

"Then you're in luck. We have everything to create the exact dish you desire. Except the deep fry pan, the grease, the cornmeal, the rice and the corn. But we have everything else, Ma'am. I recommend that you try it over an open flame."

"Let's see." Mindy put her hand on her chin. "My second choice is roasted over an open flame."

"Excellent choice, Ma'am. We should have that out in no time at all."

Wade pulled a small vial out of his daypack and unscrewed the lid. He rubbed some contents into the exterior and interior of the meat. The carcass sparkled as he applied each layer of seasoning.

"Home remedy?" Mindy inquired, trying to follow his preparation.

"Yep. I like Tony Chachere's, Slap Ya' Mama and a bunch of other Cajun seasonings, but everybody has his own taste and I have mine. It's a combination of several of them I call it Cajun Sparkle."

"Looks like it's going to be good."

"A little butter to baste it with wouldn't hurt, but it'll be okay."

Wade drove two small sticks through the ribs on each side and splayed the meat over the embers on the edge of the fire. He pierced the heart and the liver on the ends of the stick. Every three or four minutes he turned the meat. In less than ten minutes, the organs were ready.

Handing a piece of liver to Mindy, he said, "Try this. It may have a little iron taste, but it's chock full of protein. We may need that."

Mindy poked the morsel in her mouth.

"Hmm. It's good."

"When this recipe becomes world famous, don't forget the poor little chef that served it to you first."

The smile faded from Mindy's face.

"Somehow, Wade, I can't imagine ever forgetting you or this escapade in this place. Are you sure there was something wrong with the pilot or did you just want to get me out here alone with you?"

Wade looked at her with a twinkle in his eye.

"I confess. I just want to molest you over and over again. Then I'll miraculously make our cell phones start working and call us a cab."

Mindy threw a small twig at him.

"Okay, if you insist. First, hand me some of that fine cuisine. If you're going to take advantage of a naïve young lady, you have to wine and dine her first."

"Mindy, I don't think there's a man alive that'll ever take advantage of you." He paused. "Unless you want him to."

Mindy giggled while she ate the rest of the nutria. Wade was pleased that she didn't complain about the food. Even if he were unsuccessful in harvesting any other meat today, they'd both eaten enough protein to get them through the day.

Wade shoved the last of his into his mouth. "I guess I should've gotten two of them. You put that away in a hurry."

"Yep," she said, licking her fingers. "What's for lunch?"

"I'm not sure what the master chef has planned for the midday menu. In the meantime—"

Wade retrieved another soda and some cookies from Mindy's pouch.

"These will get rid of the aftertaste and give you a little sugar burst of energy."

"What about you?"

"I'm fine." Wade rose to his feet. "But first, I'm gonna rig up something to collect some rain water when a storm hits us."

"Why don't we just boil some water from the slough?"

"We could and it'd be safe. But it'll still taste like mud. If you want some water that tastes like what you're used to drinking, then I need to catch more rain water than I can catch in that little pan in my backpack. And if I boil a lot of slough water in it, everything we cook in it will taste like slough water for the whole week. Also, if we digest enough of that mud, there's a high likelihood of at least one of us getting the runs. We don't want that in this situation."

Mindy wrinkled her forehead. "Ugh. I'm with you. What do you want me to do?"

Wade pointed at her. "Stay off your ankle. We want get out of here Saturday morning and we may have to walk quite a way to do that. We'll definitely need you to walk as far as you can Saturday."

Wade prowled around the camp and searched both backpacks, searching for the most efficient way to collect the rain when it fell. His focus settled on the A-framed hut he'd constructed with the waterproof roof from the woven palmetto leaves.

He chopped down two of canes by the slough similar to the ones used for fishing, but larger in diameter. The canes were hollow inside, with only a dividing layer every two or three feet. He split the canes in halves lengthwise and removed the solid dividers. Then he secured the canes with the hollow side up to the side of the hut in an inverse-V shape. He tied a gallon plastic bag over each of the four ends of the canes.

Finishing, he stepped back to survey his work.

"Mighty good." Mindy said from the side of the fire. "I don't think I would have thought of that."

"If not that, you would have thought of something else. We all do what we need to when the time comes."

Wade hoped it would work. Theoretically, it should, but he'd seen enough theoretical plans fail he never assumed they always worked.

"Can you wait here? I need to do one more thing."

Mindy giggled.

"I was gonna practice my high jumps and sprints, but just for you, I'll stay here."

"You still have the revolver, right?"

"I do." She grinned. "Ooh, I've been wanting to say 'I do' for a long time, but under different circumstances. Where are you going now?"

"I need to get you a surprise."

"If I didn't know better, I'd say you don't like my company. You keep leaving me and going out in the swamp. What's out there that's better than me?"

Wade smiled.

"Nothing, I promise you. But what I need isn't in the camp, so I have to leave you to get it."

Wade stretched his steps while on dry land and quickly strode to the water's edge to the south of the camp. He waded across a small slough, over a ridge and into another slough. This one was bigger than it'd seemed, and soon he was surrounded by knee-deep water. About four hundred yards across the water, he found a small island amid all the murky water. The little isle couldn't have been more than ten yards long and twenty yards wide.

Along the west edge was a group of red oak saplings about six feet high. Just what he was looking for. I only took a couple of minutes to whack down the two that were almost identical, a tad over four feet tall with a wide fork at the top. He looked at them after he had removed all the extraneous branches and smiled to himself for a job well-done.

Turning to start back to camp, he froze in his tracks. Standing not twenty feet from him was a huge black jaguar, undoubtedly the one he had shared a tree with the night before. Wade's hand instinctively grabbed for his revolver, only to find empty leather. He then remembered leaving the gun with Mindy. Goosebumps rose on his arms as he realized how dire this predicament had become.

I've gone from the top of the food chain to being the next meal served in a few minutes because I left my weapon in camp. What was I thinking? What part of me will he eat first? How long will I remain conscious? Will he kill me first or just start eating after he renders me helpless? What will happen to Mindy? She doesn't have a clue where she is or how to get out. She can't even fend for herself and will starve to death when she finishes the food in her pack. Will hunters find our remains and report it? How long will it take for Sam to find out what happened to us?

25 TUESDAY MORNING
EVERGREEN

Sᴀᴍ ᴘᴀᴄᴇᴅ ᴜᴘ ᴀɴᴅ ᴅᴏᴡɴ ᴛʜᴇ ᴄᴏɴғᴇʀᴇɴᴄᴇ ʀᴏᴏᴍ with Gus and Mandy quietly watching when Bruce entered.

"Sorry, I'm late. I was talking with some volunteers and they wanted to know where to go next. I don't have a clue."

Bruce's usually neat shirt and slacks were crumpled and wrinkled. The outgrowth of whiskers indicated he hadn't shaved. His bleary eyes had trouble focusing on the three people in the conference room with him.

"Bruce, I'm sorry we haven't—I haven't been more directly in touch with you since yesterday morning. We've been talking with Mandy and every time I thought about calling you, something else came up. Mandy kept us up to date on the activities of the volunteers and your involvement with them. I want you to know, we're doing all we can do to find Mindy."

"I understand, Sam. I've been up in the forest with the volunteers, even though I don't think she's there. I just couldn't take the chance and quit looking. Mandy finally convinced me and I went back to the van. I called every friend and family member I know on the outside chance that any of them had any contact with her since Sunday night."

"Any luck?" Sam felt compelled to inquire, even though she knew the answer.

"No, but that didn't surprise me. If I know Mindy like I think I do, she'll contact Mandy before she calls anybody else as soon as she can get to a phone. I'd love for her to call me, but I'm sure she'll call Mandy first. But I have to keep the volunteers looking. I don't want to leave any stone unturned until we know what happened."

Sam slowed her pacing.

"I agree with you. I think Wade will call me first and Mindy will call Mandy first whenever either of them can."

"What do ya think happened to them?"

"I wish I knew. I'm at a loss. I'm not sure why they can't get in contact with us. It's like they disappeared into thin air."

Bruce, still standing, walked over to a window overlooking the parking lot.

"She's out there somewhere waiting on me to come help her. I'll get to her in time."

"I believe that. I also believe we'll get to Wade in time."

Sam walked over next to Bruce, gazing out on the parking lot with him.

"Do you have any meaningful leads at all?"

"I wish I could answer you differently. We have hundreds of leads already, but none that leap off the page as being the one that will give us all the answers yet. You know how it is. I've got every deputy on the staff following every lead that comes in, making phone calls and visiting with every kook within a hundred miles. Every time something like this happens, all the crazies come out of their cages and want to help solve the case. We've had alleged sightings from Mexico to Canada, but none of them have turned up anything yet."

"If we don't know where they are, does anyone have any idea why they're missing?"

"We know Mindy spent Sunday night at the Plantation with Wade. She told Mandy she was going hunting with him early Monday morning. We found her hunting clothes and rifle in the Lodge. Everything we've found is consistent with her plans to hunt Monday morning."

Sam waited for a few seconds for Bruce to say something. When he remained staring out of the window, she continued. "From there, we have no communication from either of them. They disappeared and Wade's truck was found in the forest. I believe there has to be some connection between the discovery of Kenny's body in the hunting stand and their disappearance, so we're trying to follow leads on Kenny's murder to find out what happened to Mindy and Wade."

"What's the connection, Sam?"

"Obviously, the biggest connection is that the Plantation belongs to Wade. Also, and we haven't released this information to the public yet, we found Wade's name written on a piece of paper in one of Kenny's pockets. We visited with Reba yesterday afternoon. She told us that Kenny received a telephone call late Friday night or early Saturday morning. He got dressed in a hurry and left. She never saw him alive again after that."

Bruce turned toward the conference table but did not comment.

"Bruce, this project that you guys were working on when Rachel was murdered seems to be the only connection. You, Kenny, and John were the only ones left and now Kenny is dead. Wade and I still don't know the nature of the project or who else might have been involved."

Bruce glanced down at the table and sat in one of the conference chairs. He turned his chair toward Sam.

"I still don't think the project had anything to do with any of this, but I'll tell you what I know, which isn't much."

"We'll take whatever we can get at this point. We don't have much to go on."

"Where do you want me to start? How much do you already know about it?"

Sam ran her hand through her long blonde hair.

"The only things we found out about the project is that it involves a ton of money and almost everyone involved in it is dead. That includes Ed, Bill, Frank and Rachel from before. Now Kenny is murdered. Only you and John are left. If the project isn't the connection, then there seems to be a curse on it."

Bruce shifted his gaze back down to the table and nodded. "What else do you know?"

"Only that everyone involved signed a non-disclosure or confidentiality agreement that prevents them from telling anyone about it without a subpoena. We've never had and don't now have enough probable cause for a subpoena."

"Unfortunately, Sam, the two people left are the two people that know the least about the overall project. I, and I believe John, only got involved on the periphery of the project and were assigned certain duties without knowing the entire scope. Our contributions were defined and limited."

"What contributions were you assigned, Bruce?"

"My job, if you want to call it that, was to determine the infrastructure and try to find a piece of property that might be available for acquisition by a company out of Jackson.

They gave me certain parameters and minimum requirements and was to report back to Ed. They told me not to go through the regular realtors because we didn't want everyone in Evergreen to know about it."

"What were the parameters and requirements, Bruce?"

"It needed to be large enough for a good size plant, over two hundred acres. It needed to have access to the utilities like water and electricity, and it needed to be close enough to the railroad to build a spur to it. They also wanted it to be as close to the interstate as possible. Ed even mentioned building a road straight to it from the interstate."

"What product did Ed say they would manufacture in this plant?"

"He never said, and it wasn't because I never asked. I told him on several occasions I needed to know more about the product before I could find the right place. He told me to get John to help me. I asked John, and he didn't know. Ed and Rachel probably knew, but I'm not sure anyone else did."

"Bruce, forgive my bluntness, but that just doesn't sound right. You were working on this major project for the City and you don't even know what it was about. Your daughter is missing! You need to tell us everything you know."

"I know how it sounds, Sam. I'm perfectly aware my daughter is missing." Bruce clinched his fists on the tabletop. "Don't you think if I knew anything that would help get her back safe and sound that I'd tell you, confidentiality agreement or not?"

"I'm sorry. Wade is missing with Mindy and I have this sense of urgency that we have to find them before something worse happens to them. And no, I don't know what worse means. I share the feeling with Mandy that they're alive, but in jeopardy. But beyond that, I can't feel much. I guess I'm on edge and I shouldn't have yelled at you. I apologize."

"We're all on edge, Sam. To answer your question, I did what I did on the project for two reasons. One, my boss, which was Ed, told me to work on it. Two, there was the money."

Sam arched her eyebrows.

"How much money?"

Bruce glanced at Mandy before answering, as though embarrassed.

"My share was a little over two hundred thousand. Mandy, don't get me wrong. It wasn't a bribe or anything like that. The way John explained it was that it was a consultant's fee. As long as Ed and the City Council approved it, there was nothing illegal about it."

"It's okay, Daddy. I knew you were getting extra money from somewhere. Mindy and I didn't know where it was coming from." Mandy walked over and put her arms around Bruce and then sat in a chair next to him, holding his hand.

Sam squirmed in her chair and pressed on. "Who was the source of the money, Bruce?"

"Don't know."

"Who's name is on the check?"

"An investment company out of Jackson. John and I tried to trace the company through the Secretary of State's office. The company was a subsidiary of another company, which was a subsidiary of another company, which was a subsidiary of one of the first two companies. It was a circle of companies meant to hide the real identity of the owner."

"If I remember right, Bruce, every company has to have an agent with a physical address listed with the Secretary of State. Who's listed as the agent for these companies?"

"A lady named Victoria Engle. I drove up to Jackson, and the physical address she gave to the Secretary of State is one of those mail service places. You know the type. You get a mailbox there and get to list it as a suite number at the physical location of the business. I asked the sales clerk, and he told me a lady came by once a year and paid cash for it. I met Victoria when we all went to Jackson on our one trip together."

"When was this?"

"Right before they all started getting killed."

Sam remembered seeing a picture of the group together. Reba had a picture of Kenny and the other members of the team at her house. But this lady that Bruce was speaking about was not in that photograph.

"Did you get a business card from her?"

"Sure, it's at my office. There's no address or a picture on the card. Only her name and a phone number. When I called the number, I got a voice mail that said, 'Investments. Please leave your name and number.' That's all it said, Sam."

"So you've tried to do your own investigation into this lady and whatever company she is representing."

"I wanted to know who was paying me two hundred thousand dollars for a job that any realtor would have done for the commission on the sale. It made little sense. John and I were both suspicious."

"You never said what John's job was with the project."

"I can only tell you what I know. You probably should check with him."

"What do you know, Bruce?"

"My understanding from John is that he was responsible for infrastructure and zoning type of stuff. You know, the support that the city of Evergreen and Evergreen

County would need to have to support a new plant that would take more than two hundred acres, with the influx of new citizens and businesses it would bring. The ripple effect of the kind of project Ed and Rachel were talking about would have a tremendous impact on the traffic flow, the service providers like the utility companies and the school system and others. In the private sector, the impact on the restaurants, the home builders, the clothes stores and almost everyone else would overwhelm them if we weren't prepared."

"Sounds like to me you, John and the others were all submitting parts of a report, but only Ed and Rachel knew the total picture. And I guess this Victoria lady knew about it. Does that sound right, Bruce?"

"I don't think she was acting in her own self-interest, Sam."

"Why do you say that?"

"A few times when we were in Jackson, we asked her some questions about the project and she didn't know the answers. She said she'd have to check and get back with us. So I assumed there was someone, or maybe even a group of people she was representing."

"Did she ever say what the plant would manufacture?"

"John and I speculated a lot, but she didn't tell us."

"What did you guys come up with?"

"The only thing we could come up with was a nuclear plant or a nuclear waste dump. Those are about the only things we could think of that would be so controversial that would need to be kept secret until they were ready to present it with all the kinks worked out. The only other feasible idea we had was that it could be a toxic chemical waste dump. They pay a lot and there are very few places in the country willing to accept them.

I know a lot of the folks in Evergreen that would protest against either nuclear waste or a toxic chemical waste dump, no matter how many assurances they had. And after seeing what that hurricane or typhoon or whatever it was in Japan did to that nuclear facility, I don't think most of us, including myself, want a nuclear plant in our backyard."

"Any of the three would be a tough sell for most of the old-timers in Evergreen. The last one, the toxic waste plant, would be a non-starter for almost everyone around here, including me."

"That's the only reason we could come up with for them to have to grease the skids with all the consultant fees to the city officials. If they had the support of all the officials in town, you'd be surprised how easily some things get done. A little money goes a long way."

"A little, Bruce? Really?" Sam paused. "You call two hundred thousand dollars to you a little money? There's no telling how much everyone else received."

"Sam, look at the overall picture. In any of the three scenarios we talked about, two hundred thousand would get lost in a rounding error. It's chump change in the overall scheme."

"You're right. If they pay these consultant fees and every member of the City Council and all the major officials at City Hall support any idea, there's a good chance of it getting through no matter how unpopular it is. It'd be tough for you not to support it if you'd already cashed a check for a couple hundred thousand dollars."

Bruce sighed. "I let myself get caught in a compromising situation and I'm not proud of that."

"Where does the status of the project stand now?"

"I don't know. John and I haven't talked about it for

some time and none of the investors have tried to contact me."

"They were probably taken aback when they saw over a million in their investment literally die before their eyes. They had to regroup and decide on a new plan of action."

"Either John or I could call them. It would probably look better if John called them, considering my circumstances with Mindy and all."

"Do you think he'd do that for us and try to arrange a meeting with Victoria? I'm guessing he's going to Kenny's funeral this afternoon."

"I don't know how close John and Kenny were, but I'd guess he was going to Kenny's funeral for the public image. I know I have to go as the acting Mayor. Which reminds me, I'd better get home and get a shower or nobody will stand next to me at the funeral."

Mandy put her arm around Bruce again and gave him a big hug. "I will, Daddy."

Bruce looked at Sam and Gus. "I only have one request, Sam."

"What is it?"

"You know I'll do anything necessary to find Mindy and Wade. But I don't want Mandy involved with Victoria or any of this investment group. If this murder and the disappearances are tied to the project, then I don't want to lose Mandy. She may be all I have left."

Mandy sat in Bruce's lap and put both arms around his neck. She laid her head on his shoulder started crying like a baby, not caring what the others in the room were thinking about her. Bruce could only hold her tightly with streams of tears running down his cheeks.

"No problem. We'll keep Mandy out of it. Ask John to set up a meeting for late this afternoon in Jackson. We can probably be there between five and six. We'll meet her wherever is convenient for her."

Bruce just nodded, refusing to let Mandy out of the bear hug.

Gus and Sam walked out in the hall.

"Gus, can you take care of everything this afternoon?"

"Absolutely, I'll get out my old horse whip. That thing has barely been used."

"I don't think you'll need a horse whip, Gus. Why do you have that, anyway? You're not raising any horses I know of."

"Never did."

"Huh? Then why the whip?"

Gus grinned.

"Wife number three. Man, she could make that thing sizzle when she used if for foreplay."

"Ugh. You are disgusting." Sam saw the grin on his face. "If you're even telling the truth."

"I could tell you some stories about Wife number three."

"Not now, Gus. We have to find Wade and Mindy. I wonder what he's doing right now."

26 TUESDAY AFTERNOON
ATCHAFALAYA BASIN

Wade tried to watch every twitch of every muscle in the big black cat and search for an escape route at the same time. His eyes darted left and right, but he didn't see an apparent escape route from the trap the jaguar had laid for him. The cat was slightly above him and could easily close the small distance between them in an instant.

Wade yelled at the cat and waved a stick he had just cut in its face. The black feline growled and pawed at the stick as it passed its nose, but the distance was a little too far to knock the stick out of Wade's hand. Wade took a small step to his right, and the cat mirrored his movement. He took a step back to his left, and the cat growled and mirrored his movement again. Each movement Wade made was met with an equal step by the cat and a visceral growl deep within its body, sending shivers down Wade's back.

He turned his head slightly and looked behind him, searching for any escape route. There was none.

He can outrun me. He can climb better and faster than I can. He can swim better and faster than I can. Other than that, I have him right where I want him.

Wade stared at the long sinewy body of the black cat and admired how it was constructed. It was built for speed and power, with incredible agility and balance. It was a killing machine designed by nature to dispatch its prey quickly before the prey could harm it.

That's probably why it hasn't already attacked me. It's accustomed to a deer or pig running away from it and chasing the game animal down, leaping on its back and sinking those long teeth into its neck and crushing the vertebrae.

Each time the big cat growled, he displayed the long front teeth he used to tear away the flesh from the body of his prey. When Wade waved the stick in front of its face, he showed the long talons on his paw he used to grip the hide of the prey animals. Wade knew this predator could lay waste to him in no time at all, shredding his skin and muscles down to his sinews and bones. The cat sat back on his haunches, content with letting Wade continue to wave both of the sticks in front of him.

How long is this big rascal gonna toy with me before I become his next appetizer? I know he can charge me whenever he wants to, and there's not much I can do about it. He can push aside these puny little sticks with no problem.

Wade looked down at the little fire ax trembling in his right hand at the moment. He glanced back at the cat.

Damn. This little ax is smaller than one of his paws. This won't a fair fight or a long one either. Maybe I can make one good lucky swing when he leaps and if I can time it just right.

Beads of sweat poured off Wade's head and down his back. His shirt was drenched and his pants started absorbing the overflow. His hands were trembling so badly that he could barely hold the limb in his left and the ax in his right.

Well, I can't stay here like this forever. Mindy will start getting worried. Mindy! The poor little girl put her faith in me and now I'm gonna let her down. Maybe it's too late already. The cat may have seen Mindy alone in camp and quickly dispatched her. Her body may already be hanging in a fork in the water oak tree next to the half-eaten deer. This old cat wouldn't have a bit of trouble hoisting her up the water oak. He may have a little more trouble with me. He may have to eat me, or at least a part of me down here on the ground.

Wade's legs shook uncontrollably, and his focus blurred through the sweat. He knew he didn't have much time left. He dropped the sticks from his left hand and simulated swings with the small ax with his right. He looked down at the ax again.

It sure makes a better tool than it does a weapon, but that's all I've got. Should I use the limb and try to distract him or jam it at him and try to lift him with it?

Wade glanced back at the cat and watched him lick his nose with his long tongue. He knew this helped the animal smell its prey better. Some believed it helped him smell the odor of fear emanating from the prey and told him when to attack.

Smell! Odor! I have a chance!

Wade slowing reached inside his pocket and pulled out the wad of toilet tissue he had jammed in there before leaving camp in case the occasion to use it had arisen. He quickly wrapped the tissue around the end of the stick he was holding. Reaching inside his pocket, he retrieved the lighter he had used to ignite the camp fire.

You'd better not let me down now like you have so many times in the past.

His fingers almost unable to operate, he made a swish with the lighter, but it didn't ignite. He glanced at the cat and saw the ears pinned back along its neck. He would only have one more chance. Swish! The lighter ignited and Wade moved it next to the toilet paper, causing a large brief flame on the end of the stick. Wade charged forward, surprising the large cat, which was accustomed to other animals running away from him instead of charging him.

The cat whirled to run, and Wade jabbed him with the fiery toilet paper right on the base of his tail. The black feline let out a devilish scream and sprinted away from Wade, growling every time its feet hit the ground.

Wade's shaky knees could hold up no longer. He sank to the miry murk, lifted his face toward heaven and said a quick silent prayer of thanksgiving and deliverance. Rising on steadier legs, he gathered the two sticks and almost sprinted through the bog back toward camp. Even knowing he'd hurt the cat with the flames and that it shouldn't come after him didn't completely dissipate the angst built up in his body. He wanted to slow down, but couldn't. His breathing was erratic and his pulse continued to race. Sweat continued to pour out of him like water out of a leaky bucket. Only when he came within sight of the camp with Mindy sitting calmly be the fire did he relax. He staggered into camp and collapsed by the burning embers.

27 TUESDAY MORNING
ATCHAFALAYA BASIN

"Wʜᴀᴛ ᴛʜᴇ ʜᴇʟʟ ʜᴀᴘᴘᴇɴᴇᴅ ᴛᴏ ʏᴏᴜ?"

"I had a visit from your Kitty Kat friend."

"The one we spent the night with in the tree?"

"The one and only. Except this time we were both on the ground up close and personal. I don't think he likes me anymore. I didn't play nice with him."

Wade took his time explaining his encounter with the cat, leaving out the thoughts that went through his mind while facing him.

"So you lit his butt on fire!"

"I wish. It wasn't on fire, but I burnt him enough that I hope he won't bother us again."

"You told me that cats were instinctively afraid of fire. Now, he has a reason to be."

"I brought these for you. That's what I was doing out there."

Mindy grabbed the crutches, and Wade helped her stand up and cradle one under each armpit. "Aah. You went shopping for me without telling, and it's not even Christmas yet. I'm sorry. I didn't have time to pick anything up for you. All the stores were closed by the time I dragged my body through the sloughs to get to them. I stopped at one, but I don't think you would've liked the selections. Too hip-hop for a conservative young man like you."

"Only the finest presents for our finest guests at the Atchafalaya Resort. We want to please."

"Next time, can I pick the destination?"

"Well, Ma'am. That'd be great. But if I remember correctly, when we chose this bit of paradise, our choices were somewhat limited. It was the back of a plane with a dead pilot or the exit door. I think you made the best choice available under the circumstances."

"I don't remember you arguing with my choice too much. You practically pushed me out the door. Besides, a woman has the prerogative to change her mind. I was expecting slightly better accommodations in the Presidential Suite. You paid for the Presidential Suite when you booked this trip, didn't you?"

"Yeah, but when we checked in, they saw you were all crippled up and told me we had to stay in one of the handicapped rooms. They don't have quite as many amenities as the Presidential Suite."

"It has one advantage though, Sir."

"What's that?"

"Most places won't allow you to bring pets into the room. Here they furnish their own to help you pass the idle time. They expect you to play nice with the Kitty Kat and not light its tail on fire when he just wants to be your friend. They may not let you check in again if you don't learn how to play nice with the animals."

"I'm playing nice with them. We played a nice little game of tag. The Kitty Kat is it, at least for the time being.

Although I'd understand if Management asked us to leave."

"Asks us to leave? Are you kidding?" Mindy pointed in a circle all around them. "And leave all of this? Where is the line for that? I want to make sure we're at the head of it."

"On the other side of the atrium, down by the slough. Only it doesn't start forming until Saturday. Until then, we have to get along with all of our playmates out here for the next four days."

"It's not so much the days that bother me. It's the nights. They don't play fair at night. Oh, I almost forgot. I ordered room service, but they haven't arrived yet."

"I'll go speak to the manager. What did you order for lunch, Ma'am?"

"I thought we'd have something light for lunch since we had that delicious roasted nutria for breakfast. I ordered us each a cup of chicken and Andouille sausage gumbo for appetizers and soft-shell crabs for lunch. They don't fill me up as much as most fried foods."

Wade closed his eyes and pursed his lips. "Hmm. I could eat a plate full of those things. That's my favorite seafood in the world. Two big fried soft-shell crabs with a little Hollandaise sauce dribbled over them. How did you know?"

"Are you serious or kidding me?"

"No, I'm serious about soft-shell crabs. I absolutely love them."

"Hah! Maybe I'm able to read your mind after only a day out here. By the end of the week, you won't even have to speak. I'll already know what's on your mind."

"That'd be kinda scary."

"Actually, it's gonna be real easy."

Wade arched his eyebrows.

"How so?"

"Give me a week alone with any man without his girlfriend and without me giving him any and I can tell you what is on the mind of every one of them. It's not hard at all." Mindy laughed. "What's on his mind, I mean."

Wade shook his head. "Okay, I'm going to see the manager about those crabs. If they aren't ready, I may pick something else up."

"I know they don't carry much in the kitchen, but can we have something other than nutria?"

"I'll try. But I don't want to play tug of war with the Kitty Kat to get it. Build up your fire a little while I'm gone, just in case."

"You don't have to worry about that. You'll be able to see it or smell it for five miles."

"Not too big. I have to chop the wood for it."

Wade slogged back to the east over the small sloughs and then north up a dry ridge line. About a hundred yards up the ridge, he found two large cypress logs that had fallen and formed an almost perfect V-shape on the ground. After poking the leaves to make sure there weren't any moccasins or timber rattlers in it, he settled down with his make-shift spear in his right hand and the ax in his left hand. Wade wasn't sure what affected him the most: the long night awake waiting for the jaguar to return, the morning episode with the big cat or the tremendous amount of work required to get the hut in order. It might have been any of the three or the culmination of all three, but the result was that Wade drifted into a deep sleep with his head resting comfortably against the cypress logs.

He dreamed that he and Sam were together at the Plantation fishing at the end of his pier. She was laughing and giggling too much and making way too much noise for them to catch any fish. It seemed as if her effervescent personality reflected on the top of the sparkling water in the lake. His legs dangled over the edge of the pier where he sat and soaked up the coolness from the watery depths. Sam, overflowing with non-stop energy, couldn't sit still and bounced up and down the decking, all the time talking about their future together. Suddenly, she was a blur coming from behind him and she soared over his shoulder and splashed in the water. And splashed. And splashed.

The splashing startled Wade from his deep sleep. Blurry eyes tried unsuccessfully to focus on the immediate surroundings. As the picture ever so slowly came into focus, Wade saw a huge whitetail buck only feet from him. The rippling muscles under the taut brown skin quivered in the sunlight. Wade gripped the spear with his right hand a slowly tried to raise it above the log. The end of the spear caught on the old bark of the tree and scraped it as the spear elevated. The buck wasted no time trying to figure out what the danger was. He only knew there was a noise that wasn't natural or native to his surroundings, and he crashed through the swamp. By the time Wade had raised the spear over the log, the buck disappeared into the dense swamp. Wade glanced at his watch to discover that he had been asleep for over an hour.

What a missed opportunity. That deer would have fed us for the rest of the week. What will Mindy say when I tell her? Should I even tell her I was that close to real food, the kind that we can only dream about in our situation.

A rustling noise a few feet from the log re-focused Wade's attention. Peeking over the log, Wade almost started laughing. A twenty-pound alligator snapping turtle was slowly crawling across the ridge from one slough to the other. Wade leapt from behind the log, and raced to the young turtle, although he didn't have to hurry in reality. He'd missed one golden opportunity, and he didn't want to miss another. Wade recognized this turtle as a young alligator snapper because the adults weighed one hundred and fifty pounds or more. Wade had heard of many of them exceeding three hundred pounds, although he'd never seen one that size himself.

The turtle hissed and lunged at him, at him when he neared it. Wade was surprised at the quickness of the animal in a natural box shell and pulled back, reassessing his charge-ahead strategy. Wade had seen larger turtles break a two-inch stick with ease in their powerful jaws and knew he could lose a finger or two if not careful. This slow moving reptile would have long become extinct without a formidable defense. Wade slowly moved to the other side, and the turtle whirled to face him. He circled back to his original spot next to the turtle, only to find snapping jaws inches from his ankles. Wade jabbed at the turtle's head with his spear. The quickness if the vise-like jaws clamping down on the end of his spear amazed Wade,

He yanked the spear back and examined the crushed flat end.

So much for a sharp spear. How much will Mindy laugh when she finds out that I couldn't outsmart a turtle? What will Sam say when I tell her about this? Okay, settle down and outthink this fort on legs. Somehow, I need to use its own defenses against him.

Wade moved his left hand down the spear until it was only eighteen inches from the end. He waved the spear right in front of the turtle's face, inducing it to bite. The turtle grabbed the stick, and didn't let go. Wade lifted the turtle off the ground. The stubborn turtle would not let go of the stick and his neck extended from his shell. A quick whack from the ax in Wade's right hand quickly severed the head and the turtle's body dropped to the ground. The powerful jaws, even in death, continued to clamp down on the spear. Wade had a newfound respect for the alligator snapping turtle from the Louisiana bayous.

28 TUESDAY NOON
ATCHAFALAYA BASIN

ON HIS TRIP BACK TO THE CAMPSITE, WADE STOPPED long enough to pick up some green leaves along one ridge. He crossed over one of the small sloughs early when he spotted a white oak tree on a small isle. Wading through knee-deep water was now an everyday occurrence. This trip through the muddy roil brought something he hadn't seen in the swamp before, leeches. Rising out of this slough, Wade discovered more than a dozen leeches on the skin on his leg. He removed each one and placed them in the turtle shell.

"I hear you coming. At least I hope that's you." Mindy yelled before Wade reached eyesight of the camp.

"Room Service, with your lunch, Ma'am." Wade chuckled.

Only two people as bonkers as me and Mindy would keep this charade up this long.

"It's about time. You know that with room service this slow, I'll have to reduce your tip."

"Oh, no! Don't reduce my tip. The Atchafalaya Resort doesn't pay that well. If you don't tip me, I won't be able to call a cab to take me home and I'll have to spend the night with you."

"We'll have to negotiate on that one." Mindy laughed. "The second alternative might not be too bad, depending on what you have in mind. You brought the fried chicken I ordered, didn't you?"

"I'm sorry Ma'am. The kitchen ran out of chicken earlier. It seems everyone wanted fried chicken for lunch. Very unusual, but it happens sometimes. I remembered, however, one item that you said you wished was on the menu."

"Oh, goody. A cheeseburger with extra pickles!"

Wade held up the turtle.

"Unprocessed turtle soup."

Mindy squinted her eyes.

"I don't remember saying the 'unprocessed' part of that."

"But, Ma'am. Any restaurant in New Orleans will serve you turtle soup. How many will prepare it for you in your own room? That separates the Atchafalaya Resort from all of those mediocre establishments."

"One thing I have to admit. You have a nice way of presenting any situation in its best light. You should go into marketing. Or spamming, or something like that."

"No need for compliments, Ma'am. We pride ourselves on bringing only the finest cuisine. That means we have to have the freshest meat available, and it doesn't get any fresher than what I've brought you today."

"And to just think, I was gonna settle for a cheeseburger and fries with a cherry soda. Now that seems so bland. What sides are you serving? I see something green in your little grocery basket."

"Poke Sallet, Ma'am. I'm sorry. You may know it better

as the world famous Louisiana poke salad. I know you've heard of it, but I'm betting that you've never tried it. I believe we are the only establishment for miles and miles that serve it."

"What the hell is poke salad? I've never even heard of it."

"Elvis made it famous but Tony Kenny White sang it before you were born. Most folks think it is just a legend, but it exists. The berries, roots, and mature leaves are poisonous if not properly prepared, but you're in luck. Our master chef loves to cook up a good mess of poke salad."

"Did I hear you mention poisons?"

"Yep, it's got histamines and a couple of other poisons with names I can't pronounce. But I've got a secret weapon for that." Wade pulled a few of the leeches out of the turtle shell."

"Ugh! I can't stand those blood-suckers. I'm not eating any of those, Wade. No matter how hungry I get, I refuse to eat leeches."

"I'm not too crazy about them myself. Not because they're blood suckers, but they're awful chewy. There is almost no way in the world to get them tender. The best you can do is cut them up into small pieces and swallow the small pieces whole. If you try to chew them, you'll be all day."

"So why did you bring them with you? You must've had a reason, other than you were mad at them for sucking the blood out of you."

"For some reason and I don't know why, there is a special enzyme in the leeches that help tenderize the poke salad. Without the leeches, we'd have to boil the poke salad three of four times to get it edible. With the leeches, we only have to boil it twice."

Mindy cringed.

"So let me get this straight. We're gonna take two inedible products." She held up two fingers for emphasis. "We're gonna boil the bejeezus out of them forever and a day to make one almost edible. Did I miss something in this?"

Wade laughed.

"That's real close. We have to change out the water. And don't drink or use that water to cook anything else. It might be a tad toxic."

"I'm not that thirsty right now. And what will this end product, this poke salad you call it; what will it taste like?"

"It's gonna look like a dark spinach or turnip greens with a taste similar to asparagus. It's really quite delicious if done properly. It can be tart, but I have a few packets of honey in my backpack and we'll sweeten it up a tad. It's gonna take that turtle about an hour to stew in its own shell before it's tender, anyway. So we have time to cook the poke salad."

"Any other surprises in that little bag of yours?"

"Only a few white oak acorns. When shopping for these at your local grocery store, be sure you get the white oak acorn, which is relatively sweeter and more moist than the others. I've tried them all and most are a tad bitter for my taste. But the white oak acorn is quite good. I can see why the deer and the hogs fight over them."

Mindy grabbed one out of Wade's hand and popped it into her mouth.

"Hold on."

He almost shouted as he heard the hard crack of the acorn.

"Yuck." Mindy spit the acorn out on the ground. "That thing is hard as a rock."

She continued spitting bits and pieces of acorn out on the ground.

"That's what I was trying to tell you before you so rudely grabbed one. An acorn is just like any other nut. It has a hard outer shell that you have to split and remove to get to the meat. Most people think almonds and pecans come from the tree prepackaged with just the good part of the nut. Not true with them or with acorns."

Wade demonstrated by cracking open a huge white oak acorn and removing the interior meat with his pocketknife. He handed the meat to Mindy.

"This is how they taste when they first fall from the oak. After the first hard freeze, even the white oak acorns turn bitter, forcing the animals to forage on other types of food."

He watched with satisfaction as she chewed on the acorn and smiled.

"They're also a good source of protein if you can't find any meat for a while."

"You say that about everything out here."

"Because it's true for just about everything out here that we will eat. All the meat in full of protein. The turtle and alligator eggs have protein, and the nuts have protein. I'll try to find you a starch tomorrow."

Wade pared the turtle meat off the bones, leaving only a small amount of meat compared to the whole of the turtle. He left enough fat on the meat to accentuate the sweetness in it. Compared to other reptiles, the turtle meat that he had tried in the past was delicious, but then he had a lot more condiments to add to it for enhancement.

He placed the shell next to the fire and set the little pan with the poke salad and leeches on the other side of the fire and leaned back. Soon he was fast asleep next to the warmth of the fire. Only this time, there were no pleasant dreams to amuse him during his slumber, but only snippets of the harsh reality they faced. Flashes of water moccasins, alligators, poisonous spiders, timber rattlers, wild boars and yes, large black cats flooded his mind like images going past a window. He tried to turn away from the window but was compelled to watch as they streamed by. How long he slept, he didn't know, but it was long enough for Mindy to poke him with one of her crutches.

"Hey, Wade. You're starting to worry me now. You're talking in your sleep and what you're saying isn't something a young lady should hear."

"Uh oh. What did I say?"

"Doesn't matter now. I changed out the water for the poke salad and kept stirring the turtle stew. I even added a few spices to the turtle and some of that honey to the poke salad."

"Was I asleep that long?" Wade stretched his arms and his legs and let out a big yawn.

"You must not be sleeping well at night. I can't for the life of me imagine what could be keeping you up."

"Me either. Let's try some turtle and poke salad."

Wade took some empty soda cans and cut the top out of them. He filled one with turtle stew and another with poke salad and handed them to Mindy.

"Not bad. If you ever give up ranching and detecting, you might have a future as a chef."

"If I can only get my patrons to starve themselves in the middle of a swamp for a few days before they try my food. Then they might eat it at least."

"If you keep this up, you might get back some of your tip."

"Do you mean I haven't gotten it all back yet? Even

with the poke salad? I thought that would put me over the top."

"You haven't fixed the air conditioner yet and the water for the shower still isn't hot enough. Come to think of it, you need to install another shower. I can't find the one you promised yesterday."

"I'll get right on those projects this afternoon. I'm running a little behind since I had to take your pet Kitty Kat for a walk this morning."

"What are you gonna do this afternoon?"

"First, I'll get a lot more firewood. Seems like an unending process, and I'm having trouble keeping up with it. We burn it faster than I can chop it or at least it seems that way. I'll get more palmetto leaves and get you to weave them into a water-proof basket. I've got some string in by backpack you can bind it with. Make it about twelve inches in diameter and about two feet tall."

"What is that for?"

"It's a surprise. I don't know if it'll work or not, but we can try."

"Okay, I can do that. What else do we need to do?"

"You need to stay by the fire. I'm gonna shop for supper and breakfast tomorrow morning. And I'll need to borrow the revolver. With the fire and the spear—. Oh, yeah. I need to fix the spear before I leave. That turtle kinda smashed it."

"Geez, does it ever end? I mean the cycle of hunting just to eat and all the other stuff. When do you get to rest and relax?"

"When we get out of here and back to civilization."

Wade gathered the palmetto leaves and several loads of firewood and returned to the campsite. He handed the palmetto leaves to Mindy and piled up the firewood. He took some firewood and made three little piles inside the fortified hut.

"If you hear the Kitty Kat, get inside the hut and light those. Here's my lighter. He won't bother you inside the hut with the three fires burning inside there. Just in case, make sure you take the spear with you."

"No problem there. I'll get a couple of long sticks with some moss on the ends, so I can have some fire sticks."

Wade grinned. "Good idea. Why didn't I think of that?"

"Because you'd rather play with the Kitty Kat than chase him away. I want him gone."

Wade just laughed. If only Mindy knew how frightened he had been for his life when the cat had him cornered, she wouldn't be joking about it.

"Wade, be careful out there." She paused for several seconds before continuing. "I never know if you're going to come back or not."

"I'm coming back. You're not going to get rid of me that easily."

Wade eased through the sloughs back to the white oak ridge he'd discovered before lunch. He hadn't disturbed it too much when he gathered the acorns a few hours earlier. Taking a quick visual survey, he determined a fallen treetop would make the best stand. He took a long stick and poked around in the treetop to make sure there weren't any moccasins or rattlers in there to share the afternoon with him.

A small green snake quickly fled from the treetop. Wade recognized it as a harmless garter snake, which normally would make a light meal for one stranded man in the swamp. Wade raised the ax to dispatch the snake and then changed his mind. If things went according to plan, he wouldn't need the small snake for food or for bait for fishing.

He watched as it slithered away and hid in a hollow log several feet from the treetop.

Wade trimmed enough branches of the blind to give him a comfortable place to sit and a firing lane to shoot through without interference. Then he sat back and relaxed. Being perfectly still and quiet were the keys to any success he might have in his quest this sunny afternoon.

An hour and one-half later, Wade heard rather than saw his intentioned prey. From quite a distance away, he could hear the sloshing, wading and breaking of limbs underfoot as they rushed to root out the sweet acorns. Gathering on the small knoll under the giant white oaks, the herd of pigs numbered over twenty. They ranged from over four hundred pounds down to fifteen or twenty pounds. The pigs were black or had red and brown splotches all over, which are the two primary color patterns of the swamp pigs. Wade chuckled to himself as he watched an old boar chase the younger sows and pigs around the little knoll, trying to protect as many of the acorns for himself as he could.

Wade slowly raised the revolver and took dead aim between the old boar's eyes. Realization hit him and he lowered the pistol. A sow stuck her nose in the treetop, only inches from Wade's leg. She must have smelled him and let out the biggest squeal Wade had ever heard from a hog. Pigs exploded in every direction, all of them squealing as loud as they could. In the confused melee two little piglets ended up on a couple of feet from the treetop looking around for the source of the fear, but not willing to leave the succulent acorns. Wade took time to carefully aim and placed the slug from the revolver right below the ears into the skull of the nearest piglet and watched as he crumbled onto the moist ground. The other piglet wasted no time trying to catch up with the rest of the herd crashing through the swamp on to quieter grounds. In only a few seconds after being discovered by the sow, Wade found himself on the deserted little knoll alone with the dead piglet. He sat quietly watching his surroundings for several minutes before retrieving the prey. He slipped out of the fallen treetop and picked up the dead swine with a hole square in the middle of the back of its skull. In less than five minutes, Wade sloshed back to the camp site, cradling the field-dressed swine in his arms. He had saved only the heart and liver from the innards and left the remainder on the isolated knoll for the rest of the herd to return and consume.

"Hi, Honey. I'm home."

"Good. I can't wait for some good Chinese food. You remembered to get it extra spicy, didn't you? And chopsticks? The last time you got Chinese, you forgot the chopsticks."

"Sorry. The Chinese place was out of Cajun Lobster Sauce, and I wasn't sure what else you wanted. So instead, I brought home the bacon."

Wade held up the little piglet for Mindy to see.

"Literally, I brought home the bacon."

Mindy sighed.

"I guess I'll have a BLT on rye with a touch of mayo, please."

"No problem. Let's see." He paused. "Maybe a tad of a problem. The kitchen is out of 'L' and out of 'T' for the BLT. We're also a little short on the rye bread and the mayo. Other than that, I think we have everything."

Mindy grinned.

"That's okay. That's the way I like my BLT's. Hold the 'L', hold the 'T' and forget the mayo. Just add more 'B' and I'm happy."

"You're in luck. We have plenty of 'B' tonight."

"It doesn't look like plenty to me. Didn't they have any grown-ups out there? Did you have to shoot a baby?"

Wade paused before answering.

"I could easily have taken a big boar or a big sow, and I started to do just that. Then I thought about how to store the extra meat for the rest of the week and the lack of refrigeration, and I decided not to. We could have tried to smoke a big sow, but it would have taken a few days and we would have had meat hanging in the campsite for the rest of the week. I didn't think that'd be real smart with us next to this slough with the alligators and the cat roaming around. We can eat most of this little fellow tonight and have breakfast waiting for us when we get up in the morning."

"The next time you make us reservations in a remote resort like this, remember to check to see if they have refrigeration and freezer services. Do I have to think of everything for you?"

"Sorry, Ma'am. That sorta slipped my mind when I found that dead pilot in the cockpit. Next time, I'll ask him to be more considerate and die in a more convenient place."

The grin quickly faded from Mindy's face.

"Geez, Wade. I haven't considered the pilot's family and what they must be going through. I wonder if they found him and the plane or if they're still looking for it. Either way, there's no upside for them. At least with Daddy, Mandy and Sam, we hope this will end well."

"Let's hope so, for our sakes as well. I'm still trying to figure out what happened to the pilot. I was in such a hurry to get you out of the plane. I didn't take time to look at him closely enough."

"Don't get too down. Back to the pig. I'm glad you took my instructions and shot a small one. One of us has to do the thinking around here."

"That's why you make a better chief and I make a better warrior. You can sit around the campfire and come up with ways to keep me busy all day and most of the night."

"Speaking of which. Are you gonna cook that thing or just admire yourself for killing it?"

"I thought we'd just knock the hide off and eat it raw."

"Not me. I'll have my pork chops well done and my bacon crisp, please."

"Any way you want it, Ma'am. Your wish is my command."

Wade first sliced the heart and the liver in thin slices and rubbed each slice with his special seasoning. He splayed the thin slices on the end of a stick and held them directly over the flames. The meat sizzled and spit juices for only a minute as Wade rotated it from side to side. He handed the first stick to Mindy.

"That's delicious. My compliments to the chef."

While Mindy was eating her portion of the organs, Wade rubbed down the rest of the piglet with the sauces and splayed it a little way off the direct flames above the hot embers on the edge of the fire. He left the skin attached to the meat and placed it above the coals with the skin-side closest to the fire. As the melted fat accumulated in the body, Wade scooped it out with the empty soda cans. He filled three of the cans and set them aside to cool.

Then he cut the tenderloin out and finished browning it directly over the flames before handing it to Mindy.

"For your dining pleasure, Ma'am."

"Damn. You sure know how to spoil a girl, don't you?"

"Yep, I hope so."

When Mindy finished her loin, Wade cut a small portion of ham off and browned it. He handed the sizzling pork to Mindy.

"Your third course, Ma'am."

"I didn't know the kitchen, or the chef was this resourceful. I continue to be impressed by both."

"You have seen nothing yet. You saved room for dessert, I presume."

"I don't know. Seriously, Wade. I'm getting full and it is delicious. But I don't know if I'm gonna have room for dessert."

"We'll give it a few minutes to settle. The problem is that the pork is so rich, it doesn't take a lot to fill you up. But you need all the calories you can stuff in that little body of yours to help that ankle heal. Your body is working overtime to repair the damage, and it needs all the nutrition, especially the protein, that we can get into it. So let's help it out all we can. Okay?"

"Okay, Doc."

Wade removed the rest of the pork from the fire and cut a sliver of the skin with the layer of fat underneath it and put that aside. Then he wrapped the rest in palmetto leaves and hung it inside the make-shift hut. He took one can of the melted fat and poured it in his small cooking pan. Placing the pan on a rock at the edge of the fire, the pig fat was soon roiling, so hot that Wade was afraid it would catch fire. He cut the pork skin into small cubes with the fat attached and dumped them into the hot pig grease, frying them to a crispy brown. He sprinkled a little salt and a little more spice on the cubes.

He scooped some pieces out of the grease and handed them to Mindy on a palmetto leaf.

"Dessert is served, Ma'am. The finest fried pork cracklin's in Louisiana."

"And I thought I was impressed before. You've outdone yourself this time."

"It's nothing, really. This swamp," he said, motioning with his hands all around him, "is like a huge grocery store. You just have to know what to shop for and how to shop for it. Men have survived for years out here knowing what they were doing. Others that didn't know didn't last very long."

"The aisles aren't very organized. I'd have a hard time finding what I was looking for. But then I have a hard time finding marshmallows at the grocery store in Evergreen."

"It takes patience out here, Mindy. Sometimes you go to the groceries in the swamp and sometimes you have to wait for the groceries to come to you."

"I'm afraid I'm a little short on patience. Speaking of that, what happens if we don't hear the hunters Saturday?"

"I won't lie to you, Mindy. I think I told you the Atchafalaya Basin is bigger than the state of Rhode Island and has a lot more danger in it if you try to walk across it. The problem is that I don't know exactly where we're located. If my trusty phone was working, we could get a GPS signal, and we'd know how far I needed to go to get help, but we must be a long way from the two major highways, Interstate 10 and Highway 190. If we were fairly close to either, our phones would receive a signal from a tower. That means whichever way we need to go, it'll be a good hike out."

"That doesn't sound like a barrel of monkeys fun."

"When you add in over a million alligators, several million moccasins, swamp rattlers, poisonous spiders, leeches, alligator snapping turtles that can weigh over four hundred pounds, bob cats and at least one big black cat, it makes the trip a little more exciting."

Wade gazed around him as if sizing up his chances.

Mindy sighed, "I hope that's the downside."

Wade laughed. "Yes, it is. Fortunately, there is an upside."

"And that would be?"

"Like I told you before. They don't call Louisiana 'Sportsman's Paradise' for nothing. This old swamp has some of the best hunting and fishing opportunities in the world. Generations of Cajuns have found out how to successfully navigate around in here for deer, ducks, coons, squirrels, alligators, crawfish, bullfrogs and the list goes on and on, not to mention the catfish, bass, perch, sac-a-lait, eels and gar for the guys that like to fish. This Saturday shouldn't be any different from any other Saturday in the fall around here. There should be hundreds, if not thousands of those guys out here trying to find a big buck or fill their limit for mallards. We should be within earshot of at least one. I'd rather know someone is out there before we pick a direction to go."

"That all makes sense to me. But what happens if Saturday comes and goes and we don't hear anybody?"

Wade rubbed his chin and gazed at the moist ground.

"Then we have two choices. I can leave you here by the fire and the shelter with plenty of food and hike out by myself to find somebody or at the very least a way out of here. Traveling alone, I probably can make ten to twenty miles a day, even through this bog. I may have to swim across a bunch of the bigger sloughs, so that may slow me down a little, but I figure in no more than three days, I should run across something or at least reach an area where my phone works. Either way, we could get help headed this way."

"I'm guessing choice number two involves me going with you on this little excursion to nowhere."

"Yep. But with your ankle hurt the way it is, I figure our

progress will slow to around three or four miles a day. Some of these bogs are so bad that I'll have to carry you across them. I won't be able to carry you and two backpacks, so I'll need to make two trips across them, so it'll take a lot longer. The problem lies in the uncertainty. We don't know if we're several hundred yards from finding a four-wheeler trail or access to a phone tower or several days. We just don't know."

"We don't know if you'd have to carry my little ass for half a day or for a week. Is that what I'm hearing you say?"

"That's about the size of it, Mindy."

"What do you think we should do, Wade? Which direction should we go?"

"I think we should try to keep the Kitty Kat out of our camp tonight and get some rest. We'll both be able to think more clearly if we can get a good night's sleep."

"But what about Saturday?"

"We'll worry about Saturday when Saturday gets here. Until then, let's concentrate on making the best of an unpleasant situation."

"One more thing, Wade. I can't sleep with all these nasty clothes on. Remember, Mandy & I sleep together without PJ's."

"It's all right with me, Mindy. Just spray all over with the bug spray and keep that space blanket over you and you should be fine. That reminds me."

Wade rose and took a stick that still had flames licking from one end. He entered the make-shift hut and lit a small fire in each corner and placed a small green palmetto leaf on each of the three fires. "That should keep the critters and the bugs away tonight, hopefully."

"I hate to ask this, Wade. I need help getting undressed in the hammock."

"I don't think I've ever had a young lady apologize for me removing her clothing. This is a first."

"Maybe we'll have a lot of firsts together."

"Hold on, Pony. I'll help you get undressed. After that, you're on your own until tomorrow. I'm sleeping in my hammock and you're sleeping in yours. No hammock hopping tonight. Do you understand?"

"Party pooper."

"WHERE IS VICTORIA SUPPOSED TO MEET US, JOHN?" Sam asked the City Attorney while on the road to Jackson.

"At the coffee shop off Exit 98. She said she would be there at three. We've got time. The funeral didn't take as long as I thought it would."

Sam glanced at the attorney. "How long have you known Kenny and Reba?"

"Since before they married, so ten years. Kenny had dreams, big dreams. He wanted to be the mayor of Evergreen one day and then maybe run for a state office."

"I hate to bring up a sore subject, but do you realize that you and Bruce are the only two left of the city officials from the last election? Everyone else has been murdered. And now, Bruce's daughter is missing."

"That is strange. But the others, not Kenny—the others were all murdered by the preacher because of Rachel, weren't they? Isn't the preacher still in jail or some mental institution awaiting evaluation or something?"

"I don't think the preacher has anything to do with Kenny's murder. I just find it an odd coincidence, that's all."

"I believe what you're trying to ask in a subtle way is 'Did you have anything to do with Kenny's murder?' without coming right out and asking it. Am I right?"

"Okay, did you have anything to do with Kenny's murder?"

"No, Sam. I didn't. Are you satisfied now?"

"Not yet. Where were you last Friday night and early Saturday morning?"

"I was home in bed with my wife, which I might say, after the little thing with Rachel, is my custom. After Rachel, nothing else has come close to exciting me enough to give up everything I have, Sam. And that includes my wife."

Sam nodded. "All right, now I'm satisfied. Tell me about Victoria."

"I don't know much about her other than she has a business card with no company name and no address or email, just a phone number in Jackson."

"What kind of business is she in?"

"The shady kind, if you catch my drift."

"I think I do."

"She supposedly represents an investment group and they trust her with setting everything up. I don't know what 'everything' means; you know, what she's setting up, how she's setting it up and who's involved. Those kinds of questions, only she and Ed knew. Maybe Rachel, but only she and the mayor knew for sure, and now he's gone."

"But you knew some parts of the project. According to Bruce, you were working on the infrastructure component and the impact of the project on the other parts of the city. Is that true?"

"My contribution was very generic. They would pose questions like if we brought in a two hundred million dollar project, how would that affect traffic, retail, employment and demand for city services? Then they would raise the number to five hundred million. Then they would raise the number to two or three billion dollars. After a while, I just prorated the numbers instead of spending much time on them, because they were all over the board with the numbers."

"What was the project really about?"

"I don't know. I'm sure Bruce and I concluded that it must be about either nuclear waste or toxic chemical waste, but neither one of us knows for certainty."

"Okay, tell me more about Victoria."

"I don't know much more. She's an attractive lady in her mid-thirties, I'd guess. Rather sophisticated type. She knows her way around the political circles. She's very comfortable talking about fiscal responsibility, federal assistance, local ordinance procedures, and just about anything else."

30 TUESDAY AFTERNOON
JACKSON

"SAM, PLEASE MEET VICTORIA ENGLE. VICKI, THIS IS Sam Cates, our sheriff in Evergreen." John introduced the two women inside the technology-friendly coffee house in Jackson.

Sam normally enjoyed the stimulating aroma of the unique coffee flavors, but today she barely noticed. She firmly shook hands with Vicki, anxious to find out more about the mysterious project that remained just out of reach of exposure for the last couple of years.

"Vicki, thanks for meeting with us. Under the circumstances, we need all the help we can get."

"John asked me to meet with you. I always try to accommodate John any way I can. I'm not sure what I can do to help you, Sam. Are you investigating the projected project in Evergreen?"

"Yes, and no. We're investigating the murder of Kenny Thigpen and the disappearance of Wade Dalton and Mindy Thomas. I'm not sure what, if any, connection there is to the project."

"Wade disappeared?"

Sam stiffened noticeably. "You know Wade?"

"I met him Sunday, but only for a minute. I talked to him after you left the restaurant Sunday. I guess that I assumed he told you."

"No, he didn't."

"And you say he has disappeared? John, you didn't tell me that when you set up the meeting."

"I didn't know you'd met Wade, and our interest is in the project. Why did you want to meet with Wade?"

"I had some business to do with him, John. But, like the project, I can't disclose the business due to legal obligations."

Sam's face turned to a bright red.

"So you were in the Evergreen Café Sunday? I don't remember seeing you there."

"I was there and was going to introduce myself to both of you, but your conversation was so animated. I waited until you guys calmed down. Unfortunately, you walked out before I could meet you and you didn't appear to be thrilled when you left."

"I wasn't." Sam put her head down, cupped in her hands. "I wish I had handled the situation differently."

"Anyway, we only met for a few minutes, less than fifteen for sure. He was still in the restaurant alive and well when I left. When did he go missing?"

"Yesterday. We found his truck in the National Forest, but we haven't found him or Mindy."

"So that's why he didn't show up in Houston. I thought he'd changed his mind about going and he hasn't answered his phone. I've been trying to call him since noon yesterday. I don't know anything about Mindy. I've never met her."

"What did you discuss with Wade?"

"I can't go into details, Sam. But I can tell you I had a proposal to present to him and he said he'd consider it. He was scheduled to go to Houston yesterday to discuss it with the investor that wanted to make the proposal, but like I said, he never showed up."

"That's not like Wade. He keeps his word."

"He must've canceled at the airport. I haven't heard from the charter captain either. I tried to call him twice without success. But you said you found his truck in the National Forest, so he never made it to the airport, I guess."

"The airport? Do you mean the private airport in Evergreen?"

Victoria nodded. "I arranged for a private charter plane to pick him up early yesterday morning and take him to Houston. They were supposed to bring him back to Evergreen yesterday afternoon."

"And you haven't been in touch with the charter service since yesterday?"

"I haven't been in touch with him since Sunday. I tried to call him a couple of times yesterday, but wasn't successful. I was more interested in reaching Wade. He's the one I needed to talk to about the proposal."

"Who is the charter pilot?"

"I have the information in my office. I'll get that to you. One thing I'm not getting here." She paused. "How is Wade connected to the potential project? I'm involved in both and I don't know of any connection between the two."

"There has to be some connection, Vicki. Everyone that has had any connection to the project has had something bad happen to them, it seems. Ed Moore, Frank Davis, Bill Brogan, Rachel Chastain, and Kenny Thigpen are all dead. Bruce Thomas has a daughter missing and now Wade is missing. That's why we're here. We need to know more about this project."

"I remember Kenny and Reba. We really enjoyed hosting them here in Jackson, along with all the other city officials from Evergreen. They were a great bunch of folks."

"You said '*we*' when you talked about hosting them. Who else was with you when they came to Jackson?"

They were gentlemen from here in Jackson, although they weren't part of the investor group for the potential project. They helped with logistics and coordination of the event; making reservations for hotels, conference rooms, meals, tickets to various entertainment events and things like that. I hired them from a local firm that specializes in event coordination."

"It doesn't sound like they had anything to do with the project."

"That's correct. They were event coordinators. That isn't my area of expertise."

"I hate to be abrupt, but I'm losing my patience. Who the hell can tell me what this project is all about? We've gotten the run-around for over a year now, and I don't know much more about it than I did before I ever heard of it."

Sam clinched her fist on the tabletop.

"I can give you a broad brush, but you'll need to sign a non-disclosure agreement before I can even do that. It says you won't disclose any information we discuss with anyone without our expressed written permission. I'll have to submit it to the investors and let them decide how much I can disclose to you."

"I don't believe this." Sam threw her hands up in the air. "What the hell are you guys afraid of? What is it about this project that is so secretive?"

"I'm not afraid of anything, Sam. I'm legally bound to

keep the information from the investor group confidential unless they give me permission or I get a court order requiring me to disclose it."

Sam rolled her eyes. "John, you're our city attorney. How long before we can get a court order requiring Miss Engle to answer our questions?"

John squirmed in his chair. "Sam, I find myself in an awkward situation. I've already signed one of those non-disclosure statements concerning this project, so I have a potential conflict of interest. I must withdraw myself from any of the other procedures associated with it."

"Are you kidding me?" Sam glared at him. "Please tell me you're kidding me."

"Sam, I know you're upset and I don't blame you, but I can't participate in obtaining a subpoena for a business dealing in which I have a potential conflict of interest. I could lose my license to practice law in the state of Mississippi."

"What the hell did we come up here for? A cup of coffee? I can get a cup of coffee in Evergreen."

"Settle down." John scratched his forehead with his fingernails. "Let me talk with Vicki privately for a few minutes."

Sam shoved her chair backwards and stormed out of the restaurant. She made no attempt to hide her anger with John and Vicki, slamming the door on her departure. Once outside, she paced up and down in front of the building. After a few minutes, John appeared in the doorway, motioning for Sam to return to their table inside.

Vicki spoke first. "Sam, I understand your position. If I were in your shoes, I'd be just as frustrated as you are."

Sam said nothing, but continued to stare at Vicki.

Vicki nodded and continued.

"I'll tell you everything I can without violating my agreement with the investors. Okay?"

"All right, Vicki. What is this all about?"

"Sam, this conversation is completely off the record. Agreed?"

Sam fidgeted in her chair. "Agreed."

"Two years ago, a gentleman contacted me. He asked me if I could find an investor or put together a group of investors. He told me he'd need more than fifty million and possibly up to two hundred million for a project that couldn't fail in Evergreen. When I told him I'd never heard of a project that couldn't fail, he assured me that if I could see the documentation he had, I wouldn't second guess him. I told him I could put together a group of investors that had the wherewithal to come up with that kind of money, but they were extremely conservative. He told me not to worry about that and if I could line up a meeting with them, he'd be able to convince them to invest. I told him I'd need a lot more details to get them interested in meeting, but he refused. I asked him if this investment was legal and he assured me it was. Are you with me so far, Sam?"

"Yes."

"I set up the meeting. When I got there, it surprised me when he asked me to leave after introducing him to the investors. I left the room, but wasn't thrilled about it. He told me he'd make it worth my time if it worked out. He assured me he was confident in the documentation and the investment was a good one, but that he needed to work out some details. One of these details was getting the city officials from Evergreen on board with the investment. He told me that would be part of my job."

"All right, go on."

"The investors agreed to go with the project and set aside some upfront money to help get the city officials on board. I went to Evergreen and met with the mayor, Ed Moore. His assistant, Rachel, attended the meeting as well. I believe she was actually the one that reached out to the other city officials and convinced them to sign the non-disclosure agreements and the consultant contracts so we could legally pay them."

Sam glared again at John.

"Sounds like a conflict of interest to me."

"We were assured—I say we, what I mean to say is that the gentlemen that put this all together assured us he'd addressed separate contracts for the work we required and as long as the mayor and city council approved it, there was nothing illegal or unethical about it."

Sam held up her hand with her palm facing Vicki.

"It may be legal, but it sure as hell isn't ethical. It smells. Actually, it reeks of insider trading and conflict of interest. I mean, do you want me to believe that those city officials in charge of looking out for the good of the people really have a choice? They can only vote one way."

"Sam, the consultant agreements are in force and will be paid no matter how they vote."

"Right. And I've asked the fleas on my dog not to bite him."

"We have an obligation to protect the interest of our investors."

"You're right, Vicki. You do, but not at the expense of the citizens of Evergreen with bribery. Look, I don't want to get bogged down in all of this. I want to know what happened to Wade. He isn't a city official. Why were you trying to bribe him Sunday?"

"Sam, please. I'm trying to help you find Wade and throwing around terms like 'bribery' isn't helping."

"I'll try to be more civil, but I'm not buying into all if this 'for the good of the people' BS you're trying to sell us. So let's just stick to the facts without all the self-justification."

"The meeting at the restaurant was the only time I've ever met Wade. To my knowledge, I've never met Bruce's daughter. If I remember correctly, Bruce told me she has a twin sister, but I don't remember her name."

"It's Mandy. Her name is Mandy."

"I remember now. It's Mindy and Mandy."

"Who was Wade supposed to meet with in Houston?"

"I'll have to get his permission to disclose that information, Sam."

"Sam turned toward the windows of the restaurant. The veins in her temples protruded, and her lips squeezed together. She turned back toward Vicki.

"Do you need his permission to take a dump every morning, Vicki?"

Vicki slammed her hand down on the table.

"I came here as a favor to John and I've heard all the character assassination that I care to hear today. John, call me if you need some help. Sheriff Cates, call me when you get a subpoena. But I've got to warn you. My memory gets awful fuzzy."

Vicki pushed her chair back and rushed out of the restaurant.

Sam looked down at her cup of coffee.

"I didn't handle that very well, did I?"

"Not too well."

"I don't guess I should anxiously wait for Ms. Engle to invite me to be her friend on the social networks."

John laughed. "You might be shopping on the wrong aisle for that. You wanted to be by the Valentine candy and you ended up in the vinegar section."

"I should be in the Kitty Litter section with all the BS I've heard today."

31 WEDNESDAY MORNING
ATCHAFALAYA BASIN

"Good morning, Ma'am. I trust that you slept well."

Mindy yawned, "I didn't realize how tired I was. What's on the menu for today?"

"We will begin with Pork on the Pit for our distinguished guests. Then we'll set out our traps to lure in only the freshest crawfish in the Bayou. We never serve frozen seafood. We prepare only freshly caught seafood for our diners."

"Traps?"

"Remember the basket you wove from the palmetto leaves yesterday? We're gonna weave a couple more and then we'll have our traps. All we have to do is bait them and wait for lunch to come to us."

"Basket weaving. I don't remember signing up for that seminar when I booked this exotic vacation with the agency. I may file a complaint with them. I'm here in this wonderful location and I'm weaving baskets. Can't wait to tell my grandchildren about this."

"Now don't get too excited and hyperventilate. You may

pass out and I'd have to perform mouth-to-mouth resuscitation on you. I haven't practiced in a long, long time and it may take a while to get it right."

"Sounds like you're getting horny, Detective Ranger. Are you finally gonna make a pass at me? It's only been two days with me and you alone out here. I thought I might be losing it."

Wade laughed.

"You haven't lost anything yet. You'd better quit talking like that, though, or I might take you seriously."

"That would be a change."

Wade just smiled. He glanced at the sky.

"Mindy, seriously; it looks like a storm is brewing and with the wind's picking up as quickly as it seems to be, it might be a strong one."

"That means we'll be stuck in that hut together all morning with nothing to do except think of each other."

"No, we'll be weaving baskets unless you don't care to eat the rest of the day."

"Let's see. Go hungry and harass you or get something to eat and leave you alone." She held her hands in the air with the palms up as if trying to weigh the options. "Have fun harassing you or eat. Boy, that's a tough one. Can't I do both?"

"I'm gonna make it easy for you. I'm going out to cut some palmetto leaves while you heat up the pig. Do you need some help getting to the fire with your sore ankle?"

"It feels good this morning. I may get around with these wonderful crutches the Resort furnished." She eased out of the hammock and immediately grabbed a crutch for support. "Maybe by tomorrow, anyway."

"Great, I won't be long."

Wade was only out of the camp for a few minutes

before returning with a stack of palmetto leaves. He laid them on Mindy's hammock inside the hut. The sound and aroma of sizzling pork drew him next to the fire, and he sat down by Mindy. She handed him a piece of hot, white loin on a palmetto leaf.

"Hmm. You're not an awful cook, yourself. My compliments on a job well done." He nodded towards Mindy.

"I'm great at re-heating stuff. You should see me with a microwave. I can punch buttons and zap things with the best of them."

"Too easy, Mindy. That'll spoil you."

"Speaking of easy. Wouldn't some macaroni and cheese out of the microwave be good right now? Oh, for a triple cheese mac in a can, I'd give up all the pig in the world."

"I agree it sounds good. The next time I go grocery shopping in Slough number three, I'll see if they have some on the aisles. They may have to special order the triple cheese, though."

Mindy grumbled, "If you can't find triple cheese, just bring home some regular. That's the problem with sending men to the grocery store. They think if they come back with some meat, then they've done their job. Women think about a complete meal and all you guys think about is meat."

Wade licked his fingers, trying to savor the last bits of the pork.

"This doesn't taste half bad. Save the bones with all the fat, gristle and sinews. We're gonna tie them to the bottom of the baskets for bait. I bet when those little mud bugs get a taste of your cooking, they won't be able to let go and will hang on while we pull the baskets up. At least, that's what I'm hoping."

"That sounds like a plan. That's what I enjoy about being stranded out here with you. You're always planning."

"And one more thing I'm planning on is getting washed off when that storm comes. So, I'm gonna build up two of those little fires inside the hut and tie a line across the hut. Then we'll be able to stay warmer while our clothes are drying."

"You're just trying to get me to take off my clothes, aren't you? We'll be like Tarzan and Jane, naked as the apes. Now that should get real interesting in a hurry."

"Cool your engines. I stink. My clothes stink. This shower will be a lot better and safer than jumping in the slough with the alligators and leeches. I've got some soap in my bag and I'm gonna wash me and my clothes. You're welcome to borrow some of my soap if you wish, or you can keep your stinky old clothes on for the next couple of weeks."

"I'd love to get lathered up with you, Detective Ranger."

"I'll go on the other side of the hut and you're gonna stay on this side. We won't be able to see each other that way."

"Uh oh! The rain is here." Mindy squealed as the first few big drops fell on their heads.

"Grab a fire stick and let's get those fires in the hut going better before the rain kills this one."

Wade stoked the two small fires inside the hut and tied a rope off across the hut over the fires before taking off his boots and stepping outside. Quickly removing his clothes, he scrubbed them furiously with the soap in the rain. Then he rubbed his entire body with the bar and let the rain rinse it off. He felt cleaner and fresher than since dropping out of the sky into this boggy quagmire.

"How are you doing over there?" He heard from the other side of the hut.

"Very well. And you?"

"Okay, but I forgot my razor. You don't suppose the Resort has an esthetician on staff, do you?"

"A what?"

"You know, an esthetician. That's one of those gals that pulls the hair off your legs so you don't have to shave. I'm sure the manager told you and you just don't want to pay for the service for me."

Wade laughed to himself. "I'll be sure to check with him just as soon as this storm passes."

"Would you ask him about the hot water, also? He's got the temperature of this shower a little too cool for my tastes. I'm getting goose bumps."

"I agree with you on that. Take your clothes inside and hang them over the rope right over the fire. Stand next to the fire to dry off and then use the space blanket to wrap up. It won't take your clothes long to dry out."

Wade turned his back to the hut as Mindy scurried in with her pile of clothes. He could hear her wringing the excess water out of them before hanging them on the rope. The relentless rain was making him shiver.

"All right, I'm under the space blanket and decent. You can come in now."

"I was getting a little chilly out here."

Wade wrung his clothes out and started hanging them over the rope when he heard giggling coming from the other hammock.

"What's so funny?"

"Either you're excited about being alone with a naked lady out here in the middle of nowhere. Or your little flag automatically salutes every time it rains."

Wade's face turned red, and he grabbed a palmetto leaf to cover himself.

"It's just cold and wet from the rain." He growled.

"I thought cold and rain caused most things to shrivel up. I must have always been playing with the boys instead of the men. Ya'll play with full-size flags."

"Okay, that's enough. Do you want me to talk about your body parts?"

"Go for it. Which parts do you want to start with?"

Wade jumped on his hammock and covered himself with a couple of the palmetto leaves.

"None of them. I'm too cold right now. I can see somebody getting trapped out here without a fire or proper shelter and clothing and dying from hypothermia. It doesn't take long to get cold in this rain."

"It's almost cozy under this space blanket. Care to join me?"

Wade shook his head and paused.

"Mindy, let's take care of this. Yes, I would love to join you under the blanket, but I can't. I think you're cute, sexy, pretty, exotic. Whatever term you want to use, then you're it. But I'm committed to Sam and there is no compromise in our relationship, no matter what happens. In other circumstances, then—"

"Wade, I understand, and I don't mean half of what I say. It just keeps my mind off of other things."

"No problem."

"I'll be honest with you. I'm scared to death. I don't know if I'll ever see Mandy or Daddy again." A tear formed in the corner of her eye. "I want to hug and kiss both of them so bad I don't know what to do. I can't stand it, so I shrink off a little into a fantasy world."

"I know, Mindy. I feel the same way about Sam. Even

though I'm trying to stay positive, I have my doubts. But then I look around us. We have shelter. We have water to drink and more of it coming down by the second right now. We have a fire and the ability to create more if ours goes out. We have food and know how to get more. Even though it might not taste great, it'll keep us alive for a long time. We can survive here until your ankle gets well and then if someone hasn't happened by, we'll find our way out of here."

"I believe you. I just need to vent sometimes. I don't mean to harass you as much as I do."

"I'm a big boy. I can take it."

"Yea, I saw you are a big boy all right." She laughed. "Oops. Sorry."

"That didn't last long, did it?"

Mindy shook her head. "At least it's Wednesday."

"Yep. Hump day."

"There you go again."

"Huh?"

Mindy's body gyrated under the space blanket.

"You talked about humping."

Wade reached up and grabbed a wet sock and threw it at her. She giggled under the protection of the space blanket.

Wade laughed. He knew now that Mindy was over her venting phase and was back to the person he'd come to appreciate and admire over the last three days. He closed his eyes as the rain continued to pelt down on the surprisingly waterproof hut.

32 WEDNESDAY MORNING
ATCHAFALAYA BASIN

"Hey, Sleepy Head. Thought you were going to sleep all day."

Wade yawned.

"I didn't think I'd go back to sleep. I guess with the warmth of the fire and the rain falling on our little hut, it was just too much. That was as sound as I've slept since we been on this excursion."

"You're going to be proud of me." Mindy beamed. "I set out the three traps while you were snoring. I'm getting hungry for lunch."

"You did?"

"Not sure if I did it right or not, but I know we have a least a couple. I watched them go into the trap."

"This place really is Sportsman's Paradise. If we just keep our wits about us, we'll be okay. Show me where you set them out."

"Get your clothes on first. I don't want to see your flag blowing in the breeze."

Wade hurriedly dressed. "I'm ready."

"Let's rip, Tater Chip." Mindy leveraged herself upright

between her two crutches and led Wade down the same ridge the camp was located. She picked her way on the crutches, maneuvering over the fallen logs and brush.

"Hold on." Wade edged up beside her. "Grab your crutches and hold on."

He lifted her up over his head and lowered her onto his broad shoulders.

"Our version of limousine service at the Resort, Ma'am. Don't tell the other guests about this, please. We don't want them to get jealous and we only offer this service to our guests staying in the Presidential Suite."

"I won't tell, I promise. The last time I said that was when I caught the city attorney trying to look up my skirt at work."

"Which way do we go, Ma'am?"

"Right down here. You'll see a little circular pond of sorts. I set them out around the edges of it."

Wade would have preferred she would have distributed them among three different areas, but he appreciated Mindy's angst to get them set and return to camp. She'd exceeded his expectations. Coming up on a large depression, Wade raised his eyebrows when he saw the size of the body of water and how far away from the bank Mindy set the traps. He was holding onto her pants legs and they weren't wet.

"How did you get those out there?"

"Set me down and I'll show you."

Back on the ground, she stretched with a crutch out over the water with the fork of the crutch closest to the center of the pond. Mindy then hooked the fork of the crutch into a loop of rope she had tied to the basket. Jerking upward on the loop, she raised the woven basket out of the water onto the bank.

Wade jumped next to the basket and covered the opening at the top with a palmetto leaf.

"Impressive stuff for a city girl." He raised the leaf and peaked inside the basket at the crawfish. "Dang it. That trap is half full. My compliments to the trapper du jour."

The other two traps produced similar results, and Wade smiled with approval. He hoisted Mindy onto his shoulders, grabbed her crutches and the three traps, and trudged back to camp. He gently sat Mindy down by the fire and sat down beside her. He poured the contents of the traps onto the ground between them.

"Let's put all the crawfish into these two baskets and see what we have left."

They gathered a little over three pounds of crawfish into the baskets before counting the other bounty from the pond. They sorted five small sun perch, a freshwater eel, and a soft-shelled turtle. Wade whistled at the amount of seafood they'd caught from three woven baskets. He quickly dressed the turtle and cleaned the perch. He put the eel back into the third basket.

The grease from the leftover morning pork didn't take long to heat and was soon sizzling in the pan on the flat rock. Wade placed the turtle and the bream in the pan before dumping the crawfish in the hot embers surrounding the fire.

"Ma'am, I hope you're ready for a seafood luncheon that most resorts would consider a feast. Here at the Atchafalaya Resort, we just call it service. And since you helped shop for the ingredients at our local market, I'll give you the first choice of entrée's."

"I'll take some crawfish and perch, Sir." Mindy wrinkled her nose. "I've never tried soft-shell turtle before."

"Doesn't taste much different that soft-shell crab, except

there are a few bones to maneuver around. It's a little stringier and tougher, but not bad if properly cooked."

"That's okay. I'm still gonna stick to the mud bugs and the fish."

After only three crawfish, Mindy grinned at Wade. "My compliments to the chef, again. I've only ever tried crawfish boiled or fried, never like this before. An excellent job, Sir."

Wade really enjoyed the taste of the soft-shelled turtle. There was an unmistakable earthy quality to the meat reflecting where the turtle lived and fed, but it was offset by the natural sweetness of the small amounts of fat when it sizzled in the grease. The crispness of the external shell provided a different texture than the stringiness of the meat.

He almost finished the turtle when he watched Mindy eat the last of the crawfish and the perch.

"You know. I could almost get used to staying out here if I didn't miss Mandy so much."

"Not me. I'm ready to get back to the Plantation and Sam. At least back there, the animals are behind a fence. I like it better that way."

"The food is excellent, but there is something special about a greasy cheeseburger, a bag of salty fries and a double-chocolate milk shake. Now that's hard to beat."

"Only twenty thousand calories in that little snack."

"That's all right. Those are the first things I'm gonna have when we get out of here."

"Hey, I forgot something in my bag. Boil some water and I'll be right back."

Wade returned and poured water out of the pan until he figured he had just enough left. He took a packet out of his pocket and poured it into the water. He stirred it with one of the camp spoons for about three minutes. He laid the pan on a palmetto leaf and handed it to Mindy.

"There you go, Ma'am. Instant chocolate pudding. Guaranteed to take those yearnings for a sweet away."

"You really came prepared, didn't you?"

"I guess my instincts told me to be ready for anything."

Both sat quietly, reflecting on their uncertain future.

33 WEDNESDAY
EVERGREEN

"Sheriff Cates, I'm Ben Russell with the Investigative Division of the State Police. How are you today?"

"Not that great, Ben. I would lie to you and tell you everything is great, but I don't want to insult your intelligence. Please call me Sam. Everybody around here calls me Sam. They call my dad 'Sheriff Cates'. He was the sheriff here for almost thirty years before I took the job."

"Okay, Sam. You know we get automatically involved in a case when something happens to a law enforcement official per the governor's orders. I guess he figures we don't have enough to do with our current workload."

"I understand. You won't get any push-back from me. I'd take help from the army, navy or the Bama cheerleaders if it speeds up finding Wade and Mindy."

The officer in the pressed uniform sat.

"Our purpose is officially two-fold. We need to find out what happened to Mr. Dalton and we want to help solve the murder of your councilman, Kenny Thigpen. The young lady, Ms. Thomas, is of secondary interest unless we can definitively tie her situation to one of the other two."

"Kenny Thigpen, I understand. But why Wade?"

"He's a Federal Investigator appointed by a Federal judge. I thought you were aware of that."

"I'm aware of it. Must have slipped my mind."

"And I must tell you. We aren't alone. What I mean is that some of our federal friends share our interest in Wade." Ben rolled his eyes. "A few of our friends from the Fed insisted on helping with the investigation into Wade's disappearance. They have no interest in the councilman's murder though. Just the disappearance. Most peculiar thing I've ever seen."

Sam laughed. "Damn. I forgot all about that. I bet they're interested in his whereabouts and his safety."

"Huh?"

"Ben, if something untoward happens to Wade, his death or disappearance will trigger some events the Agency would much prefer not come to light. It's an old story, but it's very much alive right now."

Ben shrugged his shoulders. "I don't have any idea what you're talking about, but when we find him, I'll buy you both a drink and you can tell me about it. I've never seen the Agency so eager to cooperate on any case before."

"It goes back a few years. Wade was an agent when I first met him. He left the agency on less than amiable terms when he uncovered some of its secrets. The agency will do almost anything to keep those secrets between itself and Wade."

"I don't want to know unless the secrets can help advance this case. I've got enough trouble in my life without pissing off the agency."

"I'll keep that in mind, Ben. With all of their help, what have you found out?"

"We understand you've intervicwed Kenny's wife, Mrs. Reba Thigpen, a couple of times, Traci Long, who worked for Mr. Thigpen and Traci's boyfriend, Rick Morgan."

"Yes, that's correct."

"You've also interviewed Bruce and Mandy Thomas, the young lady's father and sister and John Grimes, the city attorney."

"Yes."

"You've also interviewed the manager and the owner of a private airport outside of town."

"Not personally, but my deputies interviewed them."

"They also interviewed the gentleman that found the truck in the National Forest."

"Yes." Sam nodded impatiently.

"I believe it says you and Mr. Grimes interviewed a Victoria Engle from Jackson."

"Yes."

"I also see that you've checked with the various terminals; bus depot, airport, train station and even looked at some boat charters."

"Yes, we've tried to be very thorough."

"Don't get me wrong. You and your staff have been very thorough. But I'd like to go over these with you today and see if a fresh set of eyes may see something that you guys overlooked in the initial review."

"No problem, Ben. I'm really about out of leads right now."

"Maybe not, Sam. You may have more than you know."

Sam's eyes brightened. "Tell me!"

Ben looked down at his notes. "I'm not sure what it means, but according to our friends from the Fed, there is no Victoria Engle in Jackson, not one that fits your description, anyway."

"Damn. I knew it. I just knew it. She's a fake."

"We're not sure who she is, but she's not who she says she is."

"Anything else."

"Yes, and again, it's preliminary."

"I don't care. Don't keep me guessing. Tell me."

Ben again referred to his notes.

"Your deputies interviewed the manager of the airport, but he forgot to tell them something. He's been making a little money on the side, re-fueling some planes on Mondays when they are officially closed and then cooking the books."

"Yes?"

"He did re-fuel one on Monday and he helped two passengers board that fit the description of Wade and the young lady."

"But Vicki—, or whoever she is, said Wade never showed up in Houston so they must have missed the flight."

"The Feds are almost certain they boarded here in Evergreen. After that, they were kind enough to share some good news and bad news."

Sam's heart sank when she recalled the deputy sticking his head in the conference room.

"The plane crashed in the Gulf of Mexico, didn't it?"

"Yes, that's the bad news."

Sam asked glumly, "And the good news?"

Ben smiled at Sam. "The preliminary report indicates there are two parachutes missing from the plane."

34 WEDNESDAY AFTERNOON
ATCHAFALAYA BASIN

"So what's on our agenda this afternoon, Detective Ranger?"

"We should reinforce our little hut just in case your Kitty Kat pays us a visit in the middle of the night. Since we now have three fires going during the night, I'm going to have to gather more firewood."

"Seems like we need an endless supply to keep each fire burning most of the night."

"Would you rather have the Kitty Kat visit or gather more wood?"

"I think we agree with each other on that one."

"After that, I'll rig us up some fishing poles. That big slough has to have some catfish in it. We can go down there right before dark and hopefully catch a couple for supper."

"Why don't we go as soon as you get the poles ready? Fishing sounds like a lot more fun than sitting around the fire."

Wade shook his head. "Catfish aren't the most active fish in the middle of the day. They'll move around and feed some on a warm day, but they're much more active late in the afternoon or at night. With some fresh eel for bait, we should be able to catch a couple without a lot of hassle."

"I feel like we're eating the smorgasbord of the swamp. We've had every kind of wildlife out here."

"We haven't even touched the surface yet. There's plenty out here that we haven't even seen, much less touched."

"I know, but we consume so much of the day gathering firewood and finding something to eat. When do you take a day off to relax?"

"We don't. It's always better to stay busy in a situation like this. Then your mind doesn't have time to reflect on all the uncertainties and only think about survival."

"So does that mean I get to go fishing with you?"

"You're still having trouble getting in and out of your hammock. You're not in any shape to tangle with a jaguar right now."

"I hate to be the bearer of bad news to you, Detective Ranger, but you can't outrun a jaguar either."

Wade chuckled. "I don't need to outrun the cat. I just need to outrun you. By the time he finishes playing around with you, I can be in the next parish."

"That's all right. I'm not afraid."

"And why not?"

"Because if I see him, I'm gonna shoot his ass."

Wade laughed. "I wish I had your confidence. My preference is that we don't see Mr. Kitty Kat again. But if we do, I hope we have the revolver handy. We might have a slight advantage if we do."

"So explain to me one more time why we don't go fishing now. Even if the catfish are more active at night, wouldn't it improve our chances if we fished longer?"

"Our chances of catching something would be a lot

better. But that something would probably be a turtle or a gar. They're both much more active feeding during the day than catfish. We don't want either of them."

"Why not?"

"You've tried turtle. It's okay, but nothing to write home about. "

Mindy sighed.

"I won't say that I wouldn't eat a turtle again given our present situation. But I'd prefer not to and dine on the other delicacies you bring in like that chocolate pudding. That was good. The portion size was a bit small, however."

"I'll be glad to speak to the manager about that, Ma'am. Anything else?"

"Shouldn't we go fishing and be glad with whatever we catch? What if we don't catch a catfish and it gets dark on us?"

"If the catfish aren't biting, then we won't use up much bait and we'll have plenty of eel to snack on tonight."

"I believe I'd rather have the gar."

"Me too. Even though they're almost all bones, there's some fairly good white meat on them. It leaves a bit of an aftertaste, but not as much as an eel. The bones in a garfish are hard to pick through. That's why you don't see gar sold in a lot of grocery stores or restaurants. It's not because there is a shortage of them, for sure."

"Whatever we get, I'm gonna pretend it's a large deep dish pepperoni pizza with double cheese and an order of buffalo wings on the side with a cherry soda. Hmm. I can already taste it."

"No problem, except for the double cheese. Our chef used all the cheese on your cheeseburger for lunch."

Mindy laughed.

"I guess I'll settle for some catfish. But from what I've

seen so far, it wouldn't surprise me if you somehow found a pepperoni pizza out here."

"Thank you. At least I'll take it as a compliment."

Wade spent the next couple of hours reinforcing the hut, placing more palmetto leaves of the spots where rain leaked through, and made the sides stronger in case the big cat decided to get even for the burned tail. He stepped back to survey the situation. The results satisfied him except with one aspect of the hut. If the big cat burrowed underneath one side, it could do it in no time at all. Wade trimmed four dozen or more sticks, sharpening one end and leaving the other end flat. He drove these sticks into the ground about six inches apart and about two feet deep with the hammer side of the hatchet.

"That'll keep him busy enough for us to blast a few shots in his direction, anyway."

"All right, let's go fishing."

"As soon as I get some firewood for tonight and rig up those poles. Won't take long at all."

"Boy, what a party pooper. Always putting work before play. That makes for a dull life."

"But out here, at least it makes it able to live."

Wade cut some limber canes and rigged the fishing line from his bag onto them. After tying a cork on each of the lines, he positioned the hook directly above the sinker. This would insure him he was fishing near the bottom of the slough.

Wade hauled his gear back to the camp and glanced at Mindy. "Wish me luck."

"From what I've seen, you don't need much."

Wade grinned and mucked down to the slough, poles in hand. Reaching the water's edge, he separated the poles about six feet apart, jamming the handle end of each one about two feet into the bog. He set the bobs at different lengths on the lines, not knowing which one might be effective in the swirling muddy mass. This strategy was also helpful in keeping the lines from becoming entangled with one another.

After setting out the lines, Wade pushed down the swamp grass on the edge and made himself a comfortable bed to lie on in the afternoon sun. Lying prone by the slough, he stared at the Spanish moss growing on the water oak above him. Watching the moss sway gently in the slight breeze above him, his eyelids became heavier and heavier until he could no longer keep them open. Despite his struggle to keep at least one of them open, they both shut tightly. He felt his body inhaling and exhaling more deeply as the afternoon sun faded.

A combination of giggling and soft laughter startled him out of his slumber, causing his body to sit erect. His eyes had trouble adjusting, even though he widened them as much as possible.

"What are you doing down here?"

"Your job, Detective Ranger. I thought you might be down here sleeping on the job. So I came down here to check on you."

"So why are you giggling?"

"If you must know, while you were snoring instead of fishing, one of your corks went under. I grabbed the pole and there's a big ol' fish on the other end. I don't know which one of us is going to win this fight, but I'm giving him a tussle. He's huge."

Wade, his eyes now clear and alert, jumped down the bank by Mindy's side. "Do you need any help?"

"Nope, not yet. I'm gonna catch this sucker and teach him not to mess with a girl."

Wade watched as Mindy grappled with the limber cane pole. She leaned back and forth on the bank as the big fish took the line first in one direction and then in another. Simple, pure joy spread across her face when the fish rose to the top of the water for the first time. Wade couldn't help but smile as he watched this young lady find pleasure in less than ideal surroundings.

Suddenly, Wade saw one of the other corks sink completely out of sight. He grabbed the base end of the pole and jerked, setting the hook in the corner of the fish's mouth. Immediately, the fish pulled the line to the deepest part of the slough, nearly doubling the pole over itself.

"Whoa! I didn't realize how limber these poles are when they're green."

"I know. I've been fighting this baby since you were snoring and dreaming about seeing me taking a shower." Mindy laughed as Wade blushed.

"I was dreaming about getting out of here, if you must know."

"Hmm. I was sure I heard my name somewhere in those mumbling you were making. So, did you really dream about me?"

Wade just smiled. "Who else would I be dreaming about?"

"I don't know. Sometimes, I get jealous thinking you might have someone else on your mind. Maybe someone in a uniform. Personally, I think you're just attracted to her uniform." Mindy giggled.

"I don't have a clue who you're talking about."

They both laughed as they continued to struggle with the fish on the ultra-limber poles. Wade was more successful tiring out his first and hauled in a two-pound channel catfish."

He looked over at Mindy. "Are you going to play with that thing all day or am I going to have to help you? Is that fish bigger than you are?"

"He must be. Seems like I've got him, and then it seems like he's got me. I'm not sure who is winning or if either of us are."

"I hope when you do finally get him, it's not a mudcat."

"I don't know the difference between a mudcat and any other catfish."

"A mudcat feeds almost exclusively on the bottom, near the mud. It has a real oily taste to it no matter how you fix them. They also leave an after-taste in your mouth of oily fish. Not very pleasant."

"I bet some of those cheap buffets where Mandy and I eat at use them. The fried fish on them is rank."

Mindy gave a huge yank on her pole and pulled in a big catfish. "Is it a mudcat? After all of that, I don't want to throw him back?"

"Nope. This one is a flathead. They're one of the best tasting catfish you can eat, right up there with the blue cat. Great job, Mindy. Let me get this other line out of the water. We don't need any more fish tonight."

"Bet mine is bigger than yours." Mindy grinned.

"I haven't made that bet since the sixth grade. But we weren't talking about catfish then."

"So, did you win? In the sixth grade, I mean."

"Didn't you just see for yourself during our stay at this luxurious resort?"

"But you were horny then."

"So was I in the sixth grade. Not much has changed about that."

"It's only been three days, Detective. Give it another

week and you'll be all over me like gravy on rice. I won't be able to get you off of me."

"We'll see. Anyway, weren't we talking about the size of the catfish?"

"You're the one that bragged about the size of your manhood in the sixth grade. But we can talk about the fish if you like. Mine's a lot bigger than yours."

Wade laid the two fish side by side on the bank, even though he already knew the results. "Your flathead is about twice as big as my channel. You win."

"I told you! I told you! And I'm going to win the other bet too. You don't have a chance of going another week."

"I'll give you this one, Mindy. But I won't concede on the other one. Not just yet, anyway."

"We'll see. I already see cracks in the armor."

"Okay, Hop-along Mindy. If you'll carry those poles back to camp, I'll dress these fish down here by the slough and bring them up."

"No problem. I'll get the soup, salad and side dishes ready while you get these done. Don't fall asleep again. Okay?" She laughed as she swung herself up on the bank with the crutches.

"You're getting around good on those."

"Before long, you won't be able to catch me. That's the only way you'll win that bet."

"Seems to me to be the other way around. As long as you can't catch me, I'll win. I may have to take your crutches away from you."

"Fat chance on that. I'll get the fire going and be ready when you get there. Anything special for dessert?"

"Baked Alaska, please."

"Huh. Never heard of that, Detective."

"Sure you have. Three flavored ice cream baked inside a

pound cake with egg meringue on top. Bake it in one of our ovens at four hundred and fifty degrees, just enough to brown the meringue. Talk about yummy."

"Ooh, that sounds good. I'd give up one of these fish for one of those right now."

"Me too. But I'm still grateful for these fish. Let me get 'em cleaned up and I'll be there in a jiffy."

Only a few minutes later, Wade carried the fresh catfish filets to camp and rubbed them with some of his special seasoning. After folding a palmetto leaf around each one, he placed on a spit over the fire. "I sure wish I'd thought to bring some lemon juice when we planned this little excursion. Then I could serve you some world-class catfish."

Mindy's smile turned into a full-fledged grin.

"I don't have any lemon juice, but I have these."

She pulled two lemonades out if her pack.

"I'm not sure if they'll help or not. I only put them in my pack because I've never seen you drink regular soda pops and I thought you might like them."

Wade retrieved the drinks from Mindy.

"Should work. I've never used one before on catfish, but I don't see why it wouldn't work. The spices will offset by the sugar. Are you sure you don't want to save both for later?"

Mindy shook her head.

"No, I can use the sugar now. Besides, I have a lot more soda pops left in my pack."

"Why don't we use half of one can on the fish and you drink the other half of that can with the meal? That way, we can have the best of both worlds."

"Suits me."

Wade unfolded each of the filets and dribbled a little lemonade over the middle of each and then made sure the palmetto leaves didn't leak. He could almost immediately hear the sizzle of the liquid inside the leaves.

"We should be serving our world famous Catfish Acadiana at the Atchafalaya Resort in just a few minutes. Shouldn't take long at all."

Mindy licked her lips as the aroma spread from the flames.

"I'm ready."

Wade waited only six to eight minutes before retrieving the fish from over the fire.

"They're ready, Ma'am. Most chefs overcook grilled fish, but not here at the Resort. We pride ourselves on getting it just right for our valued guests, and we even prepare our fish table-side. You won't find that kind of service anywhere but here."

"Remind me to include that in our review rating. So far, you're doing all right except for the air conditioning. Did you ever speak to the Manager about that?"

"Not yet. I was a tad busy making sure your catfish were fresh. I'll be sure to add that to my list."

Wade handed a filet to Mindy with some fresh palmetto leaves underneath it to prevent the hot fish from burning her. She picked a corner off the filet and nibbled on it before eating the whole piece.

"Hmm. If you ever give up detecting or whatever you do, I might hire you as my personal chef."

"I learned the secret to serving wonderful food a long time ago. It's making sure the people doing the eating are hungry before you serve them. Works every time."

"I'm not kidding for once, Wade. This is superb."

"Thanks. I hope you remember me when you get rich and famous. In the meantime, don't forget you have another filet over here."

"Just one? I thought if I flirted with you enough, I'd get them both." Mindy laughed.

"Nope. I'm more hungry than I am horny right now."

"Let's see how long that lasts. I bet not long."

"It's gonna last at least as long as it takes to eat that other filet. Then all bets are off."

"Typical man."

"Yep."

"What's on the menu for tomorrow?"

"We can always find another snake or two."

"I had sandwiches, remember. You ate the snake."

35 WEDNESDAY NIGHT
ATCHAFALAYA BASIN

"Wade, we have company!" Mindy whispered in the dark.

"I know. He's been sneaking up on us for the last half hour."

"Is it the cat?" She kept her voice low.

"It's one of your other friends. He's not very big, though."

"Wade, it's an alligator! Quick, shoot him!"

"Relax, Mindy. He can get into our little hut if he really wants to, but my guess is that it's not worth that much trouble to him."

"Why? Didn't you tell me I would make a good appetizer for them?"

"You would, given the right circumstances, but I bet he'd prefer some fish or frogs. Maybe even a snake or a turtle, but not you right now. They prefer something smaller than themselves. That's one law of survival out here. You only attack those other animals that can do the least damage to you while you're trying to eat them."

"You may be bigger than he is, but I'm not"

"Yes, you are. I've been watching him for the last twenty minutes. He can't be over four feet long at the most. I don't think he'll bother us."

"And if he does?" Anxiety was clear in her voice.

"Then he'll be breakfast tomorrow morning."

Wade and Mindy watched the young reptile circle around the dying embers of the campfire. He stuck his long snout in the ashes of the fire and pulled out a skeleton of a catfish that had been picked clean. Feeling the heat from the hot bones in his mouth, he immediately released the bones and began hissing at the fire.

"Guess he doesn't like my cooking." Wade laughed.

"Looks that way. Oh well, you can't please all the clients of the Atchafalaya Resort all the time."

"But most of them have enough manners not to spit out my food if they don't like it."

"I think he likes his a little less done. The rarer the better for some tastes."

"You're right and it might have a little too much salt. Did you see him let those bones go? I bet that's the first and last time he sticks his nose in a fire to get some leftover catfish bones. He learned a painful lesson tonight."

"What brought him into camp?"

"Those catfish bones. An alligator is one of the few animals on earth that never quits growing. They don't hibernate like bears, so the more they eat, the more inches and pounds they add to their frames. So they're continuously looking for an easy meal."

Mindy giggled. "That one's really pissed off now. Looks like he could use a little ice. If I had some ice cream, I'd throw it to him."

The gator left the fire and circled the make-shift hut.

He waddled up to the edge and nuzzled the palmetto leaves.

"What's he doing, Wade?" The anxiety level in Mindy's voice rose.

"He either smelled your clothes or your perfume."

"I'm not wearing any."

"Clothes or perfume?"

"Neither one."

"Dang. You may get attacked from both sides if you're not careful."

"Wade, he's getting in!" Mindy screamed when the alligator placed both of his webbed front feet on the little hut.

Wade's arm automatically extended toward the gator, his gun aimed directly at its long head.

"Stay exactly where you are, Mindy. I'll only piss him off if I have to shoot him with this little pea shooter. He probably won't even feel it. I need you to stay still so I don't shoot you."

"That's easy for you to say, Wade. He's not on your side."

The ranger picked up a stick with fire on the long end. He stuck it under the reptile's snout. The alligator twisted and fell off of the hut, landing on all four feet. He waddled back toward the slough circling wide around the remaining embers sparking in the fire. When his long snout reached the perimeter of the ashes, the young gator turned toward the fire and hissed before continuing the rest of his short journey to the slough.

Wade laughed. "I reckon you just witnessed the very first lesson that young'n has ever had about the dangers of playing with fire."

"You know, that reminded me about my first lesson about boys."

"I'm not even going to ask. Go back to sleep. We've got another busy day of gathering wood and food ahead of us tomorrow when the sun comes up."

36 THURSDAY MORNING
MORGAN CITY

"I forgot how far it is to Morgan City," Sam said to Gus and Mandy. She shifted uncomfortably behind the steering wheel of the patrol car. "If we don't get there soon, I'm gonna scream."

Being in the car for over three hours and still short of their destination was frustrating for all three of them.

"Why didn't the Agency bring the plane to New Orleans or over to Gulfport? It'd be a lot easier to inspect that way." Mandy whimpered.

Gus explained, "There are only a few barges big enough with cranes powerful enough to lift and load a plane out of the sea water. Most of them are tied up on drilling jobs in Brazil or Ghana. There was one available that is headquartered in Morgan City and it has the dock space available for the Feds to perform whatever preliminary inspections they want to without the prying eyes of the media. There's also less chance of someone from offshore disturbing them because they'd have to go through a series of water locks to get to the dock.

Sam became more restless the longer the trip became and was soon reaching speeds far above the limit.

Gus cleared his throat. "Girl, we're gonna get there way before they complete their investigation. You might as well quit trying to become the next NASCAR champ and slow down a tad. I don't have much of a life left, but I don't want to spend it in a coma or a wheelchair."

"I know, Gus. I have to find out if Wade and Mindy were on that plane. If they weren't on that plane, then we're back to square one."

"If you don't quit using this squad car like one of those bumper cars at the county fair, then we're gonna be a lot worse off than square one. Slow down, dammit. That plane isn't going anywhere for a while once it gets to the dock in Morgan City."

"Do you know where Young's Road is?"

"I remember it because there's one of those unusual signs on it that caught me off guard the first time I saw it. I was down here to go duck hunting in the marsh south of town. Anyway, I crossed the railroad tracks and came to a stop sign. I looked left and saw this enormous sign that said 'Don't throw limbs in the trees.' I did a double-take on that one. Then I figured out it was a grove of pecan trees and everybody down here loves pecans."

Sam shook her head. "Gus, have you ever answered a question in less than five words?"

"Yep. And every time I do, I've regretted it. Nothing but pain and agony happens when you only use two words to answer a question."

"Huh?"

"I've answered the same question four times in my life with two words; 'I do'. Those two paltry words have caused me more misery than a mouse at a cat convention. I've learned not to answer questions so quickly."

Sam laughed. "I thought you only had three wives."

Gus shrugged. "I did. But I answered that one question to the same woman twice. I reckon I'm a slow learner. I'd probably do it again if she'd remove the restraining order she has out on me."

Mandy giggled from the back seat. "You make marriage sound like a terrible experience. I know many happily married people."

Gus nodded. "Don't get me wrong, young lady. Getting married is a lot of fun. Being married is the miserable part. It must be the cake."

"The cake?"

"Yep. One slice of wedding cake automatically adds twenty pounds that pretty bride and turns her into one of those gurus on the mountain top. Suddenly, she knows everything. I don't know what they put into one of those cakes that can change a woman so much and so fast. If I did, I'd march on the Capitol and get it outlawed."

Sam interrupted. "Are you paying attention to where we're going or just interested in spoiling any hopes of Mandy ever being happy with a man?"

"Lucky for you, I can multitask. Take a left at the light here. Go across the tracks and take a right. The dock we're looking for should be about a mile down on the left."

Sam pulled in and flashed her badge at the security guard on duty. She pulled away in her cruiser.

"Hold on there, Ma'am. I need to see some identification of the other occupants of the car, please."

"Why, Officer?"

"Following orders, Ma'am. Nobody gets to see the plane

without the proper clearance, and that includes passengers."

"Serious, aren't you?"

"Not my decision, Ma'am. This is a federal investigation and I do whatever I'm told."

Gus winked at Mandy. "Sam, that gentleman just gave you the secret to a successful marriage."

Mandy's lips formed a wry grin. "What would that be, Gus?"

"Weren't you paying attention? He told you how to have a long happy marriage."

Mandy looked at Sam, but Sam shook her head and shrugged her shoulders.

Mandy looked back at Gus. "One more time, please."

Gus turned and patted her head. "It's okay. I was young and naïve once. That officer said he does whatever the Feds tell him to do without any questions. If a husband does the same thing, you know, everything his wife tells him to do without questioning her, then they'll have a long happy marriage."

"Gus, you're playing with me again."

"I'm serious. I know a fellow that says he's read dozens of books about marriage, talked with three or four marriage counselors, and attended a bunch of marriage seminars. He said that after spending thousands of dollars and years of study, he discovered the secret of a happy marriage in his closet."

"You're pulling my leg, Gus. What was in his closet?"

"Well, it seems he and his wife had a little spat as most couples do and she had chased him into that little closet with the business end of her broom. She was beating on that door something furious when he finally found the secret."

"What is it, Gus?"

"He said 'Yes, Ma'am'. He says that now, every discussion he has with her ends in those two words and they've been happy ever since."

Mandy laughed. "I wouldn't want a husband always agreed with me."

"You say that now. You haven't had a piece of that wedding cake yet."

"That won't matter, Gus."

"Mandy, dear. It's kinda like breaking a horse. In the beginning you want him to show a little spirit, but eventually you just want him to go in the direction you got his head pointed and to go a little faster when you stick a spur in him."

Even Sam had forgotten her frustrations and was laughing when they pulled up to the ramp leading onto the barge with the plane sitting atop it. A gentleman in a dark suit me the three of them at the end of the ramp that provided the only access to the barge. They could see the small Cessna plane strapped down behind him.

"May I help you?"

Sam flashed her badge again. The gentleman took her badge and then collected Gus's badge and Mandy's driver's license. "Wait here."

He disappeared inside the plane. The trio stayed onshore at the base of the ramp, pacing up and down anxiously. Each of them were curiously eyeing the plane, searching for any answers it may share, but finding none.

The gentleman returned from the cavity of the structure. "I can't allow you to board right now. Come back in three hours and you may board."

Sam turned crimson red. "I'm getting on this barge and I'm looking at that plane. Now get out of my way."

"Sheriff Cates, your badge has no authority in Morgan

City, in St. Mary Parish or anywhere else in Louisiana. Mine gives me authority anywhere in the United States." He flashed his badge, but did not hand it to any of them.

Sam stiffened and stepped right next to the agent. Gus immediately stepped in between them. "Not now, Sam. It's not worth it. That plane isn't going anywhere. It'll be here in three hours and we'll get to look at it. But only if you're not in federal custody."

Sam glared at the agent. "What is your name?"

"Agent Bush, Ma'am."

"Well, Agent Bush. You let me know the next time you visit Evergreen County. I'd love to show you a little of our hospitality."

Sam snatched her badge from him and whirled away. She stomped to the squad car. Her whole body was still shaking when Gus and Mandy got into the car.

"Do you want me to drive?" Gus asked.

"No, I just wanta kick his arrogant ass."

"Sam, he's doing his job. Do you give relatives of a victim free access to a crime scene just because they're upset? I'll answer that for you. You don't, because no matter how much they care, they're gonna end up messing something up and contaminating the evidence."

Sam nodded, and the shaking of her body subsided. Mandy tapped her on her shoulder from the back seat. Sam looked at her in the rear-view mirror.

"When that fellow comes to Evergreen, can I watch?"

All three of them burst out in laughter, relieving the heightened tension inside the vehicle. They drove out past Lake Palourde and found a seafood restaurant between Lake End Park and Pierre Part. The menu was replete with delicacies from the various Cajun communities in and around the mouth of the Atchafalaya River.

Gus beamed. "We are on official county business, aren't we?"

Sam nodded.

"That means the county is picking up the tab for our meal today and we've got over two hours to enjoy it. If I remember right, we have a seventy-five dollar per Diem for meals when we're on the road. Is that right, Sam?"

"Yes, but there's an assumption of three meals per day."

"Does it say that?"

"No."

"Then my assumption is seventy-five dollars per day whether it's one meal or three. I like my assumption better than their assumption."

Gus examined the menu with renewed vigor. "Let's get some appetizers." He said motioning for the waitress to come to the table.

"Do you have Dixie beer?" he asked. When she nodded, he began, "Good. I'll have one, at least to start with. We can't get Dixie where we live and I love it. Then let's start with some boudin balls, an order of barbecued shrimp, an order of Oysters Rockefeller and an order of popcorn crawfish."

"Gus, we're here to eat lunch, not to horde up enough fat for the winter." Sam admonished him.

"It's not every day the citizens of Evergreen County get to show their appreciation for the fine job I do on the force by buying my lunch and I'm going to enjoy it."

As soon as the waitress placed the platters on the table, Gus started wolfing down the appetizers. Mandy did her best to keep up with him, but lagged significantly. Sam picked at the popcorn crawfish, but wasn't showing the same exuberance as the other two.

"What's wrong with you, girl?" Gus asked.

"Just feeling guilty."

"Why?"

"Here we are eating some of the best seafood in the world, and Wade and Mindy have eaten nothing since Monday. I saw one of those survival shows based in the swamp and they nearly starved to death on it."

"Yeah, but they didn't. They also didn't have Wade or Wade's revolver with them, now did they?"

"I know, but I can't stand the thought of them eating earthworms, cockroaches and grub worms while we're dining on shrimp and crawfish."

"That bothers me too." He motioned to the waitress. "Can you bring us an order of fried alligator tails, two orders of crab-boiled corn, an order of crab claws and some frog legs?" He turned back to Sam. "Yep, it almost ruins my appetite, wondering what they're eating."

"Gus, we can't eat all of that." Sam leaned back in her chair and stared out of the window. "I'm almost full already."

"Don't worry. I've got your back on this, girl. What are we looking for when we get to see the inside of the plane?"

"Evidence." Sam said firmly. "Evidence that Wade and Mindy were on that plane when it left Evergreen County Monday morning."

"I don't know about you, but I don't see where else they could've gone. We've turned over every rock in Evergreen County, and they aren't there. That fellow with the State Police told you two about the missing parachutes, at least according to the preliminary reports."

"I need the confirmation that they were on the plane and there's a good chance they're alive."

Mandy looked at Sam. "They're alive, Sam. I'm more confident of that than ever. And Mindy isn't under a lot of stress, which means she isn't alone. That must mean that Wade is alive and close to her. If she was alone out there in the swamp, she'd be stressed to the max, but she isn't. Wade must be alive and helping her."

Gus devoured the second round of appetizers. Mindy joined him in the pleasure of the seasoned food and began with the fried alligator tails. Sam pushed her chair a little way from the table and continued to stare out over the water and swampland.

"Sam! Hey, Sam! Are you ready?" Gus was almost yelling.

"I'm sorry. I guess I was lost in my thoughts."

"Let's go see your friends down at the dock. This time, promise to play nice with the other kids or I'll take your toys away and put you in time-out."

Sam laughed. "I'm okay, Gus. Not sure where my mind was, but it's back now. Let's go see what happened to Wade and Mindy."

37 THURSDAY AFTERNOON
MORGAN CITY

THE THREE OF THEM HAD TO ENDURE THE SAME identification procedures they had gone through previously when they arrived at the dock, much to the chagrin of Sam. Her body tensed and the veins in her temples pulsed when the same agent confiscated their badges and identifications and disappeared inside the cavity of the plane. Her lips pursed as she struggled to keep the words inside that were on the verge of eruption.

The agent emerged from the plane and motioned for them to ascend the ramp and board the barge. Sam raced up the ramp with Mandy only fractions of a second behind her. Gus didn't hurry and quietly ambled aboard far behind the young ladies. Sam froze immediately when she entered the small plane and Mandy bumped into her.

"What the hell? Where is everything? What happened to the seats? What happened to everything else?" She gasped while staring at the blank walls inside the cabin.

The agent did not answer and stood stone-faced looking at her.

Sam strode to him and put her face only inches from his.

"I asked you a question, Agent Bush. I expect an answer. If I don't get some answers, that information that your boss is so worried about will be public information by the time I get back to Evergreen. I know how to pull the triggers to make that happen. Unless I get a valid response in the next two minutes, I'm leaving and neither you nor him will be happy with the results. Do you understand me?" She yelled at him.

The agent appeared flustered, his eyes blinking from the verbal assault. "If you'll excuse me, Ma'am, I'll see what I can do for you."

The agent left the cavity of the plane and Sam could see him on the deck of the barge talking furiously on his cell phone. He returned and looked as calm as ever, except for a nervous tic in the corner of one of his eyes.

"My supervisor will see you now. Please follow me."

The agent led them to an outbuilding they had passed on the way in to the dock. Inside were more than a dozen agents hidden from the outside world, buzzing around like a hive of bees. Activity seemed endless and without direction.

Gus was the first to ask, "Where did all these people come from? There aren't any cars outside, and I didn't see anybody when we came earlier."

The agent didn't answer, but ushered them into a small conference room. "Agent Cook will be with you shortly." He closed the door behind him as he left.

Sam, Gus and Mandy remained silent until the door opened.

"Sheriff Cates. I'm Butch Cook. I'm the Field Agent in charge of this operation. How may I help you?"

The agent's demeanor irritated Sam again. "You knew

we were coming to look at the plane. You knew two people may have been on board that were our family and friends, but you dcliberately kept us off that plane until you removed every shred of evidence. Please, Agent. Please explain why you felt it was necessary to remove all the contents of the plane before anyone else had a chance to at least look at it."

"I assure you, Sheriff. This had nothing to do with you. It's our standard operating procedure to preserve the integrity of all the evidence of a crime scene that's in our custody. At least two of you are personally affected by the outcome of our investigation. If we had allowed you on board and some evidence became contaminated accidentally, we'd all regret it. I'm sure you have found yourself in similar circumstances as we find ourselves today."

Sam calmed down a little. "I apologize, Agent Cook. But this really is the last chance for us to have any hope that Wade and Mindy are alive."

"I understand your concerns and I also understand the unique circumstance each of us is in, Sheriff."

"What can you share with us?"

The agent paused and then pulled a file out of his briefcase.

"The plane," he pointed in the direction of the dock. "It was chartered by a lady using the name of Victoria Engle. At least that was the name that was given. We have not yet determined the method of payment for the flight, so at this point we theorize the pilot was probably paid in cash."

"That makes sense so far from our findings." Sam nodded.

Agent Cook continued. "The plane stopped over in Evergreen at a private airport on the edge of town. That airport is usually closed on Mondays. The plane picked up two passengers whose names were unknown at that point. We had sketches drawn from the descriptions given to us by the gentleman that allowed the plane to land and re-fuel. That gentleman is not the ordinary manager of the facility and at this point looks like someone that was making a little extra cash on the side of his regular job. He didn't know who chartered the plane, but was merely doing a favor for his friend, which is the deceased pilot."

The agent pulled two sketches out of his briefcase.

Sam gasped, "That's Wade! And that's Mindy!" Tears started rolling down her cheeks.

"Yes, we were told she had a twin sister and there's a definite resemblance to you Ma'am." The agent nodded toward Mandy.

"Sorry for the outburst, Agent. But this is the first definitive evidence we've seen since Monday to tell us what happened to them."

"From photographs and fingerprints, we determined with certainty that Mr. Dalton was aboard the plane. We don't have fingerprints of Ms. Thomas, but we're fairly certain she was the other passenger on the plane."

Mandy spoke for the first time in the conference room. "She was on the plane. I have no doubts about it. I could feel her presence when we were there. She's still alive, Agent."

"I can't argue with you, Ms. Thomas. When we get them back and get through all of this, we may ask you and your sister to help us out with a study we've engaged in about the sensory perception between twins. But in the meantime, we have some work to do."

"Anything else, Agent Cook." Sam sat forward on the edge of her chair.

"We're uncertain if the pilot died of unnatural causes. There are some indications of a foreign substance, but we don't know if the quantity would have been fatal or how it was introduced into his body. So we don't know if that finding is significant pending further tests."

"Excuse me, Pard," Gus interrupted the agent. "If I can unwrap some of that rope you just wound up, did you say someone poisoned the pilot or not?"

The agent smiled. "There are some indications to that effect, yes."

"Then why didn't you just say that?" Gus huffed.

"Deputy, we must be careful not to state certainty without being sure of the evidence. I hope you can appreciate our position."

"I do, Butch." Gus looked down at the table and then back at the agent. "But if you want to tell us you have a jackass, then tell us you have a jackass and not that you have a hybrid between a horse and a mule."

"I'll try to be more succinct, Deputy. Now, where were we?"

Sam replied, "You were telling us about the pilot."

"It appears a foreign substance was involved, but we don't have a conclusive determination of the chemical components or how it was administered."

Gus couldn't help himself. "So you don't know what it is, how it got there or who did it?"

Butch Cook smiled. "That would about sum it up, Deputy."

Sam glanced at Gus. "If you'll let him talk, we might find out what else he knows."

Gus just nodded and sat back in his chair.

"Thank you, Sheriff. We know when the emergency exit was opened, but we're having an unusually difficult time trying to correlate a GPS reading that corresponds to that time. We also can't say for a certainty that anyone exited. We have narrowed the location to somewhere in the Atchafalaya Basin between Baton Rouge and Lafayette."

"That's all swamp, at least most of it, anyway. Isn't it?"

"Not all of it. The first fifteen miles west of Baton Rouge up to Grosse Tete are fairly well populated. We assume that if they had exited over that area, we'd know it by now. The same can be said for the western-most fifteen miles east of Lafayette and west of Henderson. So that leaves us with a thirty mile long strip about sixty miles wide area that we need to search."

"Damn, Pard. That's twelve hundred square miles of the most uninhabitable swamp and bogs known to man. That's over a hundred and fifty thousand acres."

Sam's smile faded a little. "So how have you organized the search?"

"We've already contacted the Coast Guard. Search by air is the only feasible solution right now. They can loan us a helicopter for a couple of days. There's a leaking pipeline in the Gulf, and most of their resources are dedicated to that situation."

"One helicopter to search more than a hundred and fifty thousand acres with dense underbrush. I'm not real optimistic, Agent Cook."

"Nor am I, Sheriff. The good news is that there will be several thousand hunters in the basin over the weekend, and they might see or hear something that will help us. That's the best we can do right now."

Sam sat back with her hands up to her mouth. Suddenly, she leaned forward.

"What if you had private helicopters and pilots, Agent? How many can your people effectively coordinate?"

The agent's eyes widened. "We can't ask the private sector to help us in this situation. It's been almost a week, the area is so vast and the obligation to do it correctly would be over a week. That'd be a heavy burden to ask a private pilot to bear with the loss of revenue and carrying the expenses for that long."

"I'm not asking the private sector to donate anything, Agent."

"Are you sure you have the authority to commit the taxpayers of Evergreen to pay for the effort to cover the entire basin, Sheriff? That could amount to hundreds of thousands of dollars."

"I won't ask the taxpayers of Evergreen to pay for anything today. Except for lunch today. Now, let's get back to the question. How many private helicopters can your people manage and coordinate under the circumstances we have down here right now?"

The agent gulped hard and his gazed lifted to the ceiling.

"I would say eight to ten under these circumstances, given the lack of common communication equipment, the remote area and the terrain. If we get more than that flying around down here along with the normal air traffic, we'd run the risk of an air accident. We should be able to completely search the area thoroughly in less than a week with eight dedicated helicopters."

Sam leapt out of her chair, snatching her cell phone. "Hello, Connie. I need your help."

"Yes, we are making some progress and we can make more, but I need a favor."

"I know, Little Sis. Here's what I need. Find us eight charter helicopters that will be available for the next seven days. We want to hire them starting tomorrow morning in

Morgan City. We, at least I, will pay for the charter, including all of their expenses for a search and rescue operation."

"Yes, they need to meet us at daylight at the airport in Morgan City. Tell Bruce what we're doing or I guess Mandy can tell him. You'll be busy enough trying to find eight helicopters between now and then."

"Even if we find them the first day, we'll pay for all week. We want them committed."

"Don't worry about the rates. We want them here tomorrow."

"Hell, wire the money into their account or get certified checks. I don't care. Use my deer fund."

"Thanks, Connie. I knew I could count on you. Call me if you have any problems. Bye."

She put her cell back into its case and turned back to the agent.

"Well, Sheriff. That's quite a commitment. I didn't know Evergreen paid so well."

"It doesn't, Agent Cook," Sam smiled. "I saved my allowances when I was a child."

38 THURSDAY
ATCHAFALAYA BASIN

Wade woke up before the sun crept up over the eastern horizon. He eased off of his hammock and slipped out of the hut without disturbing Mindy. He used most of the remaining woodpile rebuilding the fire again. After a few minutes of staring into the flames, he decided to check the crawfish traps he had reset in the sloughs. He glanced over at Mindy and she was still sound asleep.

He trudged through three or four shallow sloughs before following one south for a hundred feet. He reached the wide spot in the slough where the water was deep enough to hold the mudbugs and found the traps he had previously set. He picked up the first of the traps and was surprised by its heaviness. In contrast, the second trap was very light. He carried both to the bank and cautiously sat them upright to prevent any crawfish from escaping. He returned to the water and hefted the third trap, which was very similar in weight to the first one.

He carried the third trap to the bank and deposited it by the other two. His curiosity drove him to pick up the second trap, holding it tightly to his chest with his left hand. He slowly lifted the palmetto leaf on top of the trap and peered into its depths. His eyes bulged when he saw the cotton-white mouth and dripping fangs of the water moccasin lunging toward his face. In the split second that saved his life, his left hand instinctively shoved the trap backward and the snake's thrust missed his face by a fraction of an inch. The snake recoiled in the bottom of the trap.

"Holy Cow!" Wade said out loud, even as the trap went flying. "Damn. I've got to be more careful." He said to himself since no one else was around. His rapid breathing and his shaky legs prevented him from being steady as he watched the cottonmouth slither from the now-busted trap laying on the boggy ground fifteen feet from him The snake retreated to the nearby slough and Wade sat down on the ridge to regain his composure.

Returning to camp carrying the two traps, Wade's legs were still shaking. Mindy noticed his unsteady walk immediately.

"What happened to you?"

"I had a close call with another one of your little friends," he replied.

Wade relayed the story of his narrow escape from the cottonmouth in the trap.

"Wade, you've got to be more careful. What am I going to do out here if you're dead out there and I don't know where you are?"

Wade smiled wryly. "I'll keep that in mind when I go out again."

Mindy had a tear rolling down her face. "That didn't come out like I meant it, Wade. We need each other. I need you more than you need me, but we need each other to get through this for the next couple of days. Please be more careful for both our sakes."

"I will, Mindy."

"Good. To show you my progress with the ankle, Room Service is on me this morning. Sit back and relax while I prepare—. Oops, what's in the other two traps?"

Wade laughed, easing the tension in his body. "Should be crawfish, but with the last surprise who knows?"

They emptied the traps on the ground and found nothing but crawfish, perch and freshwater shrimp in them.

Wade laid back on the ground by the fire. "I almost forgot. I have some instant oatmeal in my pack, at least two packages. It has oatmeal with berries, apples and raisins and all you have to do is add water. Has lots of calories and tastes real good to boot. I think I'll get Room Service to add that to the menu."

"Now you're getting spoiled. They say that's what happens to a man not long into a relationship with a woman. She spoils him and then he comes to expect being waited on. Just sits around all day waiting on the woman to take care of the house and kids. Besides, we're on a budget. We can't be wasting money on frivolous things like oatmeal with apples and berries."

"Don't forget the raisins. I like raisins in my oatmeal."

"Anything else, Sir?"

"Save a couple of those perch and a crawfish or two. We're going to try to catch a gar for lunch."

"I thought you said gar fish had a lot of bones and were hard to eat."

"They do and they are. But now I have help."

"That doesn't make any sense."

"I guess it doesn't. I guess the real reason is that I don't want to go back into the swamp this morning to find us some lunch. I'd rather fish for our lunch, and the only thing

I'll catch is a gar or two. So, I'm ordering gar for lunch. What will you have?"

"Boy, that's a tough decision. Gar or gar? I think I'll take the gar, please."

"Excellent choice, Ma'am. Your tastes are exquisite."

Mindy rose to get the packages of oatmeal, and Wade's gaze followed her. She wasn't using the crutches, and he was amazed at the quickness that she had progressed on her sore ankle.

"Quit looking at my butt or I'm going to have to let Sam know about your roving eyes." Mindy giggled.

"If we spend another week out here, my eyes might not be the only thing roving."

"Be careful, Cowboy. You might get your noose around a young heifer, but that doesn't mean you'll be able to put your brand on her."

"I'll keep that in mind. Gee, Room Service sure has slowed down since you took over."

"I'm a quick learner."

"Huh?"

"You said the secret to a delicious meal is making sure the diners are starving. I figure if I can kill another hour before I serve you gourmet oatmeal, then you'll like it."

39 THURSDAY
ATCHAFALAYA BASIN

THEY LAID ON THE BANK OF THE SLOUGH, WATCHING the corks bob in the water. An hour of watching had produced nothing.

"Wade, we are gonna get out of here Saturday, aren't we?"

"I'm more certain of it than ever. You're walking on your ankle without crutches and by Saturday, you'll be leaping over small sloughs."

"Man, it's gonna be nice to get back to civilization. No offense meant at all, but I'm ready for something different."

"That makes two of us. I have no complaints at all about who I'm with out here. It's just that I don't want to be out here."

"Will you put your arm around me?"

"Sure. There. Does that make you feel better?"

"Yes, it does." Mindy pulled his arm down around her waist and rolled over on it. Before long, she was gently snoring. Wade felt the warmth of the sun and the warmth of Mindy's body next to him. Soon he too was snoring, only not so gently.

A slight rustling next to his feet awakened him, bringing him out of a nice dream back to reality. Fearing that his alligator friend had returned, Wade reached for his gun. His aim was not on a reptile, however, but on one of three mallard ducks waddling on the bank next to his feet, oblivious to Wade and Mindy. The first shot startled Mindy, and she screamed as he shot the other two mallards.

"Sorry about that, but Room Service changed the menu for lunch."

"Maybe not." Mindy said, looking at a pole bent over in a long arch.

"Are you going to lay there or are you going to pull him in?"

Mindy grabbed the pole and started pulling. The gar, however, didn't want to give up so easily and headed straight for the bottom of the slough. He almost pulled Mindy in, but Wade reached around her waist and held on. He looked at the enjoyment on her face as she fought that gar, and he was reminded of a six-year-old with a new puppy. All of her fears were forgotten as she struggled to get the big fish to the bank. He put his hands over hers and together they yanked, springing the fish from the water, and it plopped right beside them. They both giggled like school kids.

"Go get the fire ready and I'll clean the birds and the fish." Wade released his arm from around Mindy.

"I didn't know Room Service ordered the clients around."

"We have different rules at the Atchafalaya Resort."

"All right, but I have a request after lunch."

"What is it?"

"You'll have to wait until after lunch to find out."

Wade yanked the skin off the gar and plucked the

feathers from the three mallards. Normally, he would have just taken the breast from the mallards because there is very little meat on the rest of the duck, but he wanted to keep the skin on them for nutrition and to retain moisture over the open flame.

"When you said these gar were bony, you weren't kidding, were you?"

"Nope, about ninety percent bones and ten percent meat. But we're going to try something different with it rather than hang it over the fire."

He pulled out the pan that was so useful in the situation they were in. Inside the pan, he rubbed some duck fat from the birds and heated the pan on the flat rock that had proven to work as a stove top since Monday. Into the pan, he tossed the duck hearts, gizzards and livers. He also put in a big white vegetable.

"What's that?" Mindy asked.

"It's the bulb from a cat reed. Takes a while to get tender, but once it does, it's good. I tried them once before and I'd forgotten how good they are."

He cut the wings and legs off the mallards and placed the breasts of the birds on spits over the flames. The wings and legs went into the pan with the rest of the food. He sprinkled the last of his spices over both the food in the pan and the duck breasts. After forty-five minutes, he cut the gar into bite-size pieces and dropped those into the pan.

The alluring aroma which began softly wafting over the campsite was now a powerful catalyst for hunger as it grew stronger and stronger, eventually overwhelming Mindy and Wade. They dug into the meal with vigor, but couldn't finish all of it.

"I guess I know what we're gonna have for supper."

Mindy laid back on the grass. "That's okay with me. That is some of the best food I've ever had."

"It's amazing what hunger does for you, isn't it?"

"If that is what does it, then I hope I'm hungry every time I eat."

"You said you wanted to ask me something after lunch. It's after lunch."

"I was going to ask you if we could start trying to find our way out of here today and not wait until Saturday, but now I'm too full to try."

"Good. I mean, it's good that you changed your mind."

"Why?"

"Your ankle is still not at full strength. That could become a problem. Also, if we start walking and get too far from here, we wouldn't be able to get back before dark. In a lot of the basin, the ridges run out and then there is only water for miles. Do you really want to sleep in knee-deep water with no shelter or fire overnight? I sure don't."

"I see what you mean."

"The other factor is the hunters. I'm counting on a lot of them being in the woods Saturday. I figure we'll try to make it a mile or so and then fire three shots into the air. That's the common distress signal for stranded or lost hunters. If we don't get a response, we try to walk another mile and repeat the process. Somewhere, we're going to find someone Saturday."

40 FRIDAY MORNING
MORGAN CITY

Sᴀᴍ ᴀᴅᴅʀᴇssᴇᴅ ᴛʜᴇ ᴘɪʟᴏᴛs sʜᴜꜰꜰʟɪɴɢ ᴀʀᴏᴜɴᴅ ɪɴ ᴛʜᴇ hanger at the Morgan City airport.

"All right, gentlemen. You understand why you're here. There are two people somewhere between Baton Rouge and Lafayette, stranded in the basin. We they're alive. Help yourself to the coffee and donuts on the house. This is Pete with the Coast Guard. He'll coordinate our efforts today. Please pay attention. We don't want anyone to get hurt because they didn't understand how Pete wants to conduct this search."

The man dressed in green coveralls stepped beside the Sheriff.

"Thanks, Sam. I know most of you and have flown with some of you. If you've never been involved in a search and rescue operation before, take what Sam told you to heart. We want to find people alive without endangering ourselves or our fellow pilots. Safety is our number one priority. We aren't looking for any individual heroes. We want a coordinated effort that gives us the best chance to find these two individuals out there. We expect you to stay within the plan we have outlined."

Sam inserted, "Pete asked for eight helicopters, but on such short notice, we could only come up with six. So we're going forward with six for at least today."

Pete turned from Sam back towards the pilots.

"Each of you will be assigned a position, one through six. The number one craft will fly in the southernmost position. Number two aircraft will fly behind and north of the number one craft. We will continue this process until all six of you are in a diagonal line from south to north. My craft will bring up the rear of the line and will be the northernmost craft. We will maintain this formation from Henderson to Grosse Tête, flying from west to east. When we get to Grosse Tête, we'll repeat the process flying north of our original search and flying back from east to west. Whoever gets the number one position; remember, this is not a race to see who has the fastest helicopter. We're looking for two stranded people, so take your time and look carefully. If you spot anything out of the ordinary, record the coordinates of the sighting and radio them to me. Keep going. I'll check out any sightings. If I don't find them, I'll catch up with you. Don't wait for me. Maintaining the discipline of the grid is imperative in a mission like this."

"Why don't we just look around if we spot something out of the ordinary? Why do we need to radio the coordinates to you and let you look around?" One pilot asked.

"Excellent question. First, let me assure you it has nothing to do with your capability as a pilot versus mine. By doing it the way we've laid it out, we'll preserve the integrity of the grid search with no gaps. Second, it is all about the equipment. There are many areas in the basin, if not most of them, that are too dense and grown over to land a chopper anywhere close to a potential sighting. Our equipment allows us to put boots on the ground, even if we can't land a craft. We also have more advanced methods of identifying and retrieving personnel without the need to land."

Pete paused for a few seconds. "Questions?"

"Is it true that we get paid for all seven days, even if we find them this morning?"

"I'll have to let Sam answer that question. As I understand it, the Coast Guard is donating its services for today and tomorrow. Sam, can you answer that one?"

"You guys will be paid for all seven days even if we find them in the first fifteen minutes. The reason we're doing that is to get your commitment to clear your schedules for the next week and show up every morning until we find them. I don't want to have to spend time trying to find helicopters. I'd rather spend the time trying to find Wade and Mindy. Speaking of Wade and Mindy, here are some photographs of each of them. To make it simple, Mindy looks just like Mandy." Sam tapped Mandy's shoulder with her hand. "They're identical twins."

"If you're flying alone, we have some volunteer spotters that'd like to ride with you. You just met Mandy, Mindy's twin sister. This is Bruce Thomas, Mindy's father. Most of you have met Gus, my friend and deputy from Evergreen. I must warn you if you take Gus with you, mute his microphone, or you'll hear every old joke ever told over the next seven days. And last, but not least, my sister, Connie. She is the one that contacted you for this job. Any other questions?"

"Where will you be, Miss Sam?"

"I'll ride in the Coast Guard helicopter."

One pilot stepped forward.

"Ma'am. I don't want to sound gross or be unkind, but you might want to re-consider. I've been on a few of these and a lot of the times, what we find are bloated bodies or bones. Are you sure you want to be in the craft that has to look at that?"

Sam stepped toward the pilot with her chin jutting out. "Absolutely sure. I need to know what happened to Wade and Mindy. And I appreciate the question. No offense taken. Any other questions?"

She waited for a few seconds, but no one else broke the silence.

"Okay, if you don't mind, I'd like to lead us in prayer for a safe mission and a successful rescue."

Sam fell on her knees and began praying. Her prayer was so intense beads of sweat formed on her brow. When she finished, she rose to her feet.

"Okay, guys. Let's find them come hell or high water."

"Mindy, get that little butt of yours out of bed. Breakfast is ready and Room Service charges extra to serve it in bed."

"I didn't hear them knock. I must have been sleeping too hard."

"I hate to complain about the snoring, but last night, you were sawing some logs big time."

"I guess it was from eating too much. But those ducks were better last night than they were for lunch. What did the chef prepare for us this morning?"

"Fresh frog legs. And I mean fresh. These bad boys were happily catching flies about twenty minutes ago."

"They smell good."

Wade picked up the pan, and turned the frog legs over to cook the other side. That's when he heard it coming.

"Mindy! Get some clothes on! We've got company!"

Wade dropped the pan not caring if the legs spilled out. He grabbed some Spanish moss and put it directly over the fire. On top of that, he added a green palmetto leaf. The moss started smoking wildly but was pent up by the leaf.

Wade quickly removed the leaf, allowing the smoke to rise in the air in strong puffs, one at a time. He repeated the process until the sound of the helicopter was directly overhead.

The helicopter paused, but only for a second or two. Then it continued on its path over the camp toward Baton Rouge. Wade could hear other helicopters in the area, but they all passed the camp without coming close. His heart dropped, and he glanced over at Mindy. She was still pulling clothes on as she exited the hut.

"I thought he was gonna stop and check us out."

"He left us, didn't he?" Tears streamed down Mindy's cheeks.

"Maybe he will report the fire when he gets to wherever he's going."

"I wouldn't count on that."

"You never—" Wade heard another helicopter headed directly in their direction.

"Mindy. Hurry. Put this leaf over the fire and then lift it real quick. Keep doing that until I tell you to quit. Understand?"

"Yes, let's get their attention."

Wade leapt and ran to the small clearing next to the camp, offering an unobstructed view to the sky free from the water oaks and bramble around it. Waving his arms above his head, he yelled as loud as he could. Logic told him that the occupants of the helicopter couldn't hear him no matter how loud he yelled, but that didn't matter. He kept yelling and waving his arms. Then he removed his shirt and started jumping up and down, wildly waving his shirt over his head.

He recognized the helicopter as a Coast Guard aircraft, specifically designed for search and rescue. More surprising was the face staring at him from the opening in the side of the craft. Sam was staring at him with a grin on her face almost as big as the opening of the helicopter. She was crying and grinning at the same time. As she waved uncontrollably, Wade was concerned she might fall out of the craft.

An officer positioned himself beside her and motioned for Wade to move to the side of the small clearing. A personnel basket began lowering to the ground. Suddenly, he saw Sam pointing behind him and he could hear her visceral screams over the whir of the helicopter blades.

Whirling toward the swamp, his hand automatically reached for his revolver even as he realized he'd left it next to the campfire after he found the frogs earlier. All he saw was a black blur and knew there was nothing he could do to prevent the assault. He lifted his hand and elbow in front of his face and neck, trying to protect the most vital parts.

The shot hit the big black cat in the shoulder, knocking him off his intended path. The cat landed right at Wade's feet. The next shot hit the feline in his neck, breaking his spine. Mindy still had the revolver trained on the cat in case it moved again. It was still growling and menacing it fangs, but couldn't move its body.

Wade walked over and took the gun from Mindy's hands. She offered no resistance. He jogged back to the cat and quickly dispatched it with one shot to its enormous head. He then jogged back to Mindy and gave her a big hug without saying anything.

Gently lifting off her feet, Wade carried Mindy to the now waiting basket, laid her in it and strapped her down. He motioned for the helicopter to take her up. Watching the basket ascend, he heard the whir of many other helicopters and saw six of them hovering in a circle around the rescue craft. Recognizing Gus, Connie, Mandy and Bruce, he joyously waved at each one of them. They were all clapping and laughing and whooping, unashamed at the display of emotion.

He jogged back to the campsite and dispersed the fire. He gathered the two packs, the ax and the pan and rushed back to the clearing, reaching it just as the basket touched the ground again. He climbed in and strapped himself to the hooks on the side. The wide grin on his face did not diminish for the entire ride up to the helicopter, and he started snatching at the straps as soon as the basket entered the cavity of the aircraft.

The embrace between Wade and Sam merged their two bodies into one seamless being. Neither wanted to let go of the other. Glancing through the opening of the helicopter, he could see the fist-pumping and high fives being exchanged in the other crafts.

42 FRIDAY NOON
MORGAN CITY

"Wade, I'm Butch Cook, the Field Agent for this operation."

"Nice to meet you, Butch. I'm glad your operation came along. My playmates from the swamp were wearing on my nerves. Your guys couldn't have come at a better time."

"It really wasn't my guys, Wade. The sheriff put together the resources for the search and rescue. She organized it and funded it. That was a first for me. You'll have to thank her for that."

Wade turned to Sam and gave her another hug and kiss, one of many since he had boarded the helicopter and returned to the offices next to the dock in Morgan City.

"Thank you," he whispered.

"You guys have a seat and let's have a little talk."

"Is this on the record?"

"Yes, Wade. It is being recorded for our records. You can start by letting us know how you ended up on that plane."

Wade recounted his meeting with Victoria at the Evergreen restaurant, his discussions with Mindy and the boarding of the plane in Evergreen. He talked about his mid-air decision not to sell the Plantation and the discovery of the dead pilot in the cockpit. He gave them a brief overview of the exit from the plane and the days spent in the middle of the swamp.

"Interesting." Butch Cook looked down at his notes. "So no one knew Miss Thomas would be getting on board prior to you arriving at the private airport in Evergreen Monday morning."

"That's correct."

"And you invited her to accompany you to Houston, even though you are engaged to Sheriff Cates."

The agent pointed toward Sam.

"She sorta invited herself, Butch. The twins, Mindy and Mandy, differ from most people. They're a tad eccentric, I guess is the correct word. They're also very persuasive. When they want something, they usually get it."

"I see."

"No, I don't believe you do. If I understand your implication correctly, it couldn't be farther from the truth. We had no intention of spending the night in Houston. I'd planned to call Sam as soon as we landed in Houston to let her know where we were. I would have earlier, but I wouldn't have been able to hear her over the noise of the plane."

Agent Cook frowned. "If you didn't plan on spending the night in Houston, then why did both of you bring packs with you on the plane?"

"I always bring mine when I get on a plane or a boat. Other than that, it stays in the truck with me wherever I go. So it would be more unusual for me to be without it than it was for me to have it."

Butch rubbed his chin. "And Miss Thomas? Why did she have a pack with her?"

"I can only tell you what she told me. She didn't know how long the trip to Houston would take, and she didn't want to get hungry on the way over there or on the way back. She also wasn't sure if we'd have time to eat lunch in Houston. So, she packed some sandwiches, soda pops, chips and cookies. As it turned out, we were most fortunate to have the food she packed. It made our stay out there much easier to endure."

"I see. So could Miss Thomas have been planning an extensive stay in the basin without your knowledge?"

Wade laughed out loud. "So you think Mindy planned the death of the pilot, figured out that I was going to accidentally discover him and planned to jump out of the plane without me. Butch, you've got to be kidding me."

"You have to admit, it is a bit odd that Ms. Thomas invited herself along on a flight when something untoward happened to the pilot leaving you and her alone on board and she has a pack full of food with her."

"A pack full of junk food, Butch. She didn't have any of the essential equipment with her to start a fire, build a hut or gather water. She didn't even have some insect repellent. Without that, I don't know how anyone could endure the hordes of mosquitoes in the swamp. You'd be miserable."

"We have to follow every lead. She was with you when the two of you discovered Kenny Thigpen's body in your hunting stand. You and she seemed to be more than prepared to spend time in the basin together."

Wade leaned forward.

"So now you think Mindy and I are in cahoots together. We murdered Kenny for some reason beyond my imagination and then killed a pilot that neither of us had ever met. And why? Because we could then spend a week in a quagmire filled with alligators, poisonous snakes and more bugs and spiders than exists in the rest of the world combined. Hell, yeah. That's a great theory, Butch." Wade rolled his eyes.

"There are coincidences here that are unusual. You've been through the same training I've gone through. They taught us never to believe in coincidences."

"I can tell you one thing, Butch. Following this lead will get you nowhere and waste your time. You're gonna get to the end of it and be back at square one."

"I have to ask. Are you and Ms. Thomas more than just friends? Are you romantically involved?"

Wade paused and looked at Sam.

"I'm gonna be honest here. Yes, we are more than just friends. I don't think two people can spend the time together that Mindy and I spent under the conditions we spent them, and not have a bonding beyond normal friendship. But that bond is more like she's my little sister. The answer to your second question is an emphatic, '**No**'. There's not now, nor has there ever been any kind of physical or romantic relationship between us. I won't sacrifice my relationship with Sam for anybody or anything in the world."

Wade grasped Sam's hand and held it tightly.

"What was your relationship with Kenny Thigpen?"

"I met him during our investigation of the murder of the young lady that worked at City Hall, Rachel Chastain. We, meaning Sam and I interviewed him twice. As I recall, he had an iron-clad alibi for the time of her death. So we didn't spend an inordinate amount of time with him."

"And Sheriff Cates, you knew Kenny Thigpen prior to the investigation that Wade referenced, didn't you?"

"Not in the way you're suggesting, Agent. I knew Kenny professionally."

"And your relationship with the Thomas twins, Sheriff. How well do you know Mindy and Mandy?"

"We're friends, Butch. They inadvertently became involved in the investigation you mentioned, or at least inadvertent on our part. I believe they enjoyed being a part of it."

"Do you often engage private citizens to help you in your investigations, Sheriff?"

"No, but the twins aren't ordinary private citizens, Agent. They, as Wade said, are eccentric and hard to say 'No' to."

"Do you have a romantic involvement with either of them, Sheriff?"

Sam laughed. "Sorry. Nobody has ever asked me that before. No, I'm not a lesbian, Agent. And I can assure you, the twins are not lesbians either."

"You've discussed this with them?"

"I've had discussions with them that have convinced me beyond a shadow of a doubt that Mindy and Mandy are heterosexuals, Agent."

"Okay, Wade. Back to you. Do you know anyone that has any reason to want to see you dead?"

"I've had a long time to think about that out there laying in that parachute and sitting around the campfire not knowing if I would ever get to see Sam again. I haven't been in Evergreen that long. The only answer I could come up with is your people."

"My people?" Butch's eyebrows arched noticeably.

"Yes. Your guys. There are some pissed off folks at the Agency, and they are pissed off at me for what I did a couple of years ago. Some of them were demoted and some of them had friends that were fired. The Agency has more than the wherewithal to eliminate the pilot and me at the same time in an unfortunate accident."

"Wade, I don't have a clue what you're talking about. I know there was a big reorganization because of an extremely large cut in the budget, but there ended up being a large cut in everybody's budget at the Fed. What did that have to do with you?"

Wade assumed the Agency would have briefed Butch on the Porcelain Doll operation at the Plantation when they assigned him to this field operation. But he now realized they hadn't, and the file would probably never see the light of day again.

"It's not important, Butch. I would leave this part out of the official record for now. If you leave it in, you might be the one stranded in the Atchafalaya Basin next time, both figuratively and literally."

Agent Cook scratched his head. "I don't believe I want to know what you're talking about, Wade."

"That's a wise decision, Butch."

The air of confidence Butch Cook entered the room with was much more subdued now. His demeanor did not possess the steadiness it had when the questioning began.

"Please tell me what each of you know about Victoria Engle."

Sam began. "I only met her the one time in Jackson. I've already discussed that with you previously, so I won't re-hash that. She was protective and less than forthcoming with information about the investment group she represented. Supposedly, this investment group was gonna make a huge investment in Evergreen, but nobody knows what it is."

"What is the focus of the project, Sheriff?"

"Not a clue," replied Sam. "Anyway, our conversation was short, and we parted on less than favorable terms. She offered to have John, that's John Grimes, our city attorney to call her."

"We may have to use John to contact her. From what we've found out so far, she doesn't exist."

"That's what the State Police detective, Ben Russell, told me."

Butch continued, "We are trying to develop some leads to find her, but she must be clever. So far, she's been under the radar and has done a good job of hiding her tracks. Our best guess is that she's from south Louisiana, but we're uncertain of that. We don't know. You may find out later."

Wade sat up. "Are you telling us we need to find out? Does this mean the Agency is scaling down its investigation in the matter?"

"Wade, you know the Agency is goal oriented to a fault. In this operation, for whatever the reason, our primary goal was to find you alive. That seems a little odd to me, but I have my orders. Hence, this was my exit interview for the case and I'll turn everything in to my supervisor and close my end. I have no idea if they'll pursue anything else in the investigation. The murder of Mr. Thigpen is strictly a matter for the local authorities, meaning you Sheriff Cates. As far as the death of the pilot, we don't know if it was murder or an accident. I understand you're a Federal Investigator, Wade. I assume you'll be charged to find the answers to those questions."

"What access will we have to your files, Agent Cook?"

"We can't reveal all the contents of our findings, but you'll have our cooperation."

Butch Cook paused and looked around the room. He

reached inside his briefcase and Wade heard the distinctive sound of a recorder being turned off.

"We cannot officially reveal our findings so far into the investigation."

He picked up four boxes and laid them on the conference room desk.

"I can't be responsible if in the excitement of finding you alive, we left a copy of our findings behind."

"Thanks, Butch."

"We'll pick up everything and get out of here. This is my card. Call me anytime. Wade, as you know, anytime you call me on this number, it'll be recorded. If you need to speak to me privately, ask me how my golf game is. I don't play, so I'll know to call you back on a private line."

Within an hour, all traces of the Agency had disappeared from the building. The Federal Transportation Safety Board occupied the offices and had custody of the plane. Their agents were buzzing around like wasps around a nest that had been hit with a stone. Wade checked with them, but they had very few questions for him.

"Did you notice any sluggish behavior on behalf of the pilot prior to your departure from Evergreen?"

"No, Sir."

"Did you witness the pilot eating or drinking anything during the re-fueling at Evergreen?"

"No, Sir."

"Did you see the pilot eat or drink anything after boarding the plane?"

"No, Sir."

"Could you tell if the plane was ascending or descending when you discovered the pilot disabled?"

"My impression was that it was descending, but only slightly."

"Did the safety equipment, meaning the exit door and the parachutes, work properly and easily when you used them?"

"Yes, Sir."

"Did you hear anything unusual from the operation of the plane?"

"No, Sir."

"Thank you. We will call you if we need anything else."

Sam put her arm around Wade. "Let's go home."

Inside the car on the way to Evergreen, Wade took a big bite of the big greasy double cheeseburger with extra mayonnaise and pickles.

"I'm not sure why, but I've been craving one of these."

Sam shook her head.

"I thought you might crave something, but I didn't think it'd be a cheeseburger. I've lost the attention of men a lot of times, but never to a cheeseburger."

43 SATURDAY MORNING
EVERGREEN

"Boy, did that feel good? There is something about sleeping in your own bed that makes a huge difference." Wade looked over at Sam as the two of them sipped on some dark roasted Community Coffee on the back patio of the Lodge.

"It's good to have you home. I was worried sick about you out there in that swamp."

"I can't even begin to tell you how much I missed you and the Plantation. There were a couple of times out there that I wasn't sure I'd be back. Now that I am, I'm not sure I ever want to leave here again."

"Do you want some breakfast?"

"Not right now. Thank you again for putting everything together to get us out of there; the helicopters, the Coast Guard, the Agency and everything else. I still can't believe you paid for everything. You didn't have to do that."

"And leave you out there alone in the middle of nowhere with one of the twins. That's like putting a hog in charge of watching the feed corn. Eventually, there won't be any corn to watch."

"The only things I bit were the critters that had a tendency to bite back."

"That's doesn't exactly eliminate Mindy, does it?"

Wade laughed. "No, that doesn't eliminate Mindy. At least she wasn't planning on having me for lunch."

"Not in that sense, maybe."

"Sam, you're impossible. Here you are, the envy of every woman in Evergreen, and you're jealous of Mindy. She is a wonderful kid, but she'll never come close to you."

"I'm not jealous of Mindy. But you never invited me to go camping with you for a week."

Wade almost spit his coffee out.

"Invited her to go camping? This was more like the IRS deciding to do a spot audit and then deciding to spend the next six months pouring over every record you have. I didn't have a lot of choice in the matter."

"I know, but I bet you picked her fresh flowers every day to take her mind off of her sore ankle. If I remember correctly, when I was in the hospital, I didn't get any flowers or candy, at least not from you."

"It was a tough choice every morning. Even tougher was picking out the vase to match them with given the limited selections available. You know what? They didn't accept credit cards either."

Sam laughed. "So did you serve her breakfast in bed?"

"Nope. We ordered Room Service. That way neither one of us had to get up."

"So when are you going to take me camping and bring me flowers every morning?"

"As soon as we find out who tried to kill me and who killed Kenny Thigpen. So let's do that before an early lunch, shall we?"

"Good. Then I'll have the afternoon off without worry

about where you are. I may even take time for a manicure and a pedicure. Shoot, I might even go for a leg-waxing."

"We'd better hurry then. I'll get us more coffee before we start in on these reports."

Two hours and a pot of coffee later, Sam closed the last of the files. She looked over at Wade sitting in one of the other rockers.

"So, who did it?"

"Don't know, but at least we can eliminate some suspects from acting alone."

"Who?"

"The women: Kenny's wife, Reba; Traci, Victoria, you and John's wife. Kenny weighed too much for any of you to have carried him from the road to the stand by yourselves. You guys would have needed help to do that."

"Gee, thanks for eliminating me. That's nice of you."

"No problem," Wade laughed. "At least we're being thorough. I suggest that we start back at the beginning of all of this. That seems to be with Victoria and whatever this mystery project is all about."

"Did you see anything in the files that would help us find her?"

"The only firm conclusion from the file is that Victoria Engle doesn't exist, at least not in Jackson."

Wade rubbed his hand on his chin. "What I can't figure out is why she'd want to kill me. I've never met her before Sunday. Heck, I never even heard of her before then. How can I make somebody that mad at me without meeting them?"

"You have a special knack." She giggled. "Only kidding. Let's go talk with John. He's the only person in town other than Bruce that's met her previously."

"That we know about."

"That's true, Wade. There may be more folks that know a lot more about everything than they are saying, at least to us."

44 SATURDAY

EVERGREEN

"John, thanks for seeing us on a Saturday."

"No problem. I'm glad you and Mindy are okay. You had us all worried for a while there. Sam, I understand you were there at the rescue. Congratulations."

Sam smiled. "Thanks. We're all grateful to find them safe and sound. Can we ask you a couple of questions about Victoria Engle?"

John nodded. "I don't know a lot about Vicki. She was primarily in contact with Ed. I guess I assumed that since she knows Bruce, then she probably knows he's the acting mayor and would use him as her primary point of contact for Evergreen."

"All right, we'll check with Bruce again. But from what I understand, she hasn't tried to contact him at all. Tell us what you know about her."

"We met in Jackson. I believe I've already told you that, though. She coordinated the entire event and made sure we were where we were supposed to be and met with the people we were scheduled to meet. I met with some consultants about the contracts that would be required by the city for expansion. We even discussed how we should contract for the law enforcement given the split duties now between the city and the county."

"What did you learn from these consultants?"

"Mainly that we couldn't and wouldn't get it right the first time. You can't absorb a huge project the size of the one they were discussing. Whether you're talking about Dallas or Evergreen, there are too many variables to cover everything completely the first time you attempt it."

"Did you ever meet the actual investors?"

"That privilege was left to Ed and Rachel, and both of them are dead now."

"When we met with her Tuesday, she mentioned that someone in Evergreen contacted her to get all of this set up. Do you have any idea who that person is?"

"I remember her saying that and I was a surprised. I'd always assumed that Rachel organized all of this. But when we met with Vicki, she definitely referenced her contact in Evergreen as a male."

"So you don't know who that may be?"

"Not a clue, Sam."

"Have you tried to call Vicki since we met with her Tuesday, John?"

"No. If you'll recall, she wasn't in the best of moods the last time we talked with her. In fact, I'd say she was more than a tad agitated at you."

"I didn't think she was being straight-forward with me and I wanted to find Wade." Sam glanced over in Wade's direction.

Wade suggested, "John, why don't you try to call her now and see if she will to talk to you?"

John dialed the number from the business card he

pulled from the desk beside him. He almost immediately put his cell phone down.

"Out of service."

Wade sighed. "Do you have any other way to contact her?"

"No, only that phone number."

"Who were the consultants you met with in Jackson?"

John pulled another card out of the desk.

"Wilbert and Associates. I met with Jacob Wilbert, one of the brothers."

"Did you ever feel like they knew more about the project than the general size and scope?"

"I did, but I'm not certain of it. They kept information of that type close to the vest."

"Is there any way we can get a subpoena for their records, John?"

"Based on what, Sam? We'd be laughed out of the court trying to get one because we're curious about a project that never happened that may or may not have anything to do with anything."

"You're right. I'm frustrated and I don't know where to find answers."

"Find a solid connection between the two, and you won't have any problems getting a subpoena. Until then, there isn't a judge in south Mississippi that will authorize one."

Wade stood and looked out of John's window. "What I can't figure out is how I'm involved in any of this."

"I only remember your name coming up once in all of our discussions. Somebody, and I believe it was Rachel, mentioned that your land would be the perfect location for the project."

"I'm not going to sell my land to them or to anyone else, John."

"I believe that was the consensus of the group, but then Rachel said something odd."

"What was that?"

"She said you owned an option to buy the six hundred acres next to you."

Wade shook his head. "I don't know anything about an option to buy any other land than the Plantation. Sam, have you heard about this before?"

She shook her head.

John paced around his large home office.

"What I'm about to tell you is hearsay. Do you understand that?"

Wade laughed. "That means to me it may all be BS and you'll never repeat it to any judge or in any court. Does that about cover it?"

"That's about the size of it. My understanding is they basically gave the title to the Evergreen Plantation along with all of its assets by the Agency for reasons known only to you and the Agency. When the transfer was ultimately completed, one asset was the right to buy the six hundred acres that abuts your property. The Agency had got this right when they obtained the Plantation to preserve their privacy and protect against anyone knowing of their involvement with the operations at the Plantation. When you took over, you automatically assumed that asset as part of the transfer since it was part of the estate. The weird part of what Rachel said was that the price listed in the option was some ridiculous figure, something in the hundreds of dollars per acre instead of the thousands. The price of land around here hasn't been that low in decades."

"Who would know if any of this is true?"

"The only person in town that might know would be Collier Templet, the estate attorney. I'm fairly certain he handled the transfer of the estate for the Agency when they moved it to you."

"They sent a stack of papers taller than me to sign. I met him a few times, but his assistant showed me all the places I needed to sign. She told me he'd reviewed the entire package, but I knew he hadn't. There were papers in there that no one had read in years. But she never mentioned an option to buy more land to me that I recall. That's something I probably would remember."

John looked thoughtfully at his desk.

"He may have considered it inconsequential compared to the entire package. The title search and the transfer of the legal deed without liens were his primary focus, I would assume, although I'm not a real estate attorney. I know if I had been assigned the responsibility, those are the two responsibilities that I would have taken most seriously."

"Thanks. I'll find the documentation and go through it."

"I know you've been a little indisposed, but has the investigation made any progress on the other side, the murder of Kenny Thigpen?"

Wade looked up at John. "We assumed, or at least I assumed all the events are somehow related. So to answer your question, we've made very little progress."

"In my opinion, the events are undoubtedly connected. Let's keep in touch. I'll keep trying to get in touch with Vicki."

45 SATURDAY
EVERGREEN

"Reba, sorry to bother you on a Saturday, but we're trying real hard to put some information we've gathered together."

"Please, come in. Wade, I'm glad to see you're okay. It must've been scary being out there in that big ol' swamp."

They took the same seats they'd occupied during their previous visit.

"Yes, Ma'am. It was. I'm sure glad to get back to Evergreen and Sam. He glanced over at Sam, who had taken a seat on the sofa next to Reba.

"May I get you some coffee? I just made a whole pot out of habit and I can't drink it all by myself."

"That'd be great." Sam smiled. "Let me help you."

Sam rose to help Reba with the coffee while Wade stood and looked at the pictures around the room. He was only half paying attention to the pictures when one of them made him freeze. The picture in the frame was of two couples on a beach. One of the couples was Kenny and Reba Thigpen. The other couple was Collier Templet and a lovely woman that appeared to be his wife.

What a coincidence? Butch Cook reminded me of something I learned at the Agency. Never believe in coincidences.

Reba and Sam returned with the coffee and some pound cake. Wade eagerly took both and began munching on the cake. Sam took the lead in the interview.

"Reba, I met with Traci. How well do you know her?"

"Kenny always spoke well of her. I think she was finally learning the ins and outs of the business. She was in a better position to help Kenny run the company than I was. I'm not a risk-taker and Kenny was. So it was better for me to stay away from the business as much as possible. Kenny was more relaxed recently than I've seen him in years, and I think a lot of that had to do with Traci coming on board and helping him."

"Has Traci contacted you since Kenny's death?"

"She told me you went by the office, and she also offered to buy the business from me. She only wants the files and to transfer the phone number to her. I don't have any use for them. I have no desire to get into the business adviser business, so I agreed to sell them to her. I wished her the best of luck."

"How well did Kenny do in the business, Reba?"

"We've had our ups and downs over the years. It's been great for the last couple of years, despite the economy. I guess more people need help running their business in a poor economy than they do in a good economy. We also seemed to do well on the trip to Jackson, although I don't know what that was all about. They escorted most of the wives to different restaurants for lunch and only got to see our husbands at night. Then they paid for our entertainment, and we didn't discuss business much. I did a good bit of shopping and Kenny didn't complain a single time."

"While you were in Jackson, did you talk with Vicki Engle at all?"

"We had lunch together one day. I'm not sure why, but everybody else went one direction and the two of us went the other and had lunch at a quaint Italian diner. The food was absolutely delicious."

"What can you tell us about her?"

"She's a professional businesswoman, and she's very personable once you get to know her. She said the deal she was working on with the city was the biggest one in which she has participated."

"Did she say where she lives?"

"Right there in Jackson, I believe. She told me she loved to sit on her balcony of her town home and watch the steamboats go up and down the Mississippi. She said it gave her goose bumps when they tooted the river horns."

"Did she tell you if she is married?"

"Not directly. I noticed she wasn't wearing a wedding ring or an engagement ring, so I assumed she wasn't married. I got the feeling or sense she had a boyfriend though."

"Why is that?"

"She used the word 'we' when she talked about going out or eating out. So I assumed she had a steady boyfriend, but again I don't really know."

"Did she mention any restaurants she enjoyed?"

"Several of them, but I don't remember the names. The only one I remember she called '*Columns*' or something like that. The only reason I remember it is she said they have the best spicy shrimp with grits or shrimp with spicy grits. I can never remember which one is spicy, but I want to try it one day. I've never had shrimp with any grits before."

"Anything else?"

"They enjoyed going to the football games together. I wish Kenny would have taken me to a game. It seems like a lot of fun."

"Did she mention any of the team names?"

"Not that I recall. We were just making girl talk, you know. I wasn't digging for any information."

Wade and Sam nodded.

"Anything else?"

"I got the impression she knew someone from Evergreen."

"Why is that?"

"She asked me questions like 'What part of town is the best to live in?' When I mentioned a few of the upper scale neighborhoods, she seemed to have already heard about them."

"I see. Any particular places?"

"It was as if she'd heard of all of them, but had never seen any of them."

"Let's talk about you."

"I have to warn you. I lead a boring life."

"No problem. Tell us about your relationship with Kenny."

"We had some great times together, and some that weren't so great. But I guess every couple goes through some of that. His business had its difficulties. When it went through the down times, Kenny would get stressed with the finances and all. A couple of times, he nearly had to close the business, and it stressed Kenny to the max. When he got stressed, I wasn't far behind him."

Sam sighed. "I understand."

"Thanks, Sam."

"Okay, the next questions are going to be a little tougher."

Reba nodded. "Okay."

"Did Kenny have a relationship outside of your marriage?"

Reba started laughing. "Goodness, no. Kenny wasn't the romantic type, you know."

"Was he romantic enough for you, Reba?"

Reba reddened. "I don't understand the question."

Sam smiled. "Reba, we already know that you were having a relationship with someone outside of your marriage to Kenny. Do you want to tell us about it?"

Tears streamed down Reba's face.

"Are you gonna tell anyone?"

"Not now. And we won't if we don't have to."

"How did you find out?"

"The Agency told us about it."

"The Agency was investigating me?"

"It's normal to look at the spouse as a person of interest in any murder case."

"What did they find out? What did they tell you?"

"We can't reveal everything in their files, Reba. That would violate our agreement with them. Do you want to tell us about the relationship?"

"I think I'd better talk to an attorney, Sam. If I'm being investigated, I probably need some legal advice."

"No problem, Reba. You're entitled to the advice as long as you're aware that it puts you in a different light in the investigation."

"I understand."

46 SATURDAY AFTERNOON
EVERGREEN PLANTATION

"I wonder what that was all about." Wade said to Sam when they returned to the Lodge."

"I don't know if she's involved in something or just scared her secret affair will come to light. If she's involved, I can't figure out how, other than she was tired of living with Kenny. But how would that include you if that was the case? Unless, of course, you got tired of playing with children like the twins and moved on up to the adults like Reba."

"That would mean I first would take one or both of the twins over you and then take Reba over one or both of the twins. Now that makes a lot of sense."

"Stranger things have happened."

"I'd advise you to never take the Detective's test with that kind of reasoning."

"For you information, I took it and passed it."

"They must have left out the deductive reasoning portion if that's the best scenario you can come up with. Besides, it was a compliment to you."

"And I thank you."

"I got one thing out of the interview."

"What's that?"

"Victoria Engle, or whatever her name is, wasn't living in Jackson when she and Reba talked. She was living in New Orleans."

"Why do you say that?"

"Miss Engle told Reba she liked to sit on the balcony and watch the steamboats sail up and down the Mississippi River. The Mississippi doesn't go through Jackson. It goes from New Orleans to Baton Rouge and up through Natchez and Vicksburg. It doesn't go anywhere near Jackson."

"Then she could live in one of the other cities. Why New Orleans?"

"Reba mentioned the Columns, which is probably the Columns Hotel down on St. Charles Avenue in the Garden District. One of their specialties is the spicy shrimp and grits. I've had it and it's great. It's definitely not in Jackson."

Sam sighed. "I feel a little slow. I didn't catch either of those."

"That's because you never lived in New Orleans. I lived there when I was with the Agency. That helped."

Sam took a sip of her coffee. "So where do we go from here?"

"Do we really have a choice?"

"There is one other lead we need to follow. I forgot to tell you."

"What is it?"

"Andy Netterville."

"Who the hell is Andy Netterville?" Wade asked.

"Ann Clement's boyfriend. Collier Templet said Andy walked in the office and found you making a pass at Ann. Said he got upset."

"I know I've been through a lot, but I don't remember flirting with Ann or meeting her boyfriend. Ann is kinda cute though."

Sam threw a napkin at Wade. "Cuter than the twins?"

"Different kind of cute. But neither is as cute as you."

"If I find out you made a pass at Ann, you won't find me so cute."

47 SATURDAY NIGHT
EVERGREEN

WADE COULD NOT SEE AROUND OR OVER THE HULK standing in the doorway.

"We're looking for Andy Netterville. From the description, I'm guessing you're him."

The big fellow grunted. Other than that, he did not move.

"Can we come in? We need to talk to you and I hate to do it out here." Wade nodded in Sam's direction.

Netterville took a step backward. Wade moved to the side to allow Sam in first. And to access the mountain of a young man. Tree trunks for arms and legs. No fat. All muscle. Powerful, but not too quick on his feet. That might be all the advantage Wade would get if things turned for the worse with the conversation.

Andy remained standing after Wade and Sam sat on the sofa. Still, he had said nothing. Just glared at Wade like the ex-agent was a piece of meat ready to eat.

"Andy, is it true that Ann Clement is your girlfriend?" Wade asked.

A small grunt sufficed as an affirmative answer.

"Were you told that I flirted with her?"

Another small grunt.

"I can assure you I didn't. Ann was professional and kind during the time we spent together during the transfer of the Plantation. I did nothing inappropriate."

No grunt this time.

"I'm not sure where the rumor started, but I can assure you nothing happened," Wade said.

"Don't believe you," Netterville growled.

Wade stood. He was not accustomed to being called a liar.

"I don't —"

The mountain moved. More like an avalanche. In a fluid motion, if one could call a mountain toppling over fluid, Netterville charged. Wade braced for the impact, knowing he had little chance against the sheer power and weight of his opponent.

The mountain fell short. Wade had to look twice to figure out why. Then he saw petite, little Sam wrapping plastic cuffs around Andy's' huge wrists.

"What happened?" the agent asked.

"I tripped him. He was looking at you and paid no attention to me. I wanted to let you boys do your thing and play rough, but we don't have the time for you to spend at the hospital." Sam grinned, standing over the young athlete.

"I guess we've found our culprit," Wade said. "He was ready to kill me."

"He didn't kill Kenny," Sam said.

"And just what makes you so sure of that?"

"Because he would have broken every bone in Kenny's body with his bare hands. Andy isn't the type to use a gun."

Wade nodded. "I'd have to agree. So where to we go from here?"

"I don't think we have a choice," Sam answered.

48 SUNDAY MORNING
NEW ORLEANS

WADE SAT THE TRAY OF BEIGNETS WITH CUPS OF chicory coffee on the table at Café du Monde between Jackson Square and the mighty Mississippi River. Never had he felt better about being with Sam on a gorgeous Sunday morning.

"There you go. Special order for the Sheriff of the Year for her role in the rescue of a poor farmer boy from the swamps of the mysterious Atchafalaya Basin. My compliments, Ma'am."

"Why thank you, Sir. Now tell me the truth. Did you miss me or the food more?"

Wade laughed. "Let's see. I had Roasted Cottonmouth, Turtle Stew simmered in its own shell, Piglet in a Pan and Squirrel on a Spit served by a voluptuous young twin on one hand and on the other hand I have you. No contest. I missed you more."

Wade nipped the corner of a hot beignet, fresh from the hot grease. The pent up explosion of the grease captured within the beignets combined with the crispness of the fried dough and the sweetness of the deep coating of powdered sugar almost always surprised him and never disappointed him. He leaned back in his chair, wiping his mouth and chin with one of the stack of napkins in front of him.

"I've tried these everywhere. I've seen them for sale and even tried to make them at home. They never taste as good as the originals they make right here. I wonder what they do differently here at Café du Monde than everywhere else. These are so good."

"Might be the temperature of the grease or adding something to it. I wish I knew." Sam agreed. "If I did I'd market it and sell it across the world and make millions. I've bought the mix before and tried it at home. No matter how close I follow the instructions, it just doesn't taste the same."

"It must be the view of the river, the bustle of Jackson Square or the Farmer's Market next door. I don't know. I guess it could be the combination of all of them."

Wade looked around him and smiled.

Sam nodded. "Isn't that it? The aura of New Orleans, I mean. People will do things on Bourbon Street or Jackson Square they'd never do in their hometown."

"You're right." Wade agreed. "It's a little like Vegas in that respect, but a lot more mysterious. People check their inhibitions at the city limit and pick them up on the way back out of town. It's amazing to watch normally conservative folks act so bizarre down here. I think it's voodoo or something."

"I wouldn't want to be a cop down here for anything. There's so many lines that are blurry. People do things on Bourbon Street that would get them arrested on Canal Boulevard and one runs into the other. They can do things during Mardi Gras they can't do the rest of the year. I like things black and white, not blurry."

"Sam, it's not hard to figure out."

"Okay, explain it to me." Sam's steady gaze challenged him.

"It's all about the money."

"The money?"

"Who brings money from outside the city and spends it in the city?"

"Tourists."

"Exactly. And where and when do most of these tourists spend their money?"

The conclusion hit her, and she acknowledged his logic.

"In the French Quarter during Mardi Gras."

"Yep. Tourism is a huge factor in the city's economy. After Katrina, a lot of people predicted the downfall of New Orleans, but despite everything it's rebounded and tourism is flourishing."

"So the cops don't want to do anything to hurt the tourist industry, so they let things within reason go when tourists may be involved that'd get a local arrested."

Wade nodded. "Better for their careers if they look the other way, depending on how it may look to the tourists."

Sam changed the subject. "I love these beignets myself, but I wish I could eat them without getting the powdered sugar all over me."

Wade grinned. "I don't mind brushing it off. I'd have to be thorough."

Sam rolled her eyes. "Do horny boys ever grow up?"

"Yep, we become horny guys." Wade paused. "Then we become dirty old men. Simple progression of time."

"Now isn't that the truth?"

"And you girls have been taking advantage of it forever."

"I beg your pardon."

"If women don't want to take advantage of the instincts

of men, then why do they spend so much of their time and money trying to look beautiful and sexy?"

"We're not trying to look beautiful and sexy. We're trying to look professional."

Wade laughed. "Yeah, right. If looking professional means weighing the perfect weight with an hour-glass figure, then I agree with you. And if looking professional means spending zillions of dollars at Victoria's Secret, then I agree with you. And if looking professional means spending half of your paycheck on the latest colored water they call perfume, then I agree with you. See, I agree with you."

"It's all part of the secret plan."

"What secret plan?"

"If I told you, it wouldn't be a secret. Only women know the secret."

"And why not share this secret plan with men?"

"Because you wouldn't understand it, anyway."

Wade laughed out loud.

"You're probably right. I can only speak as one man. I never understand a woman's logic, even though they're right most of the time. It's how they get to the conclusion that I don't get. Doesn't seem like logic to me."

"Speaking of plans, do we have one or do we wait here all day and hope Vicki walks by?"

"You have to admit it. This isn't a bad place to wait. Great view of the river and close to the French Quarter. Some of the best restaurants in the world are within walking distance."

"And Mr. Logic. What are the chances that Vicki will come ambling along as we sit here?"

"About one in several hundred billion, I'd guess. Although that may be a tad optimistic. What's the population of the earth again?"

"So what do you suggest as a course of action?"

"Let's take a stroll if you're through with your beignets."

Wade led the way past the horse-drawn carriages into Jackson Square, pausing in front of the statue in the center of the plaza. They briefly scanned the plaque on the statue of the likeness of "Stonewall Jackson", nicknamed that because of his fierce leadership in defense of the Crescent City. They continued across the plaza and stopped in front of the St. Louis Cathedral.

Wade looked around. "He's usually right here."

"Who?"

"The guy who draws caricatures of the tourists for twenty bucks. He's been down here forever."

Sam pointed him out. "There he is. On the corner over there."

Wade and Sam walked over to the artist and watched him finish a drawing of a teenage girl. Her boyfriend was watching over the artist's shoulder with a grin as wide as the Mississippi itself spread across his face.

"Man, you're good. That looks just like her."

The proud young man held up the finished sketch, alternating his focus between it and his girlfriend.

"She's pretty, don't you think?"

The teenager held the drawing in front of Wade and Sam.

Both of them smiled and nodded. "She sure is. Second prettiest girl in Jackson Square, I'd say." Wade said.

The teenager responded, "Heck, she's the prettiest girl in New Orleans."

Wade just laughed.

The artist had already shifted his focus to Wade and Sam, with his focus resting on Sam.

"It'd be a pleasure, Ma'am."

"I'm sorry, but we're not here for that."

"But that's the only thing I do."

Wade stepped forward.

"We'd like a drawing of my friend here. Her name is Sam. But we don't want the regular version. We want the deluxe version."

"What do you mean? I only do face drawings, nothing else."

"I want to see just how close you can get to the real thing, not just a caricature. We want every curve and every line and every hair, just like she looks as close as you can draw it. I know you like to change the symmetry on your drawings to make them fuller or thinner in the face and you get a bigger tip for making them look better than they are, but we want reality."

"That will take some time, Sir."

Wade grinned. "I understand. Time is money."

"For me, it is. I can't spend all of my time on one drawing. The only way I make money is drawing people's faces and I need to draw as many as possible during a day."

"No problem. We're willing to compensate you for your time. How much for a deluxe version?"

"Fifty dollars."

The artist looked at Wade as though he was expecting him to balk at the number.

Wade shook his head. "We don't want the fifty dollar version. We want the two hundred dollar version."

The artist gulped.

"Okay, I'll do the best I can. But it's gonna take a little while."

"No problem."

Sam spoke up. "I don't want to sit for that long."

Wade chuckled. "Think of it as part of your job. You'll see."

He turned to the artist.

"If you get this right, then we have another job for you. But first, I want to see how close you get to drawing Sam as she really is. Remember, you're not trying to flatter her, just get down on paper what she really looks like."

"This is one of the few cases where drawing her as she is will flatter her. I hope you're pleased when I get it done."

Sam blushed and looked away quickly.

"Ma'am, if you don't mind, just sit in the chair and turn slightly towards the statue. That's it. Now lift your chin slightly."

The artist removed his hat and scratched his head. He walked around to the other side of Sam and then back again. He peered closely at her face from every angle possible before beginning.

"Here goes. I've never done this before, so wish me luck. Portraying the depth in two dimensions is the tough part."

"Just do the best you can. You impressed me with the last sketch you did for the little lady before."

"Thanks. Now, Sam. Can you hold that pose for a bit, and then we'll give you a break?"

One hour later, the mirrored image of Sam reflected on the canvas paper.

"Excellent job. I mean, that is terrific."

Sam looked at the sketch and frowned. "Oh my God, is my face really that fat? And look at the lines in the corners of my eyes. Wade, that looks nothing like me!"

"Sam, that's exactly how you look. He couldn't have done a better job and no, he couldn't have changed anything about it to flatter you. At least not in my eyes."

"Ma'am, if I can say so myself. That's the best drawing

I've ever done. Do you guys mind if I take a picture of you and the sketch together? I'm going to use that one in my advertising."

"She'll be glad to do that for you. After that, we want you to do what we're really after."

The artist took the photograph of Sam holding up the drawing while Wade took out the Agency's sketch of Victoria Engle. He handed the sketch to the artist.

"Now, what we want is for you to make a drawing of this drawing. The only thing is that we want to make some changes to it. We've both seen this lady up close and personal and know there are some flaws in the drawing. Sam can describe them better than I can. I'd like for her to tell you about the flaws and see how much closer you can get this drawing to reality. Same as before, but you won't have to worry about your model squirming so much in the chair."

"I've never done this. All of my models have been three dimensional. But if you can describe the changes in as much detail as you can before I start drawing, that'd help. Again, depth is the tough part, especially from a drawing."

"Just do the best you can and I'm sure it'll be okay."

"All right, first let me draw an outline in light pencil and then we'll start making the changes."

In less than ten minutes, Wade could hardly tell one sketch from the other.

"Okay, Sam. Tell him what you remember differently from the sketch."

Sam studied the newly drawn sketch for a few minutes. "The cheek bones need to be more defined. The eyebrows were slightly higher and there was just a tad more space between them. She had a stud earring, and it was a good bit lower in the lobe than most. Yeah, down there."

Sam looked at Wade.

"I'm not trying to be mean. I'm just trying to remember her exactly as I saw her."

"I know. Do your best and it'll be fine."

She looked back at the drawing. "There were some little crow's feet starting to form in the corners of her eyes. They weren't too pronounced, but they were noticeable. Her hair was bleach blonde, and it had some black streaks in the roots. When she smiled, her lips weren't symmetrical. This side of her mouth was a little crooked."

The artist re-drew each meticulous adaption to the approval of Sam. When he finished, Sam stared at the drawing.

"That's her! That is exactly the way I remember her looking sitting across the table from me in Jackson."

Wade smiled. "Looks just like I remember her."

He gave a large tip to the artist as he gathered the three sketches. One of Victoria by the agency and the two the artist completed in the plaza.

Turning to Sam, he said, "This will save us a lot of time. It's as close to having a picture of Victoria as we can get without having one. I'm still amazed that neither Reba nor John had any photograph with Victoria in it from their trip to Jackson."

Sam now understood the plan. "So we take this down to St. Charles Avenue and start showing it around the street."

"We'll start with the town homes and condominiums that are tall enough to have a view of the river. If we don't have any luck this morning, we'll have a leisurely lunch at the Columns Hotel and see if anyone there can help us."

49 SUNDAY NOON
NEW ORLEANS

"MAY I SHOW YOU TO YOUR TABLE?" THE HOSTESS AT the Columns Hotel, dressed in the traditional white top and black vests and trousers, was both professional and pleasant.

"Sure, we'd like to have a seat by the window, please."

Sam almost fell into her chair. "Pretty discouraging so far, wouldn't you say?"

"Yeah, but it's early yet. We can't let the disappointment of a couple of hours discourage us."

The waitress poured some water into the empty glasses on the table. "What else can I get for you to drink?"

Wade looked up at her. "Two unsweetened teas, please."

The waitress disappeared into the depths of the kitchen.

"I guess we keep going. I truly believe Reba, either on purpose or by accident, pointed us down here on St. Charles. The things she told us couldn't lead us anywhere but the Garden District in New Orleans. I forgot how many town homes and condominiums there are down here though."

"Who's Reba's boyfriend? She sure sealed up like a clam when we tried to ask about him." Sam said out of frustration, more than expecting an answer.

"That's what has me confused."

"What?"

"It looks to me like Reba is somehow involved. But it also seems like Victoria is also involved somehow. But they don't seem to be working together, or Reba would have never mentioned the conversation they had that led us here. So how can they both be involved, but not working together?"

The waitress re-appeared with two glasses of tea. "What can I get you for lunch?"

Wade hadn't glanced at the menu.

"We have a special with stuffed Mirlitons. They're stuffed with either ground beef, shrimp, or crab dressing. You can get one stuffing or a combination of all three. With those you get a house salad and a side order of fries or chips. Today, we also have a half and half order of Fried Crawfish tails and Crawfish Etouffe. With it you also get a house salad and your choice of fries or chips. Is this your first time here? If so, you need to try our Spicy Shrimp and Grits or our Crawfish "Monica" Mac. Those are two of our signature dishes."

Sam glanced up at her. "We had a late breakfast. I'll have the stuffed Mirlitons with crab. The house dressing will be fine for the salad."

Wade nodded. "I'll have the same. Those basin crawfish were good, but I'm ready for something else."

He and Sam laughed at their inside joke as the waitress gathered the menus and ambled back toward the kitchen.

"Where were we?" Wade scratched his head. "Oh, yeah. Reba and Victoria. I was so sure Reba pointed us in this direction, but now I'm not so sure. I could've been wrong."

"Do you want to stay down here and keep looking, or do you want to go back to Evergreen and see if we can get Reba to talk to us?"

"I don't know."

Wade pulled out the artist's sketch of Victoria and studied it closely.

"Who are you? Why do you want to kill me?" He directed the questions toward the sketch, but the answer came from the side of the table.

"That's Emily. It looks just like her."

The waitress returned with the two house salads and stared at the drawing. She stood dead still for more than ten seconds before placing the salads on the table in front of Wade and Sam.

Wade's mouth dropped open.

"Who is Emily?" He stammered not so eloquently.

"Emily, you know. The one that used to come here."

"Do you know her last name?"

The waitress regained her composure.

"Uh, no. And looking at it again, I'm not sure it's her. I'm sorry. I shouldn't have been looking at your private papers. It just that the drawing reminded me of someone that used to eat here, but doesn't anymore."

"What is Emily's last name?"

"I don't know. I only knew her as Emily, but that's not her now that I look at it."

"Would you have any records for Emily, you know like how she paid?"

"I'm sorry. I've got to get the rest of the orders out or the chef will get upset." The waitress turned and re-entered the kitchen.

Wade leaned over the table.

"Is there any doubt she recognized the lady in the drawing and her name is Emily?"

Sam shook her head. "No. She definitely recognized her and then tried to deny it. I wonder what else she knows."

"We've got to find out." Wade pressed his fingers against the tabletop. "We need to know."

"Hold on, Batman. We can't go barging into the kitchen. Let's eat and then the restaurant won't be so busy and we'll have time to talk to her then."

"All right, but she will talk to us before we leave."

Wade and Sam nibbled on the house salads, waiting for the waitress to re-appear with the main entrees. They were disappointed when another waitress brought them the stuffed Mirlitons. Wade looked around the room for the first waitress without success.

They finished the delicious dish and waited for the waitress to bring the check. Again, they were disappointed when the second waitress brought the check to them.

"Anything else?"

Wade looked around again.

"Where is the waitress that began serving us?"

"She said she wasn't feeling well and went home."

Wade rubbed his eyes and said quietly to Sam, "Emily is already packing, I would guess. We might as well go back to Evergreen."

"Let's at least enjoy our lunch. This is such a beautiful restaurant and hotel."

"Okay." Wade said without a lot of enthusiasm.

The second waitress was patiently waiting.

Sam looked up. "We'll have one Crème Brûlée and one Bananas Foster, please."

"It'll only take a second." The second waitress left the table.

Wade looked at Sam and shook his head.

Sam grinned. "Let's forget about all of that and enjoy this gorgeous weekend."

"How could I refuse a suggestion like that from such a lovely lady?"

"Admit it. You can't. Now I'm ready for some dessert."

"Bet it isn't as good as the Cottonmouth Pie we made in the basin."

"Oh, yeah. You're going to have to demonstrate some of those fabulous recipes you keep bragging about. It seems to me that you almost never cook at the Lodge. Of course, you aren't trying to impress any vulnerable young ladies at the Lodge."

"Not when you're there, anyway." His glass of tea stopped halfway to his lips. "Oops. That didn't come out right. That's not what I meant to say. What I meant to say—"

"Forget it. We're gonna enjoy the rest of today."

50 MONDAY MORNING
EVERGREEN

"Welcome, Wade. Have a seat."

Wade observed the nattily clad man on the other side of the desk. "Thanks, Collier."

"What can I do to help you today?"

"A couple of things. You're the attorney that prepared the documents for the Agency when it transferred the Plantation to me. You got to look at all the paperwork."

"That's right."

"I was talking with John Grimes, the City Attorney."

"I know John very well."

"John said he thought there should have been a document in the package that gave me the option to buy the piece of property that abuts the Plantation. I briefly looked through the stack of papers, but I didn't see one that appeared to be an option, but I'm not sure what I'm looking for in there. So I guess my question for you is if there is an actual option and if so, can I get a copy of it?"

Collier took a deep breath of air.

"I don't recall an option to buy another piece of property. Hold on."

Collier pressed one of the large buttons on his desk phone. "Ann, can you bring the entire document file transferring the Plantation to Mr. Dalton into my office, please?"

"Yes, Sir." Wade heard the feminine on the speaker.

"She'll be a few minutes. It's quite an extensive file. Is there anything else I can help you with while we're waiting?"

"I guess you've heard about my mishap in the basin."

"It's hard to keep a secret in Evergreen."

"Being out there reminded me I don't have a will in case something untoward would happen to me. I'd like to draw one up."

"I'd call what happened to you 'untoward'. Everybody in Evergreen started at least one rumor. Some started three of four so they could be right no matter what happened. But I don't remember anyone saying they thought you and the young lady were trapped in the middle of a swamp. The most prevalent one was that you and the Thomas girl eloped and were in Vegas having a great time."

Wade rubbed the back of his neck.

"No, Sir. I assure you that wasn't the case. I don't know if you know or not, but I'm engaged to Sam. What happened last week was the strangest situation in which I've ever been involved."

"I talked with Sam Monday after the waitress at the Evergreen Cafe told me you asked about my firm." He paused. "I can only hope I'm never stranded like that. Rumors, however, say you should start a Survival school the way you took care of everything. Some of them say you wrestled alligators and wild cats at the same time."

Wade blushed. "You can't believe everything you hear. I

only did what I had to do for survival. Most guys would have done the same."

"Is it true you wrestled a man-eating alligator?"

"No, but I wrestled a two ounce crawfish. Mindy didn't want to let it go."

Collier laughed. "You gotta be careful with those little boogers. They fight back."

"So did most of the things we ran into in the Basin. But we coped with what we had available. We were fortunate we each a backpack with us and that made the situation a lot easier to manage. Without them, I would hate to think about trying to stay out there for almost a week."

"I guess you're glad to get back to the Plantation."

"I am. There's no place like home. Although Sam and I took some time off yesterday and went down to New Orleans. Some of the best scenery and best food in the world. Beignets and Stuffed Mirlitons never tasted so good."

"Aah. Café du Monde and the Columns. Two of my favorite restaurants. But you can't really pick a bad restaurant in New Orleans."

"We didn't eat that badly in the swamp, but when you compare it to world-class cuisine, there really isn't any. The biggest things we missed were all the modern conveniences like cable television, computers, internet cell phones that work and things like that."

The attorney leaned forward.

"My idea of roughing it is standard cable, without the premium channels. That's as far as I ever want to go on the roughing-it scale."

The curvy assistant wheeled in a steel cart with more than a dozen boxes stacked on it. She handed Collier a manila folder about six inches thick. Collier briefly scanned the first few pages inside the folder.

"Good to see you again, Mr. Dalton." Though the girl's voice was pleasant, it did not have the same friendly tone. Ann must not have appreciated the short time Andy spent in custody.

"Thanks. I appreciate all the help you were when I got the Plantation."

"Don't mention it." Still not friendly.

"According to the paperwork, there are four more carts of documentation. Do you want to see them?"

Wade stared at the boxes on the single cart. "No, that's okay."

The attorney nodded at Ann. "That'll be all for now."

Wade watched the view from the other side of Ann as the exited the office. For some reason, she did not have the same allure as before.

The attorney picked up a folder from the top of the stack.

"You should have received the executor summaries of everything necessary to transfer the property. Might have been fifteen to eighteen inches thick or so."

"That seems about right."

Collier placed the manila folder on his desk before addressing Wade. "The Agency took a few shortcuts when it obtained the property from Teddy and setting up Dave as the public owner on record. We had to trace back more than a dozen loops to find out how they hid the true identity of the owner. Dave didn't own six square inches of the whole place."

"Anything else?"

"There was an unresolved tax lien on the property from the 1940s. We found a clever way to deal with that to keep the greedy folks from capitalizing, though."

"How's that?"

"The law requires us to advertise in two major newspapers in those circumstances. We assumed if we advertised in the Evergreen Weekly and the Jackson paper, we'd get hundreds of descendants interested in getting a share of whatever they could get, no matter if they were descendants or not. Now the law is not very specific in the term 'major' when it defined newspapers several decades ago. So we advertised in the Frog Level paper in Arkansas and the Star Weekly in Sleepy Cat, Colorado. Didn't get a single response."

Wade laughed. "I can see why the Agency chose you for the transfer."

"That's only one example of the hoops we had to jump through to accomplish what the Agency wanted us to do. I'm showing and telling you all of this to let you know how something as simple as an option to buy another piece of property could have slipped through the cracks and been overlooked. It could be in one of these boxes and the paralegal could have missed it or considered it unimportant in the goals they gave us."

"Is there a way to find out without re-creating the world? I can't afford for you guys to go through every box."

"You don't have to worry about the fees. The Agency is on the hook for any unresolved issues. I'd like to thank you."

"For what?"

"Because of your deal with the Agency, I billed more on that one transaction than I did on all of my other cases combined for the last three years. And the best part is that I got paid." Collier let out a hearty laugh.

Wade shifted in his chair. "You're welcome, I guess."

"To answer your other question, there may be a way to find out if there's a valid option out there without going through every box."

"That'd be nice."

"I don't know. We may go through every box, anyway. I could use another good paycheck from the government."

Wade laughed. "You'll just have to pay more taxes on it."

Collier frowned. "You obviously aren't aware of the grievous expenses we have in the legal profession. Speaking of roughing it, a legal conference in Paris or Oslo can be onerous. They're also extremely expensive and I wouldn't go unless I expect that one day I might get an international case here in Evergreen."

Wade shook his head. "And how many international cases have you handled so far?"

"None, yet. But if I get one, I'm ready."

"That's pretty much what I figured. When will you know something about the option?"

"Give me a couple of weeks and I'll call you on that."

"Okay, how about the will?"

"No problem. Tell me about your situation: assets, liabilities, relatives and all that stuff."

"Relatives don't really matter. I want to leave everything to Sam."

"You guys aren't married yet. Correct?"

"No, we're engaged, but not married yet."

"For estate purposes, get married."

"Why?"

"You'd be surprised how many relatives come out of the woodwork if they smell any amount of money. Nephews, nieces, aunts, long-lost cousins all want a piece of the estate. Former girlfriends will show up claiming the deceased promised them something in the estate. Those claims aren't that easy to contest if the beneficiary isn't married or has a direct heir."

"I see."

"The other side of that is that Mississippi is not a community property state, so Sam would not automatically inherit your estate. I recommend you have a will filed plainly stating your objectives. You both should also agree on some pre-nuptial agreement saying which assets will become part of the marriage and which ones won't, depending on how long the marriage lasts."

"We plan on the marriage lasting."

"So did every other couple I've talked to about it. Unfortunately, about seventy percent of them are wrong."

Wade laughed. "We plan to be in the other thirty percent. But it really doesn't matter."

"Why is that?"

"She's worth a lot more than I am."

"No way, Wade. Not on a Sheriff's salary."

Wade just smiled, saying nothing.

"I never would have guessed."

Wade nodded his head, but remained silent.

"All right, I need a list of your assets. That includes land, house, equipment, animals, furniture, fixtures, brokerage accounts, savings accounts, checking accounts and anything else you can think of. Same thing for liabilities, but only long-term debts."

"No problem there. You have the list of the assets in your file there. The number of animals on the place is impossible to count. I can tell you how many I buy and how many are harvested, but I can't tell you how many the predators kill or how many die of natural causes. I also can't tell you how many are born on the Plantation each year."

"Give me the best estimate that you can."

51 MONDAY
EVERGREEN SHERIFF'S OFFICE

Sam picked up her office phone. "Sheriff Cates?"

"Yes."

"This is Emily. You know me as Victoria Engle."

"Yes, Emily?" Sam's body stiffened and her grasp on the phone tightened.

"I understand you were looking for me in New Orleans."

"That is correct."

"I don't live in New Orleans anymore, Sheriff."

"Where do you live, Emily?"

"I'd rather not say. Not yet, anyway."

"We need to talk to you. You could be in worlds of trouble."

"I realize that. At least now I realize it. But you have to believe me. I didn't know what he was up to. I'm still not sure of all of it, but I know enough to be sure I don't want to be part of it anymore."

"Why don't you come to my office in Evergreen and we can talk about it?"

"Because the first thing you would do is arrest me, Sheriff. You know that and I know that."

"So what do you propose?"

"I want to meet you in Louisiana. As I understand it, that's outside of your jurisdiction and you can't arrest me in Louisiana. You have to come here, Sam. I only want to talk to you."

"Where do you want to meet?"

"North of Baton Rouge. There is a newly incorporated city called Central. It only has one law enforcement officer. They have a sheriff's station, but it's for all of East Baton Rouge Parish. You'll find Jackson Park off Sullivan Road next to the new elementary school. I'll meet you there."

"Okay, I've got all of that. When do you want to meet, Emily?"

"I can't meet until tomorrow, Sam. There're some things I need to do before we meet."

"Okay, what time tomorrow?"

"Can you meet me at eight in the morning? The kids will all be at school and we should have the park to ourselves."

"Eight o'clock tomorrow morning. I'll be there."

"Come alone, Sam."

"Emily, are you safe?"

"Yes, but if he finds out I'm gonna talk to you, I won't be. He'll make sure we never talk."

"Why is that, Emily?"

"Because I know too much."

"Do you want to tell me anything now?"

"Not over the phone. You never know who might be listening."

"I hate to agree with you, but it's true. I'll see you in the morning."

Sam punched a familiar number on her cell after she hung up with Emily.

"Hey, can we meet for lunch?"

52 MONDAY
EVERGREEN CAFÉ

"Wade, what do ya think she's going to tell me?"

"I wish I knew, Sam. This whole thing has me baffled."

"Me too. I still don't see the connection between you and Kenny Thigpen."

"I don't know of one. I barely met the man before any of this started and I didn't have a reason to kill him."

"Why do you think Reba asked for an attorney?"

"Hey, guys." The simultaneous greeting could only come from the Thomas twins. "Mind if we join you?"

"Please do." Wade said unnecessarily. The twins were already pulling their chairs out before he said anything.

"Have you guys ordered, yet. If not, try the special."

Wade shook his head.

"Nope, we haven't ordered yet. I don't remember seeing anything on the special board. What is it?"

Mindy beamed, "Catfish Atchafalaya Resort. It's catfish roasted over an open flame with just a pinch of salt and a dash of mysterious spices. Crusty on the outside and raw on the inside. Can't resist it."

Wade smiled. "Seems like I've heard of that before. You

don't think they stole the recipe, do you? We may have to get a restraining order."

Mindy giggled. "I don't think they stole that one. But you know, it really wasn't that bad given what we had to work with. Everything was good."

Mandy sighed. "I'm jealous, you know."

"Of who?" Sam asked.

"Mindy, of course. She got to spend an adventure-filled week with Wade in the basin and I was stuck in Evergreen worrying about her and trying to find them."

Wade glanced at Sam. "I wouldn't call it an adventure, Mandy."

"What would you call it?"

Wade thought for a few seconds. "I'd call it a misadventure."

"But all she talks about is you fighting with the black jaguar and the alligator and the snakes. Plus the meals. She said the meals were delicious."

Wade laughed. "We also discovered the secret of serving a delicious meal."

"What's that?"

"Make sure you're starving before you eat it. If you're hungry enough, then it tastes fairly good."

The waitress stopped by the table. "What can I get you today?"

Wade grinned. "What are your specials today?"

"Let's see." She checked the list on her pad. "We have fried oysters with fries. We have a six ounce rib eye with a baked potato, and we have stuffed green peppers over rice pilaf."

"I'll take the rib eye." Wade's stomach started growling in anticipation.

"Me, too." Mindy squealed.

Sam was much calmer. "I'll take the oyster special."

Mandy echoed. "Sounds good to me."

Wade's stomach continued to rumble even as he chewed on the perfectly cooked steak. But his eyes weren't on the fresh meat. They stared at the window to the outside, trying to focus, but unable to see clearly.

"Wade, what is it?"

"I don't know, Sam. I should know and that's the problem. Something hit my brain, but it won't sink in. It's like I have an idea, but I can't get it to come together."

53 TUESDAY MORNING

CITY OF CENTRAL, LA

Sam parked next to the cinder block restrooms at the small city park. Pulling into the parking lot, she saw a lone figure sitting on a bench behind the swings and silver monkey bars. Sam inspected the area suspiciously, checking the shadows for lurking danger. She exited the vehicle and strode toward the lady seated in the middle of the park, trying to scan the entire scope of potential danger around her.

"Good morning, Emily."

"Good morning, Sheriff. Please have a seat. You know my first name. What else do you know?"

Sam shook her head. "Honestly, not too much. We know you aren't Victoria Engle. We know you once lived in New Orleans. We know you used an untraceable phone when talking to the officials in Evergreen."

Emily nodded. "I see."

"We know you were involved in setting up huge payments to city officials in return for their support of a large project in Evergreen. Your people think the contracts are legal, but I'm not so sure. But we'll leave that up to someone else to decide."

"I can only tell you what I was told."

"Who else was working with you, Emily?" Who are the investors you represent?"

"That's what I want to talk to you about, Sam."

"Okay, let's talk."

"I want you to promise me immunity for anything we discuss today."

Sam arched her eyebrows. "You've taken part in at least two counts of attempted murder and probably at least one count of murder. You don't want to pay the consequences for your actions. Is that what you're saying?"

"I didn't know he was gonna try to murder Wade and the girl. I still don't know what happened to the pilot."

"Convince me, Emily."

"I will. I'll provide everything I have, but I don't want to spend the rest of my life in jail."

"So far, you've given me nothing."

"Okay, let me tell you this much. He—"

Sam heard the impact of the bullet hitting its target before she heard the quiet report of the muzzled rifle from behind her. She immediately fell on the ground in front of the bench, grabbing Emily in the process, pulling her slumping body off of the bench onto the ground beside her. One look at the gaping hole in Emily's forehead told Sam everything she needed to know about Emily's chance of survival. Sam leapt to get behind the merry-go-round. A bullet bounced off the metal about six inches from Sam's face.

She yanked her pistol from its holster and three quick shots in the general vicinity of the shooter and then squirmed in the sand to fit behind the large iron plate at the base. Sirens began blasting through the air and police cars from the East Baton Rouge Sheriff's station fill the tiny park. Tires screeched on the street in front of the park and slid in the gravel parking lot. Officers jumped out of their cruisers with shotguns, pistols, and rifles aimed in Sam's direction, ready to fire.

"Throw your weapon on the other side of the merry-go-round. Stand up. Put your hands in the air. Turn away from me. Walk backwards toward the sound of my voice. Get down on your knees. Lay down on the ground. Cross your legs. Put your arms straight out." The officers were yelling over each other, the verbiage so familiar to Sam. She complied with each request.

Suddenly, she felt the impact of a knee being driven into the small of her back, temporarily knocking the wind out of her lungs. The officer on her back slipped a pair of handcuffs over one tiny wrist and then the other.

"We've got a body over here!"

One deputy helped Sam to her feet. She inhaled and exhaled deeply.

One officer pulled out a card. "You have the right to remain silent. You have the right—"

"I know the drill, Officer. I'm the sheriff of Evergreen County, Mississippi."

"You may or may not be. But you have rights either way." He read the rest of her rights from the card. When he finished, he yelled at one of the other officers, "We need to get a female officer down here on the double to pat her down."

"If you guys will just listen to me."

"I'm sorry, Ma'am. We have to get a female officer down here before we do anything else." He escorted Sam to the rear of one of the patrol cars and leaned her over the trunk.

Sam watched as the officers placed her weapon in an evidence bag. Other officers roped off almost the entire park.

The female officer arrived and frisked Sam, revealing her badge from Evergreen County.

"So you work for the Sheriff's department up there?"

"I'm the Sheriff."

"What brings you to East Baton Rouge Parish?"

"I'm working on a case involving the victim over there. Her name is Emily. She was using the name Victoria Engle. She asked me to meet her here to discuss some matters in that case."

"Was she a suspect in that case?"

"She was a person of interest."

"Tell me a little about the case."

"A City Councilman, Kenny Thigpen was murdered in Evergreen. Two others disappeared in the Atchafalaya basin last Monday and were rescued last Friday. The pilot of the plane they had been flying in was discovered in the Gulf of Mexico; its pilot was dead."

"I read a report on that. So you're that Sheriff Cates. You look so much different than I imagined from the reports. Let me get those cuffs off of you."

One of the other officers stepped near and whispered something in the female officer's ear.

"As you probably guessed, there's no identification on the victim. Where did the shots come from?"

"From the wood patch across the road."

"Did you see him?"

"No."

"What were you shooting at then?"

"When I came in, I noticed the Sheriff's substation was only a few hundred yards up the road. I figured the shots might get your attention and I could get some help down here fairly quickly."

The officer laughed. "It definitely got our attention. It's not every day we hear gunshots from our desks."

"Sorry about that, but I needed help."

"Do you have any idea who the shooter was?"

"No."

The officer jotted some notes on her pad. "Do you have any other suspects in the case?"

"We have no other firm suspects."

"Who is 'we'?"

"The FBI, the Mississippi State Police, my department and the city detectives. There's also a Federal Investigator involved with the case."

"Unfortunately, since this shooting occurred in East Baton Rouge Parish in the city of Central, you now have at least two other jurisdictions involved."

"Welcome aboard the merry-go-round."

"I'm glad he missed." Wade clutched Sam's hand in his.

"Yeah, me too." Sam told Wade about all the events surrounding the shooting in Central, including her brief stint in the back seat of the patrol car.

"I bet you were scared. I know I would've been if someone were shooting at me with a high-powered rifle."

"The bad part was that I knew he could hit where he was aiming. I was trying as hard as I could to squeeze down behind that merry-go-round."

"I know I wouldn't have fit behind it."

Sam laughed. "Do you want to know what I was thinking?"

"What is that?"

"Do you promise not to tell anyone or laugh at me?"

"I promise."

"I was afraid I'd get shot in my butt. Then I'd have to admit it was bigger and wider than any other part of my body. How embarrassing would that be?"

Wade guffawed. "Of all the things to be thinking about

when you're being shot at, that's the last thing I would have imagined. Just the image of it is funny now that you're safe. I bet it wasn't funny then."

"No, but it's the truth. I had everything else hidden, but my butt was sticking up above the merry-go-round. It seemed like it was two feet high. You promised not to say anything to anyone about it, remember."

Both of them were still laughing when the waitress appeared at their table.

"What can I get you?"

"I'll just have the special, Agnes."

"We have two of them tonight, Sam."

Sam arched her eyes, but remained silent.

"We have the chicken-fried steak and we also have stuffed peppers tonight."

"I'll have the steak, Agnes."

"Me, too." Wade echoed. Even as he said it, the gleam of the thought he had unsuccessfully tried to get to come to the surface struggled to enter his consciousness.

"I'll have those out to you in no time."

What is it? What am I trying to recall? It's important. What is it?

"Are you okay, Wade?"

"I have something rolling around in this thick mind of mine and I can't get a focus on it."

"Don't try so hard. When that happens to me, somebody will say something or something will happen and it'll just pop out."

"That sounds like an idea. I've been trying to force it out and all I'm getting is a headache."

Sam laughed.

"What's so funny?"

"If you guys would think about something other than

sex every once in a while, it wouldn't give you a headache when another idea pops in there."

"At least we don't use a headache as an excuse not to have sex."

The waitress placed the plates of chicken-fried steaks in front of them, saying nothing. But she had a big smile on her face.

"Anything else?"

"Can I get some pepper sauce for the turnip greens? I forgot they were one of the side orders or I would have asked earlier."

"No problem."

He looked over the table at Sam.

"Do you remember our first meal together? It was the chicken-fried steak right here at the Evergreen Café."

"I remember. I love the steaks here. The stuffed peppers are always good, but I prefer the steaks. There's no other restaurant that makes them the same as here."

The waitress returned with the pepper sauce and had two of the stuffed pepper specials in her other hand for another table.

A wide grin crossed Wade's face, and his eyes sparkled.

Sam looked at him. "I take it the idea popped."

"I know who tried to kill us. I don't know why or how I can prove it, but now I know who did it."

55 WEDNESDAY MORNING
EVERGREEN

"Come on in Wade. I wasn't expecting you back so soon." Collier Templet rose to greet the agent.

"Sorry to bother you, but I have the list of assets you wanted. I didn't want you waiting on me."

"I appreciate that. It gets awfully frustrating sometimes when someone wants everything rushed and I work nights and weekends only to wait on them to furnish some information I need."

"Look through it and let me know if you need anything else."

"I will. I heard about Sam's close call yesterday. Everybody at the café was talking about it this morning. Is she okay?"

"It shook her up, but she's a strong young lady. She's gonna be fine," Wade said.

"Please pass along my good wishes. She is a special young lady."

"I'm very fortunate and very glad the shot missed."

"Do you have any idea who shot at her, Wade?"

Wade paused, "We don't know exactly who, but it won't be long before we know."

Collier's body stiffened in his chair. "What do you mean?"

Wade had a big smile on his face. "They recovered a bullet from the scene yesterday."

"Do they have a gun to match it? Don't you need both?"

"Not anymore. The Agency has a new ballistics application. It's so simple, I don't know why they didn't think of it before."

"What is it?"

"You're familiar with ballistics, right? Every rifle barrel has lands and grooves inside it to make the bullet spin in a tight spiral when it's fired. Each barrel leaves a unique pattern on the bullet, so it's accepted in court now to match a barrel and the bullet through this pattern."

"Of course."

"Now, and for many years, the barrels have been cut with lathes that are controlled by a computer chip. Right?"

Collier nodded.

"Now, they don't need the actual barrel. They can match the bullets to the records of the computer chip to determine which barrel matches it. They can trace the barrel and recover it once they know who has it. They still need the actual barrel for evidence because the new application hasn't been tested by the court system."

Collier shook in head. "That's amazing technology. They can go back and match a barrel to a bullet without physical possession of the barrel."

"It's fast too. They should know where the barrel was manufactured, what gun it went on, and where the gun was sold before lunch today. Then they just need to pick up the physical barrel and we'll have our suspect. I hate to take up all of your time, but I'm excited about this."

"You should be after everything you and Sam have been through."

"Collier, I shouldn't have told you all of this. It's just that I'm really blown away with it, but Sam promised she wouldn't tell anyone, so I don't want word to get out on the street. You know how hard it is to keep a secret in Evergreen."

"Your secret is safe with me."

"Okay, and let me know if you need anything else for the asset list."

"I will. Thanks, Wade."

Wade crossed the street and jumped into the back seat of the twins' waiting car. In less than five minutes, Collier Templet's car exited the parking lot and turned in the opposite direction toward his house. Mindy was driving the blue sedan and remained back in traffic. Wade couldn't contain his excitement.

"It worked. I can't believe it actually worked. He's going home."

Collier reached his home and raced inside his house, not bothering to shut his car off or closing his garage door. They watched as he returned with a long packaged wrapped in a blanket under his arm. His tires screeched as they left marks on the pavement in front of his house. When he stopped at the first intersection, Sam's patrol car pulled directly in his path. Three other patrol cars surrounded his automobile. Officers from each of the cars crouched behind the doors of their automobiles with their weapons pointed directly at Collier.

Collier Templet, his hands cuffed, sat across the interrogation table from Sam and Wade.

"Why did you kill Emily?"

"She was about to tell everything."

"Everything?"

"How I killed Kenny and put him in that old stand to implicate Wade. How I spiked the pilot's coffee and had her drive Wade's truck to the National Forest."

"Why Kenny? Why kill him?"

"He knew about the land option I stole when they transferred the Plantation to you."

"You stole it?" Wade shook his head in disbelief.

"I never thought you'd miss it. While I was doing the deed work for the Agency, I went out there and discovered that old stand way in the back of the property. When Kenny told me he knew about the option, I knew I had to eliminate him. I thought nobody would find his remains out there for a few months and then everybody would forget where they were and nobody would ever get around to questioning me. Everyone should have shifted their focus to you."

"Bad luck for you, I'd say. What is this big project all about?"

"I think I'll save that for later."

"Why did you want the option so badly?"

"Are you kidding? You really don't know, do you?"

"I guess not. Anything else you want to tell us now?"

'I'd like to ask you a couple of questions."

"Okay."

"All that you told me about the Agency developing a new ballistics application. That was all BS, wasn't it?"

"Me and Gus made it up last night. We had to get you to show us where the gun was."

"So how did you know it was me? Did Emily tell you something before she died?"

"No, you did."

"I never told you anything."

"Remember when I told you that Sam and I had gone to New Orleans, and we'd enjoyed the beignets and stuffed Mirlitons?"

"So?"

"You said you liked the Café du Monde and the Columns Hotel as well. I never mentioned which restaurants we went to in New Orleans. You might have deduced Café du Monde because it is famous for its beignets. But the Columns is famous for a lot of things, but not its stuffed Mirlitons. You can get Stuffed Mirlitons at more than two dozen restaurants in New Orleans. The only way you would have known we were at the Columns Hotel was if Emily told you about us asking about her there. So, you gave yourself away."

Collier dropped his gaze to the table.

"About the big project? You really don't know?"

"Not a clue," Wade responded.

"The option for the section of land next to yours. It was worth its weight in gold."

"Why?" Wade asked.

"A seismic survey shows a reservoir of sweet oil bigger than the one they found in Midland. The fault is directly beneath that land."

"And the big facility was a refinery to process all the oil," Wade sighed. "How much is it worth"

"Billions. Lots of Billions." Collier whispered.

"More than a human being? More than your future?"

"What happens now?" Collier asked meekly.

"You go to jail for the rest of your life and we're going to the Evergreen Cafe. Their special today is stuffed Mirlitons.

The End

Dear reader,

We hope you enjoyed reading *Stranded In The Swamp*. Please take a moment to leave a review, even if it's a short one. Your opinion is important to us.

Discover more books by Jim Riley at https://www.nextchapter.pub/authors/jim-riley

Want to know when one of our books is free or discounted? Join the newsletter at http://eepurl.com/bqqB3H

Best regards,

Jim Riley and the Next Chapter Team

NOTES

Stranded in the Swamp is the third of four books in the Wade Dalton and Sam Cates series. It features the dynamic duo with even greater challenges.

I have taken great literary license with the geography and data of south Mississippi. They are wonderful and a great way to experience the deep South culture. I lived there for over five years and found it to be one of the most desirable places on earth if you enjoy the outdoors, great cuisine and remarkable people.

There are so many people to thank:

My family, Linda, Josh, Dalton & Jade

David and Sara Sue

C D and Debbie Smith

My brother and sister-in-law, Bill & Pam

My sister, Debbie

My sister-in-law and her husband, Brenda & Jerry

The Sunday School class at Zoar Baptists

Any and all mistakes, typos and errors are my fault and mine alone. If you would like to get in touch with me, go to my web site at http://jimrileyweb.wix.com/jimrileybooks.

I thank you for reading **_Stranded in the Swamp_** and hope you will also enjoy the rest my books.

Lightning Source UK Ltd.
Milton Keynes UK
UKHW021855050321
379874UK00012B/1172/J

9 781034 502456